CRISTOBEL

Diane Guest lives in Connecticut with her husband and children. She is also the author of *Lullaby* and *Forbidden Garden*.

DIANE GUEST

Cristobel

A BERNARD GEIS ASSOCIATES BOOK

Fontana
An Imprint of HarperCollins Publishers

Fontana
An Imprint of HarperCollins*Publishers*
77–85 Fulham Palace Road,
Hammersmith, London W6 8JB

Special overseas edition 1992
This edition published by Fontana 1992
1 3 5 7 9 8 6 4 2

A catalogue record for this book is
available from the British Library

ISBN 0 00 637780 7

Set in Linotron Palatino

Printed in Great Britain by
HarperCollinsManufacturing Glasgow

Prologue

I can hear her, she thought in wonder. I can hear her but no one else can. 'Mother?' she whispered, hearing the voice again from a long way off.

'Come along, Justine.'

She would have been frightened if she hadn't known that this was only a dream. 'But where are we going?' she asked.

A soft laugh. 'You'll see.'

In her bare feet Justine drifted along the hall, following the sound. Down the great staircase she went, across the marble tiled floor, past the exquisite tapestries, stopping just outside the dining room door. Inside, on one of the long mahogany sideboards, a single four-branched candelabra burned dimly, and beyond, the doors to the veranda stood open. She slipped out, feeling the sweet, humid air, like rain upon her skin. All around she could smell fragrances of cinnamon and ginger and clove. 'Mother?' she said.

The little soft laugh came to her again on the back of a breeze and she ran to follow, puzzled, wondering why her mother had come back now, after being dead so many years. Her bare feet whispered along the path, and just ahead – always just ahead – danced the sound that was her mother.

In the moonlight she could see clearly the path

ahead. 'Where are you?' she called. 'And why are you here?'

'You'll see.'

And all at once she was afraid. She stopped dead in her tracks and shivered in the darkness. I want to wake up, she thought. This is enough. I want to wake up.

'But you *are* awake, my dear,' the voice murmured, so close that she could feel a cool breath brush against her cheek.

Justine froze. 'This is madness,' she said. 'I'm dreaming. I know it.' She closed her eyes tight, then snapped them open and stared. Just ahead in the moonlight she could see where the path ended and the sea began. She looked down at her feet, then at her hands, then at the thin gauze of her nightdress. 'What am I doing?' she said aloud. 'Am I awake? And if I am, what in the world am I doing?'

As if in response, haunting laughter filled the air. Not sweet or soft as before, but cruel now, mocking.

She didn't try to make any sense of it. She couldn't. She had only one thought. To run back to the house. Run back to Marcus and the safety of his bed. But to her horror she couldn't move. Only her hands were alive, clasping themselves together in painful spasms of panic.

'Poor, pathetic wretch,' the voice echoed.

Justine screamed out loud. 'Who are you? What do you want?'

'Come along. I'll show you.'

And suddenly she was moving forward, walking slowly but deliberately down the path towards the ocean.

Clouds drifted across the face of the moon, but even in the periods of darkness she could still see. She stopped at the very edge of the steep cliff where the land joined the wild, surging Atlantic. She could see the waves crashing in upon the gigantic boulders that lined the shore.

I'm going to jump. The thought came into her mind as clearly as if someone had spoken it out loud. *I have lost my mind and I am going to kill myself.*

For one moment she stood paralyzed, hearing nothing but the pounding of her heart inside her chest and the pounding of the surf far below. 'But why?' she whispered. 'Why?'

And then she heard her name. 'Justine!' Insistent still, but different somehow. A deeper voice, more concerned, more agitated.

It's too late, she thought, looking down from the dizzying height. Too late.

The last thing she heard as she slipped into a dark fathomless void was her name being called over and over and over.

1

All his mountain climbing gear was packed and ready, waiting just inside the door for an early morning pick-up. Stefan Leyland took a last check of things, then set the alarm, and crawled into bed. He was exhausted and fell asleep almost at once, but it was a light, uneasy sleep. He kept coming awake abruptly, wondering if there was anything important he had forgotten to tell Jon before he left. Any small detail that might distress one of his patients while he was away.

'All you have to do,' his partner had said as he was cleaning up his desk, 'is go out the door, close it quietly behind you, and don't look back. For two whole weeks, don't look back. And for Christ's sake, don't fall off the mountain.'

Reluctantly he had left the office, not because he felt comfortable about it, but because he knew that he needed to get away. After three years of constant pressure he had finally accepted the fact that he needed a vacation. But it didn't make him any less concerned about his patients. He knew that some of them considered his taking time off a betrayal. And for a psychiatric patient, betrayal – real or imagined – could trigger a whole mess of things.

That was why, when his phone rang at three-thirteen

in the morning, he sat straight up and answered after only one ring, as if he had been sitting at his desk the whole night waiting for the call. 'Doctor Leyland,' he said. Calm. Professional. Wide awake.

'Stefan?' The voice was distant. Unrecognizable.

'Yes.'

'Stefan, it's Marcus.'

'Yes, Marcus. What's the matter?' he said, doing a mental flip through his card file of patients and former patients, trying to identify the caller.

'Jesus Christ, Stefan, I need your help.' A faint, cultivated accent.

Something clicked in Stefan's brain and he was shocked into silence. It wasn't a patient at all. It was Marcus Leyland. His brilliant, eccentric younger brother. He hadn't heard a word from Marcus in more than three years.

'Stefan, are you there?'

'Yes. I'm just surprised to hear from you.' An understatement at the very least. He glanced at the clock on his nightstand. 'It's almost three-thirty.'

'I know, I know.' Impatience. Marcus's trademark. But beyond the impatience there was another sound that Stefan Leyland heard all too often in his profession. It was the sound of panic.

'Calm down,' he said gently. 'Tell me what's wrong.'

'It's my wife. I need your help.'

In spite of his brother's tone, Stefan couldn't keep from wondering which wife Marcus was talking about. According to mutual friends he was on number three. He waited.

'It's Justine.' There was a pause, followed by deep, laboured breathing, and Stefan could tell that his brother was fighting for control. How odd, he thought, to hear Marcus sound so . . . so human. 'Stefan, I think she's gone mad.'

'Marcus, you know I'll help if I can. What's she done?'

The reply was muffled but the fear was unmistakable. 'She tried to jump off a cliff into the goddamned Atlantic Ocean, that's what she did.'

'When?'

'Just now. An hour ago.'

'Where is she?'

'Right here. Upstairs in bed. I stopped her, but Jesus Christ . . .'

'Marcus, listen to me. She should be in a hospital,' Stefan said quietly.

Marcus's reaction was predictable. His tone grew hostile, full of scorn. 'So they can lock her up? I might have known you'd suggest something like that.' He must have had second thoughts because when he spoke again the tone had changed, become more conciliatory. 'She doesn't need a hospital, Stefan. She needs a doctor. Someone she can trust.'

Stefan didn't reply at once. 'Someone *she* can trust?' he said finally. 'Or someone *you* can trust.'

There was no response for so long that Stefan thought they had been disconnected. 'Marcus? Are you there?'

'I'm here.' All trace of anger was gone, and for the first time in his life Marcus sounded helpless. 'You *are* my brother, Stefan. I'm asking you to come.' A pause. 'No, I'm not asking. I'm begging. Will you?'

Stefan glanced over at the equipment piled by the door, thought about the mountain, the group of old friends waiting for him in Switzerland, the thrill of the climb. He took a long, deep breath. 'Isn't that what big brothers are for?'

There was another pause, then three quiet words. 'Thank you, Stefan.'

Stefan had never known Marcus to thank anyone for anything in his life. He must really love this lady, he thought. 'Before you hang up, I guess you'd better tell me where you are.'

'I thought you knew.' The cool arrogance was back in his voice. 'Everyone else does. We're at Cristobel.'

Stefan raised an eyebrow. So Marcus was back in Barbados, living with his new wife at his ex-wife's family estate. How convenient, he thought, to have such a rich and understanding ex-wife as Caroline.

It was raining when he arrived at Grantley Adams Airport, a sudden torrential downpour, but by the time the battered cab had made its way to the eastern side of the island, the rain had stopped. Past seemingly endless fields of sugar cane and along narrow, winding lanes, the road wandered east then north, through valleys extravagant with colour and hillsides lush with waxy-wet foliage.

Stefan had given the driver no directions at the airport except to say that he was going to Cristobel. That was all Marcus had told him to say, and it seemed to be enough. At least he hoped it was since he had no idea where the place was.

Inside the cab the air was stifling and he cursed himself for not having checked to make sure it was air-conditioned before getting in. He leaned back and rolled the window down, trying to get a breath of fresh air now that the rain had stopped. 'How much farther?' he asked the driver.

He thought the answer was, 'Just ahead,' but the man's accent was so heavy he couldn't be sure, and suddenly they were out of the rain forest, curving along the edge of a high cliff with the restless Atlantic far below. The dramatic change in scenery took him by surprise, but before he had had a chance to absorb it, they turned away from the sea to follow a lane so narrow that Stefan could have reached out and touched the trees on either side.

There was something meticulously contrived about this stretch of road, as if someone had deliberately planted each flowering shrub, each tree according to a master plan. But curiously, in the midst of order, Stefan sensed a wildness about the place, as if no matter how valiant the attempt to tame it, ultimately nature was going to triumph.

The lane curved around a hill and in the middle of nothing, the driver stopped and pointed towards a shaded opening in the vegetation, an archway too narrow to allow a car passage. 'There be no road,' he said.

'You're kidding.'

The driver shook his head. 'Not too far, mon. Up on the hill.'

Stefan paid him, grabbed his bag and climbed out, wondering what the hell Marcus had gotten him into. He knew that ex-wife Caroline was richer than God and so he had always assumed that she lived accordingly, but by the looks of things here, he had been wrong. You should never assume anything where Marcus is concerned, he told himself.

The thought was barely articulated when, abruptly,

the path ended and he found himself on the edge of a vast, velvet lawn – and just beyond stood Cristobel, with its gleaming white walls and tall, jalousied windows lining the verandas. A high roof extended on all sides, shading the galleries, and from an open window somewhere above, Stefan could hear the light strains of music. 'My apologies, Marcus,' he said softly. 'I don't understand how you've managed, but this time you've really outdone yourself.'

As if in response, the front door opened and his brother stepped out onto the porch. 'It's about time,' Marcus said in an annoyed tone, and it brought Stefan up short. Why in hell, he wondered, had he allowed himself to be talked into coming to this overripe steaming jungle to help someone he never really had liked anyway, when he could have been breathing in the cold, pure air of the Alps with some of his dearest friends? 'It's nice to see you too, Marcus,' he said and brushed past his brother into the house.

2

Stefan found himself standing in a spacious, marble-tiled entry hall that ran from the front of the house to the back, opening onto a wide, shaded veranda in the rear. Through the open doors he could feel a cool rush of air, and he guessed that the temperature inside the house had to be at least twenty degrees lower than it was outside.

'Trade winds,' Marcus said, coming in behind him. 'Leave your bag right there by the door. One of the servants will take it up.' He led the way through a wide arch to the living room where the air was even cooler than in the hall. Two huge ceiling fans circulated silently above.

The room was furnished in simple but dramatic fashion, a perfect blend of white wicker and rich, dark mahogany. The only colour came from masses of cut flowers and giant decorative plants. There was a casual elegance about the place, with the emphasis on the casual, and it surprised Stefan. The word casual had never been in Marcus's vocabulary.

'Decorated by Justine,' Marcus said, as if he realized that an explanation was necessary. The explanation only made Stefan more puzzled. Decorated by Justine? What about Caroline? Marcus crossed to the sideboard where a bar had been set up. 'You could probably use a drink.'

Stefan nodded. 'Vodka and tonic,' he said, then suddenly realized how parched he was. 'But first a glass of iced water, if you don't mind.'

While Marcus made the drinks, Stefan had a moment to study his brother unobserved. Marcus still moved with the same fluid grace that Stefan remembered. Their mother used to say that her younger son was like a cat, cool and premeditated in everything he did. And she was right.

Even at thirty-seven there was little evidence that Marcus had aged. His body was trim, athletic, his face unlined. Physically the two men resembled each other, with the same build, the same colouring, but where Stefan's hair was streaked with grey now, Marcus's was still the colour of pitch. Nonetheless, they were clearly brothers until you looked into their eyes. While Stefan's were deep blue, reflecting a warmth of spirit and natural good humour, Marcus's were ice-green, feline, at times exhibiting arrogant disapproval, at others, simply vague indifference.

Except, Stefan thought, when Marcus was with those he loved. Like their mother. Like Caitlin, Marcus's first wife. Then that frigid expression would vanish, leaving Marcus an irresistibly handsome man.

Stefan wondered what he was like when he was with Justine.

'How was your trip?' His brother handed him a frosted glass, then turned and crossed the room, motioning for Stefan to sit.

'Uneventful,' Stefan said, stretching his legs out in front of him. 'So tell me, Marcus. How is it you're here at Cristobel? Where's Caroline?'

Marcus shrugged. 'Who knows? Somewhere in

18

Tibet. Or was it Mongolia? But more to the point, who cares?'

Stefan's eyebrow went up a fraction of an inch. 'It just seems odd, that's all. That you would be staying here. With a new wife.'

Marcus seemed genuinely amused. 'Why shouldn't I be here? Cristobel is mine.'

Stefan was astonished. 'Caroline gave Cristobel to you?'

'Of course she didn't,' Marcus laughed. 'The judge did. One of the prices she had to pay for deserting her husband and her children.' He took a sip of his drink. 'An interesting twist, don't you think? I adopted her sons to please her, and now because of them, Cristobel has been taken away from her and given to me. The judge thought the boys would be better off staying in the only home they've ever known, and since I am now their father, it meant turning Cristobel over to me.'

Stefan had been watching his brother closely, looking for some clue as to Marcus's true feelings about all of this, but as usual his expression was inscrutable. The only detectable emotion was amusement.

'I take it you don't care that Caroline left,' Stefan said quietly.

'I used to. But no longer. Not since I met Justine.' At the mention of his wife's name, his attitude changed abruptly. He became agitated.

Stefan waited.

Marcus stood up, crossed to the sideboard and poured himself a fresh drink, then said almost to himself, 'I don't like other people knowing my business.'

An understatement if I ever heard one, Stefan thought. If ever there was a private person, Marcus Leyland was it. Resentful of any intrusion, no matter how well-meaning. What little Stefan knew about his brother's life had always come from other people, like their mother, and after she died, Stefan lost all contact with his brother, not that they had ever been close. Oddly enough it was Marcus's first wife, Caitlin, who had made the few feeble attempts to keep in touch.

Stefan smiled to himself, remembering Caitlin. A kooky little girl, as brilliantly eccentric in her own way as Marcus was in his. But where Marcus was arrogant, reclusive, Caitlin was eminently likeable. Stefan was sorry when the two drifted apart. She had been good for Marcus. He had been almost human when she was with him, always kept slightly off-balance trying to anticipate her next move.

Even after their divorce, Stefan still heard from Caitlin from time to time – unpredictably, with years passing in between. A potted plant delivered to his office one day, simply signed, 'To the doc from Cait.' Months (or was it years?) later, a call at ten in the evening. She was in New York. Was he free in an hour for cocktails? And whenever she came, she brought whatever news she had of Marcus. That he was broke, that he was rich, that he was living in the Costa del Sol, that he was in New Zealand. Now, even though they were divorced, Caitlin still knew more about her ex-husband and probably loved him better than anyone else in the world. When he married Caroline it was Caitlin who told Stefan. She made no bones about the fact that she didn't approve of Marcus's choice. 'The woman is a self-indulgent brat,' she said. 'And a dolt into the bargain.' Stefan would never forget the hilarious imitation she did of Caroline, mimicking her perfectly, from the imperious toss of her head right down to the peculiar way she rolled her Rs.

Stefan always listened when Caitlin talked about Marcus, but with little real interest. He had long ago come to grips with the fact that he would never have a relationship with his brother. It was Caitlin he liked, and he was always happy to see her, however unorthodox her values.

As for Caroline, Stefan had met her only a few times and each time he had to bite his cheeks to keep from laughing, remembering Caitlin's outrageous imitation. Caroline was every bit as self-centred as Marcus himself, but where Marcus had a purpose in life – to create perfection in everything and everyone around him – Caroline had only one concern: To do exactly what she pleased no matter what the cost. Stefan wouldn't have cared one way or the other except that he knew she had two sons by a previous marriage, two sons who, on Caroline's list of priorities, came just before eating oysters, which she loathed, and just after watering her Spider Orchids of which she was quite fond. She had all the maternal instincts of a stone.

At his practice he had seen enough children damaged by neglect to make him dislike her intensely. He wasn't sure how good a father Marcus was, but he knew one thing for sure: Marcus wouldn't have to go very far to be a better parent than Caroline. How typical that she had flown the coop without a backward glance.

But in a small way, Stefan thought, sipping his drink, justice had prevailed. Now Cristobel belonged to Marcus, so at least the boys had a home. He wondered if Caroline had any regrets. Probably not.

Stefan suddenly became aware that he and Marcus had been sitting in silence, his brother staring vacantly into his empty glass, and Stefan decided to get on with the business in hand. He was here for only one reason: To make a primary evaluation of Justine's condition, and then to decide, whether Marcus liked it or not, if she needed hospitalization. 'Where is Justine now?' he asked.

As if in answer, faint strains of music drifted in from somewhere above. 'She's upstairs in her studio,' Marcus said. 'But before you meet her, I think there are some things you should know.'

Stefan shook his head. 'Right now I have only two concerns. One, is your wife still in a dangerous state of mind, and two, can I help her? Anything else will have to wait.'

Marcus looked irritated but he said nothing. 'As you wish.' He stood up. 'Come then, and let me introduce you to her.' He crossed to the door.

Stefan set his glass back on the sideboard and was turning to follow his brother when all at once he stopped, held in place by the weirdest feeling that he was being dissected. Not just scrutinized. Dissected. And it made his skin crawl. He turned, not towards Marcus, but to the opposite side of the room where the doors opened out onto the veranda.

A woman was standing in the shadow and it was her stare that was making Stefan feel as if he were being skinned alive. She was a tall, strikingly handsome black woman of indeterminate age, with hair the colour of coal, cropped close to her head. She wore a loose-fitting dress of deep crimson, heavy gold earrings, and around her neck a primitive gold pendant shaped like a hand. There was something regal about her and, Stefan thought, narrowing his eyes, something disturbingly pagan. For a moment she stood motionless, then stepped into the room, her study of him ending abruptly.

22

'Have you seen the children, Marcus?' The accent was French. Her voice was low, modulated but void of expression. She might have been addressing a passing stranger.

Marcus turned, his tone equally remote. 'Should I have?'

She ignored the question. 'They are late for their French lesson.'

'I'm sure that if anyone can find them, Amalie, you can.' Cool dismissal. He turned to Stefan. 'Shall we go?'

Stefan cast a sidelong glance at the woman, wondering who she was, wondering why he felt so uneasy. He crossed the room and could feel her watching him again. He was almost to the door when she said, 'Welcome to Cristobel, Dr Leyland. I hope you'll be most comfortable here.' It was as if she were the mistress of the manor, scrupulously polite but none too pleased to see him.

'I'm sure I will be,' he said, smiling, the evenness of his tone masking his discomfort.

Marcus was already across the hall, waiting at the foot of the stairs, and Stefan hurried to follow. 'Who was that?' he asked.

'That, my dear brother, was Queen Amalie.' There was annoyance in his tone. 'Years ago she was given to Caroline's mother by a well-meaning friend. She was Caroline's nurse and after that, the boys'. She thinks Cristobel belongs to her.'

They walked down a long, high-ceilinged gallery with doors open to rooms on either side, allowing the cooling breeze to blow through. At the far end, just outside the one door that was closed, Marcus stopped. 'Amalie tries my patience from time to time, but I'm a

23

reasonable man as long as she does her job. She takes care of the boys when they aren't away at school. And for that, I'm grateful.' He reached out to open the door. 'Still,' he added in an off-handed way, 'I'd avoid Queen Amalie if I were you. They say, among other things, that she likes to turn princes into frogs.'

Stefan smiled, then saw his brother's expression and the smile faded. For one moment, beyond Marcus's mask of cool control, Stefan saw something more than just irritation over the eccentricities of a high-handed servant. In his brother's eyes Stefan saw hate – and fear.

3

Stefan's first impression as he stepped into the room was of cold. Not the breezy cool of the rest of the house, but good old New York City air-conditioned cold. His next impression was of whiteness. Whiteness from ceiling to floor, reflected endlessly in the full-length mirrors that lined the walls behind the dancers' *barre*. Now he recognized the music he had heard earlier. It was something by Tchaikovsky but he wasn't sure what.

He didn't see her at once, but when he did, a single word came into his head. Exquisite. He couldn't see her face clearly but even so, the word described her perfectly. As the brothers watched, unobserved, she continued to dance with unaffected grace. There was sweetness, innocence in her movement, but at the same time such elegance, such authority, that something clicked in Stefan's head. He had seen her before. But where? Who was she? He racked his brain, trying to place the name. Justine. And then it came to him. Justine Powell.

Some years ago the teenage Justine Powell had taken the New York City Ballet by storm, then had disappeared almost as quickly as she had come. He frowned, trying to catch the memory. Something about a knee injury. Or an ankle. Something. He wasn't sure he had ever known, since ballet had never been one of his passions. But he did remember her name because for one brief season the sheer brilliance of her performances had put her on the cover of *Time*. He had actually been persuaded to see her in a superb production of *Coppelia*.

She hadn't seen them yet, so absorbed was she in the dance. She moved not *with* the music but as if she *were* the music.

'I never tire of watching her,' Marcus said softly, and he sounded so unlike himself that Stefan turned to look at him.

Well, that explains everything, Stefan thought. This time Ice Man is truly in love.

At the same moment, the music stopped and he heard her voice, low, melodic. 'How long have you two been standing there?' She came down the length of the room to greet them, and as she drew closer, Stefan realized with a start that this exquisite creature was not very pretty. Her eyes were hazel, an unremarkable colour, with dark shadows underneath. Her hair was brown, her nose straight but overlong with a faint sprinkling of freckles. She had a wide, full mouth. Not that she was unattractive, but from the way she moved, the turn of her head, the perfect lines of her body, he had expected a matchless beauty. Justine was no more than average.

She gave Marcus a quick kiss on the cheek, then turned to Stefan and met his gaze directly, her expression one of open relief. 'And you, of course, are Stefan. Welcome to Cristobel.' Unlike Amalie, she said it as if she really meant it.

She held out her hand and he took it. It was small and thin, like a child's. 'You dance brilliantly,' he said, and instantly regretted it. It was so obvious that it sounded ridiculous. Like saying, 'My, but the water is wet.'

'You'd never know that every step is a painful effort,' Marcus said.

'Hush!' She put a slender finger up to her husband's lips. 'You know you exaggerate. It's just that I need to be careful, that's all.'

'Justine has had three knee operations in two years,' Marcus said. 'Before that she was the darling of the ballet world.'

So I was right, Stefan thought. She *is* Justine Powell.

'Well, the operations are all behind me now,' she said. 'And with hard work and a little luck I'll be back in New York by September.' She looked at Stefan and a shadow flickered across her face. 'That is, unless you decide that for some medical reason I'm not able.'

He didn't answer. At this point he couldn't. But clearly she didn't seem to be suffering from any acute disorder. She seemed concerned. That was all.

There was a moment's awkward silence, then Marcus put his arm around her. 'Haven't you put yourself through enough torture for one day?' he asked softly. 'Are you ready to quit?'

She glanced at the clock on the wall. 'Another half hour. Then I'll shower and change and join you two for cocktails.'

'I suppose there's no point in arguing.'

'None.'

'Very well, darling. In the meantime, I'll show Stefan the aviary.'

To hell with the aviary, Stefan said to himself. At this point the thought of a shower and a quick nap was almost narcotic.

'Poor Stefan,' Justine said, seeing his expression.

'Why don't you let him relax for a few minutes? I'm sure he's tired. Besides, aren't you supposed to meet Jack Thomas at four?'

Marcus looked startled. Could he be so concerned about her, Stefan wondered, that he has actually forgotten something?

'Of course,' Marcus said smoothly, kissing her gently on top of the head. He turned to Stefan. 'Justine is right. You must be tired. I'll show you to your room.'

They were almost to the door when Justine spoke again. 'Thank you for coming, Stefan,' she said, and there was the slightest tremor in her voice.

He turned to look at her and saw a face clouded with anxiety. 'I hope I can help.'

'Of course you can,' Marcus said sharply. 'Why else do you think I called you?'

We're becoming well-acquainted, panic and I, she thought. She wondered if it had shown on her face or if she had managed to hide it. But you aren't supposed to hide it, Justine, she told herself. If he is to help you, you have to be honest with him. Have to let him know how frightened you are.

She crossed the room and flicked the switch on the CD player. Soft strains of Tchaikovsky came again but she didn't move, didn't go back to the endless process of retraining her body. Instead she stood looking at herself in the mirror. Slowly she put her hands on her face. 'A sorry sight,' she said, tracing the faint purple smudges under her eyes, and the single word that had haunted her since that night came clearly into her mind. *Why?* In the nightmare of her memory she remembered it exactly as it had happened. The candles

28

burning, the smell of the evening air, the moonlit path that she had followed to the edge of the cliff. And the voice. Her mother's voice. But no. Not her mother. Someone else. Someone vicious. She shivered. But none of that really mattered, did it? What mattered was what had come after.

'You tried to kill me,' she whispered to her reflection. 'You tried to jump off the goddamned cliff.' And hearing herself say it out loud, she shuddered with renewed horror. It was true. She had tried to kill herself. She was standing here right now only because Marcus had saved her, pulled her back from the edge of the cliff, carried her home.

But why had she done it? Why? She didn't want to die. She had worked too hard, struggled with every ounce of strength to develop her talent, and then, after her injuries, to regain her skills. More than anything in her life she wanted to dance again. And she was almost there. Almost ready. In September she was going to work with Marina again. Her brilliant mentor, Marina. And Marina would polish what flaws Justine couldn't see, help her feel again what she had lost. And then she would be ready to try a comeback. She knew she would never be the same kind of dancer she had been; the spontaneity was gone. Now, because of her injuries, she was forced to be more deliberate, more controlled. But there was a depth to her work that hadn't been there before. She had suffered, and she hoped that Marina would know how to use that suffering to Justine's advantage.

Never for one moment had she doubted that she would succeed.

Never.

Until now.

Anger welled up, pushing the fear away. You jack-ass. You crazy jackass, she choked. Why did you go and do something so stupid? What in the name of God is the matter with you?

That's what Dr Stefan is going to tell you, a voice in the back of her head whispered, and the fear came back with a rush. She took a deep breath, put her hand on the *barre* to steady herself, then began her exercises, but in her mind the single question still lingered. *Why?*

And the dreaded answer. You're crazy, that's why!

4

J.C. watched intently as his elder brother made a small circle in the sand with the twigs they had gathered. Then he crumbled a handful of old leaves until they were no more than powdery bits and placed them in a pile inside the circle. When everything was ready, August took the magnifying glass from his pocket and held it exactly right, so that a single beam of concentrated sunlight was centred on the pile.

Neither boy moved.

J.C. felt the prick of a bug on the back of his neck but he didn't dare brush it off. August would kill him if he ruined the experiment one more time. He stared at the spot of hot light in the leaf dust as hard as he could, trying to forget the bug.

Nothing happened.

And then, in the midst of the dust pile, a small dark spot appeared, then a wisp of smoke, and a single tiny red spark.

August crouched closer and began to blow very, very gently.

'You did it!' J.C. said, falling forward onto his knees.

Instantly the flame went out.

For a minute neither boy moved.

'You cockroach!' August yelled, turning on his brother.

'I didn't do it,' J.C. said, jumping to his feet. 'It wasn't my fault your stupid fire went out.'

'It was too. I told you I didn't want you around, didn't I? You always ruin everything.' He made a menacing motion with his fist. 'Now bug off before I smash your face in.'

J.C. didn't need to be told twice. Not only was August two years older than he but he was a whole foot taller. 'I hope you set fire to the whole world,' J.C. shouted. 'Then *you'll* be the one who gets your face smashed in. And don't ask if you can use my kite either.' He hitched up his shorts and stomped away through the underbrush. August would be sorry. Just wait until he wanted J.C. to go with him to the cave and he said no. Then he'd be sorry.

He trotted through the palm grove, past the ruins of one of the old sugar houses, stamping on clumps of grass as he went, hoping to catch sight of a snake or a lizard. Normally he would have stopped to see if anything had crawled into the stone foundation but right now he was too mad. I hate that shitty brother of mine, he thought. I know why nobody likes him. It's because he's a rotten craphead.

But in truth, J.C. really didn't know why nobody liked August. Except that he kept to himself most of the time. And always acted like he knew something no one else knew, with that shitty secret smile of his. As a result the other boys usually avoided him. But it didn't seem to bother August a bit. The only one it bothered was J.C., because he wanted desperately to be included and never was. Just because he was snotface August Leyland's little brother.

Well, not any more, J.C. thought grimly. Just wait until school starts again. They can ignore his ass all they want. I'm going to pretend I don't even know him. Then I'll get to go on all the fun trips and August can just stay at school alone.

But as much as he wanted to, he knew he'd never be able to abandon August because deep down he loved him. August was all the family he had. Oh sure, they had a mother who phoned them once in a while, but what good was that? She hadn't come home to Cristobel since J.C.'s eighth birthday and that was almost two years ago. As for their real father, he was dead. Not that that meant they didn't have a father. They did, because Marcus had adopted them and that made him their real true legal father. But even so, he was way too busy to bother with them.

J.C. was almost to the gate when he heard Amalie call, but it wasn't until he saw her coming down the path, carrying her big straw bag, that he remembered their French lesson. Ugh.

For a minute he considered hiding, but only for a minute. With Amalie it wouldn't do any good. She would find him instantly. You couldn't hide anything from Amalie, at least not for very long, because Amalie was magic. Everyone knew that. Most of the servants kept clear of her, except sometimes when they brought her presents. And once, one of his friends, a native boy named Best, told J.C. that Amalie could change herself into a ball of fire. Later, when J.C. asked Amalie if it were so, she laughed. 'Young Master Best had better be cautious or he may wake up one morning covered with boils.' J.C. told Best what she had said and Best ran home crying. He never came back to Cristobel.

Now, J.C. stood by the gate and waited for her to come.

'*Mon petit,*' she said and her eyes were very black,

the way they got when she was upset. 'Where is your brother?' J.C. pointed. 'Up above the cane fields.'

'Doing what?'

He looked down at his sneakers. Amalie would be furious if she knew about the fire-making. 'Just hanging out.'

She frowned. 'Have you two been fighting?'

'No. At least, not me.'

'And August? Has he been fighting?'

'No. But he would have if I hadn't gotten out of there.' He met her eyes. 'Why is August so rotten mean?'

She smiled, showing strong white teeth, but there was seriousness in the smile. 'Your brother loves you, Jean-Claude. More than that. You and I both know you are his only friend.' She took his hand. 'Come. Let's find him. And just for today, we will forget our French lesson. Today we must go to the Place of the Monkeys.'

J.C. felt a chill. The Place of the Monkeys. Amalie's secret place. August loved to go there but not J.C. He wasn't sure why, but there was something about the place that scared him real bad. He never told anyone. Not Amalie because she would have been displeased with him. Certainly not August because he would have called him a crybaby wimp.

They found August exactly where J.C. had left him, still kneeling in the sand, but there wasn't a trace left of the pile of leaves and twigs. 'Come along, August,' Amalie said, her voice very quiet. 'You've been home from school for more than two weeks. It's time we went to the Place of the Monkeys.'

August jumped up, his eyes bright with excitement.

'Have you remembered this?' From the straw bag she pulled a small silver flute and handed it to him.

August nodded, smiling. 'I remember.'

'Can I play it this time?' J.C. asked.

Amalie shook her head. 'Not yet, *mon petit*. You aren't ready. Someday, perhaps.'

But J.C. knew she'd never let him. He didn't have The Gift. He didn't even know what The Gift was. But August had it. Amalie said so. 'I will teach you,' she told August. 'Then you will be stronger than all those boys who tease you.'

Teach him what? J.C. wondered, but whenever he asked his brother, August simply smiled that mysterious smile. 'You'll see. Someday.' And the way he said it made J.C. think that maybe he didn't want to know.

The path they followed disappeared and as they moved deeper into the rain forest the light changed, becoming tinged with green. The trees here grew so closely together that at times he lost sight of the sky.

As many times as J.C. had been to the Place of the Monkeys, he never could remember how to get there. Not that it mattered. Even with Amalie and August along for protection he didn't like going. He would never dream of going by himself.

He kept up with them, although there were lots of things along the way he would have liked to investigate. A rotten log swarming with black bugs. A small clear pool of water. A huge spider with babies on its back. But he didn't stop. No way did he want to lose sight of Amalie and August. Don't even think about stopping, he told himself, feeling a touch of panic. You'd get lost for sure.

And then suddenly the tangle of underbrush thinned out and J.C. knew they were there. In the Place of the Monkeys.

It was a small clearing surrounded by monstrous

trees that grew up on huge, exposed roots, spreading their branches thick and tangled to make a dark green canopy overhead. High in the trees monkeys chattered, then sensing the strangers, were still.

J.C. looked around, wide-eyed. Everything was exactly as he remembered: on one side of the clearing was a long, low table made of stone, and on the other side, casting its long, eerie shadow, was the cross. A huge, pointed thing made out of two wooden stakes lashed together.

He didn't dare speak. He knew he wasn't allowed to.

Amalie took three small straw mats from her bag, placed them on the edge of the clearing directly across from the stone table, and motioned the boys to sit. August put the flute to his lips, and as he played, Amalie arranged a number of candles, some on the stone, some in the dirt at its base, and lit them. Then she drew some wavy lines around everything. When she was finished, she reached once again into her bag and took out the loathsome thing that had always frightened J.C. the most. It was the head of a snake. It was the Lord Damballah, and Amalie said it was her greatest treasure. Carefully she placed it between the lighted candles; she then set in front of it a small black box shaped like a coffin. Amalie said some strange words, none of which J.C. understood, and she drew a large circle in the dirt. Then she sprinkled cornmeal all around in intricate, mysterious patterns.

Finally, after what seemed like hours, she took her place between the boys. 'Strangers have come to Cristobel, and I feel a great uneasiness,' she said in a dark voice. 'When Marcus brought his new wife here I came to the Place of the Monkeys. I called upon the *loa*. I prayed for them to bring our Caroline home. To save Cristobel for us.' She bowed her head. 'But they have not answered. Caroline has not come. Instead Marcus has brought his brother here. So now together we must pray. Together we must beg the *loa* to bring her home.'

August set the flute down, and all was quiet. No chattering of monkeys, no peeping of tree frogs. No sound at all. Then in a hushed tone, Amalie began her incantations.

J.C. stared down at his outstretched legs, not daring to look across to the place where the candles burned, the place where he knew the snake's head sat, its hideous, dead jaws half-opened, waiting. He knew he was supposed to be praying to the *loa* but he couldn't imagine why they would listen to him. After all, they were Amalie's gods, not his. At his school the boys were taught that there was only one God. That to believe in any other was the most wicked sin. Besides that, Amalie's *loa* were scary creatures, and J.C. understood nothing about them except that they frightened him to death. There was Papa Nebo and Erzulie and the dreaded Baron Samedi who was the spirit of the graveyards. But as far as J.C. was concerned, the worst, the most terrifying of all was the Lord Damballah, Amalie's serpent god, whose head sat on the altar in front of him.

He closed his eyes tight, trying to forget the thing on the table, but now he could hear it hissing, soft, menacing. He remembered a story he had heard at school about a boy whose breath had been sucked out by a snake. He felt hot tears slide down his cheeks. He drew his legs up to his chest and rested his head on his knees, covering his ears with his hands. He was sobbing now, quiet, hitching sobs, but no one seemed to notice. He guessed they were too busy praying. Almost at once he felt an overpowering drowsiness creep over him. Still resting his head on his knees, he fell into a deep undisturbed sleep.

Justine stepped out of the tub and wrapped herself in a soft, thick bath towel. She was feeling much better. To hell with gloom and doom, she said to herself, drying her hair with a brisk motion. What happened that night was a freak. It will never happen again. I'm happy. I love my husband. And I'm going to dance in New York again. What more could I ask?

Aware now that she was late, that Marcus and Stefan would be downstairs waiting, she left the bathroom, crossed to the closet and pulled out a cinnamon silk blouse with pants to match. She felt festive. She was going to dress accordingly. As she applied a touch of lipstick, she smiled at her reflection. 'We're going to be just fine, you and I. Don't you worry.' She drew a comb through her hair, swept it back behind her ears, and tied it with a cinnamon and grey silk scarf. 'There. I think we'll pass inspection.'

She was almost to the door when she heard it. Not for a second did she wonder if she was imagining it. Horror-stricken, she knew she wasn't. Her name, soft, gentle, came to her from somewhere outside the open windows. 'Justine. Come here.'

'No,' she said aloud. She reached her hand out to turn the knob. Get out of here, she thought wildly. Get out of here! But her hand wouldn't move.

'Justine.' Still soft, but insistent.

Slowly, against her will, she felt herself turning

around, felt herself going back across the room to the window.

'It's peaceful where I am,' the voice said. 'So peaceful.'

Shaking with fear, Justine looked out across the roof of the lower veranda. Through the bougainvillea vines she could see only a small corner of the lawn, but beyond it, hidden in the shadow of a huge mahogany tree, she could make out the figure of a woman. Barely able to catch her breath, strangling, she half-whispered, 'Who are you? What do you want?'

And the answer. 'You, my dear Justine. I want you.' So quiet, so distant. Yet she could hear every word clearly.

She let out a low moan, and at the same time, from behind, she felt hands on her shoulders. 'Justine. Darling. What is it?'

She made a gasping noise in her throat and pointed, the words coming out in a tumble. 'Marcus. Look. There by the tree.'

He moved beside her, still holding her with one arm.

Justine stared. The woman hadn't moved. She was still standing motionless in the shadow. 'There. She's the one, Marcus. The one who called to me. You see? I'm not crazy. She's real.'

Marcus followed her line of vision, and she felt him stiffen beside her.

'Who is she?' Justine whispered.

'There's no one there, Justine,' he said gently. 'Come away from the window. Stefan is waiting downstairs.'

Incredulous, she whirled around to face him, almost swooning. Didn't he see? 'Marcus – ' Her eyes ricocheted back to the place where the woman still stood.

'She's right there, for God's sake!' she screamed, on the verge of hysteria. 'Are you blind?'

Marcus looked as if she had slapped him. 'Justine,' she heard him say. 'Sweetheart. Please. Calm down.'

'Oh, God.' Hot tears burned her cheeks as they fell. She blinked hard. 'Just look,' she said, fighting for control. 'She's right there. At the edge of the lawn.' She jerked away from him and pointed, but where the woman had stood only moments before now there were only patches of light and dark. Justine moaned and covered her face with her hands.

'Jus,' Marcus said tenderly, putting his arms around her. 'You saw someone. I didn't. It's nothing to be upset over. It was probably one of the servant girls. I just didn't see her, that's all.' He tipped her chin up. 'Come on now. Poor Stefan will think we deserted him.'

'Of course. Stefan,' she echoed. And for one terrifying moment she couldn't imagine who Stefan was.

How long J.C. slept there in the sand he wasn't sure. He knew it must have been a while because when he opened his eyes, the sun was gone, the clearing in semi-darkness. His first reaction was one of panic. They had left him alone. And then he felt Amalie's hand on his shoulder. 'Come, *petit*,' she said. 'We are done here. It is time to go.'

Later, when he thought about it, he still wasn't sure what it had all been about. He asked August, but his brother seemed sort of out-of-it, like he wasn't sure either but didn't want to admit it. And that night, when J.C. finally crawled between the cool white sheets in his own safe, familiar bedroom, he folded his hands over his heart and said his real prayers. The ones to the real God.

He prayed that his mother would come home, and that he'd never have to go to the Place of the Monkeys again.

5

They sat in wicker chairs on the long veranda at the rear of the house, sipping brandy. Candles on the tables cast a flickering glow and along the paths leading towards the sea small hidden lights allowed Stefan a glimpse of Cristobel's exotic gardens.

The air was heavy with the scent of flowers – night flowers, Marcus said – and the warm breeze made a faint, mysterious rustling as it passed through the trees. For some eerie reason it made Stefan think of Amalie.

'There must be a storm coming,' Justine said, and the nervousness was back in her voice. All through dinner Stefan and Marcus had tried to draw her into the conversation, but she had seemed distracted, anxious, her thoughts clearly elsewhere. Not only did she have very little to say but she ate next to nothing even though the food was superb.

Stefan watched her closely, wondering why she seemed so withdrawn. Certainly she hadn't seemed so earlier.

For his part, Marcus was determined to create a congenial atmosphere. He did most of the talking, asking questions about Stefan's practice, describing his own latest project. He had finally finished a series of photographs for Jack Thomas, the British naturalist.

'Just in time,' he said to Stefan. 'I've too much else on my mind right now to be concerned about work.' A shadow crossed his face. 'In any case, tomorrow you must let me take you through the aviary. I think you'll find it fascinating. Justine does, don't you, darling?'

She looked up from her plate, startled. 'I'm sorry, Marcus,' she said. 'Forgive me. I guess I was day-dreaming.'

'I was just telling Stefan about the aviary.'

She made an effort to look enthusiastic. 'Oh. Yes. The aviary. The birds are beautiful, and Marcus assures me that they are much better off there than they would be in the wild. They're well fed and kept safe from predators . . .' Her words trailed off, and she fell silent again, lost in her own private thoughts.

For a few moments no one spoke.

Then Stefan heard her whisper under her breath, 'Oh, damn.' She inhaled, straightened up in her chair and cleared her throat. 'Well,' she said with a cheer-fulness he could tell was forced, 'I think I've behaved badly enough for one night, don't you? What do you say we begin again, and this time I promise to be better company.'

From that point on, the conversation flowed smoothly. Not brimming with hilarity to be sure, but smoothly. Justine tried to be sociable, but to Stefan she was like a child whistling in the dark. Behind her smile and expression of interest, she was still very much on edge.

Now, sitting on the veranda with dinner behind them, the sound of tension was back in her voice. Marcus reached over and took her hand. 'And how do you know a storm is coming?'

She pointed. 'See how the leaves on the tamarinds have turned?'

'I've never heard of such a thing,' Marcus laughed.

'That's what they say about maple trees,' Stefan said, 'so maybe the same holds true for tamarinds.'

Justine shrugged, an elegantly expressive gesture like all the rest of her movements. 'I don't suppose it makes any difference.' She pulled her hand away from Marcus and stood up. She walked to the edge of the veranda and stared out across the gardens. 'You can hear the ocean from here. But then it's not very far away. Just down that path.' All attempts to hide her anxiety vanished. 'That's where I tried to kill myself. Just down that path a little way.'

Marcus set his glass on the table. 'You might as well know, Stefan, that Justine had a fright earlier this evening. She saw one of the servants standing on the edge of the lawn and she thought it was the same woman who called to her that night.'

In the dim light Stefan couldn't see his brother's expression but he could hear the concern.

'I didn't just *think* it, Marcus.' There was anger in her voice. 'I saw her. I heard her. It was the same woman. And now, if the two of you will excuse me, I think I'll retire. It's turned cold and I'm tired. Maybe I'm coming down with something.' She moved to Marcus's side and kissed him on the cheek. 'Thank you for your patience.' She turned to Stefan. 'I'm sorry I've been such a bore. Tomorrow we have to talk.' It was impossible not to hear the urgency in her tone.

She was gone before either of them had a chance to respond.

Halfway up the stairs, Justine was suddenly filled with dread. What was she thinking of, going to bed? She

44

knew she wouldn't sleep, wouldn't be able to click off her brain, and the worst thing she could imagine right now was being alone. And yet here she was, rushing up to an empty room, running away from two people who might be able to keep her from feeling so frightened.

She took a deep breath, then continued up the stairs. She was afraid to be by herself, but for some reason every muscle in her body ached and the desire to ease herself into bed was overpowering. Maybe she really was coming down with something. Besides, if she needed company, she could always slip through the passageway that led from her bedroom to Marcus's. Not that she liked being there. Once it had been Caroline's room, and Justine couldn't forget that, even though Marcus now claimed it as his own.

She had almost reached her own door when all at once she stopped. Whether it was because of a sound or simply a feeling, she wasn't sure, but she knew without a doubt that someone was in her room. She pressed herself against the wall just to one side of the open door and waited, her heart pounding, her hands clenched together.

For a moment all was still. Then, like a shadow, a tall dark figure slipped out into the hallway.

'Amalie?' Justine knew she sounded terrified but she couldn't help it.

Slowly the black woman turned to face her. 'I was looking for August,' she said, her face dispassionate, her voice calm.

'In my room?' It was a reasonable question, and yet incredibly she felt foolish asking it. For some reason she always felt foolish in the face of Amalie's unnerving self-confidence.

45

'I've looked everywhere else, Mrs Leyland.' The tone
was polite, not the least patronizing; still, Justine felt as
if Amalie was humouring her.

'I hope you find him.' Dumb. What an incredibly
dumb thing to say. Justine felt the colour touch her
cheeks. She turned and fled into her room, closing the
door quickly, leaving a cool, unsmiling Amalie behind
her. Without any effort the woman had succeeded in
making her feel like a simpleton, and somehow Justine
suspected that Amalie was pleased.

She was so upset by her own lack of composure that
she never thought to wonder if Amalie had been telling
the truth, if she really had been looking for August.

'Go to sleep,' she whispered to herself. 'Please.' But
she didn't. Couldn't. She was so tired and yet precious
sleep eluded her. Her mind kept sliding over and over
the events of the past week, trying to make some sense
of them, trying not to let fear engulf her, make her
doubt her sanity.

And yet how could a sane person not know what
was real and what wasn't?

But it was possible. She knew it was possible because
it had happened to her once before.

She was fourteen years old and it was winter. She was
asleep in the house she had lived in with her parents,
the house her mother had been born in. It was a safe
house, a happy one. But that night she woke up out
of a deep sleep to find a snake on the headboard of
her bed. A gigantic brown reptile with bluish-purple
bands and a body that stretched from one side of the

46

room to the other. Panic-stricken, she had fled down the hall and wakened her mother, refusing to go back until the snake had been found and destroyed. Her parents humoured her. They searched behind every piece of furniture, every article of clothing, but there was never a sign of a snake. The next morning they all laughed about it over breakfast. Everyone, that is, except Justine, because in spite of what her parents said, she knew without a shadow of a doubt that the snake was real. She knew it was still there, somewhere in her room, hiding, and each night she lay breathless, waiting for it to come.

But as the days passed, a slow, trickling doubt began to form in her mind. How could something so huge hide all that time? And how, in a pitch-dark room had she been able to see its colour? And why had she never been able to identify it in any of the reference books?

For a long time she fought the doubts, because to admit that the snake had not been real was to admit that her mind had played a terrible trick on her.

Now, remembering, she wondered if it was happening again.

She sat up in bed and held her hands out in front of her. 'Justine Powell,' she said sternly, 'this is you. These are your hands.' She clenched her fists and held them to her temples. 'These are real.' It gave her some small comfort. She sighed and lay back down. But as soon as she closed her eyes, the questions began again, whirling around and around in her head. How do you know what's real? The voice? The woman? And what if none of it is real? What if you find out that it's all in your mind? What will you do then? And the final question that made all the rest seem meaningless. Why do you want to die?

If only she knew more about insanity.

She closed her eyes tight and as methodically as she could she began to review everything she had ever known about the mind and the cruel tricks it could play on itself.

Gran. The only person Justine had ever known whose love was unconditional, immutable, ironclad. Gran had lived with them then, and in the sweetness of her smile, in the softness of her voice, Justine had grown to believe that nothing could ever hurt her.

But when Justine was nine years old, Gran began to change. Almost imperceptibly, she began to forget things. Gran, who had never forgotten anything before. And she became confused. Sometimes not knowing where she was. Or even who.

At the end, Gran still smiled but it was a smile that no longer was reserved for her grandchild. Now she smiled for the strangers who had come to live in her imagination; or maybe it was for some long-forgotten memory. Whatever the reason, Gran's eyes, once keen and sharp-sighted, saw less and less of the little girl, more and more of her invisible friends.

When she died, she recognized no one.

Justine never forgot what happened to her grandmother, never forgot the terror of seeing her lose her mind.

Is this how Gran felt? she wondered, staring up at the ceiling. Is this how it started? Is this how she went insane? She rolled over and covered her head with her pillow and prayed for sleep, but something kept nudging her awake. Another memory. Something she was supposed to think about that couldn't wait.

Leah.

Leah Cleves lived three doors down from her when Justine first moved to New York. She and Leah were both enrolled in the School of American Ballet, and in those days, although they all worked as if possessed, none practised with more passion than Leah.

She was the most beautiful girl Justine had ever seen, and that autumn her days were filled with a wistful longing to be exactly like Leah. Justine remembered her teacher's amusement when she confessed her secret ambition. 'But my dear Justine,' Marina had said, 'don't you know? *You* are the star here.'

But Justine never believed it. There was this thing about Leah. It wasn't just her incredible looks. It was her mysteriousness, her remoteness, as if she had another life somewhere that nobody knew about. Sometimes she would go off for days and no one would know where she was.

One day right in the middle of rehearsal, Leah stopped dancing. She walked across the studio to face the mirrors that lined the walls and stood staring at herself for what seemed to Justine an eternity but for what was, in fact, only a minute. So still, so intense was she that the rest of the company, Marina included, was struck dumb. Then without a word Leah left.

An hour later she jumped in front of a subway train at the Fifty-ninth Street station.

No one ever talked about her after that. They never discussed her, never asked what happened. It was as if the girl had never existed. Justine decided that it was because deep down they were all afraid. Afraid that maybe what Leah had was catching. Like measles or chickenpox.

Now Justine wondered if her long ago wish had

come true. That finally she was going to be just like Leah. She rolled over and stared at the clock beside the bed. *It's three in the morning and I'm still awake. Will I ever sleep again?*

She felt desperate and yet the thought of leaving her room, going to Marcus for comfort made her feel more hopeless than ever. As hard as Marcus was trying, he had been no help to her at all. She found herself praying for morning to come, praying for the time when she could talk to Stefan. Maybe *he* could tell her what was happening to her.

6

Marcus and Stefan sat at a table by the pool, eating breakfast. The light shining through the trees was green-gold, the air fresh and cool, and Stefan decided that it was about as idyllic a spot as he had ever seen.

The pool itself was an irregular shape, edged with rough, uncut stone, surrounded by masses of exotic flowering shrubs. It gave the impression that it had always been there; that the gardens, the slate-paved terraces, even the house itself were simply afterthoughts.

'Coffee?' Marcus said.

Stefan nodded and said a silent prayer that it would be American coffee, not the strong, bitter island variety. It proved to be a mixture, stronger than he liked but not undrinkable. 'Is Justine joining us?' he asked.

Marcus frowned. 'I'm surprised she isn't here. She's usually the first one up in the morning.' The words were scarcely out of his mouth when his wife appeared on the edge of the patio. The purple smudges under her eyes had deepened, making her seem more vulnerable. And lost somehow. Like a street urchin.

'I'm sorry I'm late,' she said, sitting down. 'But there's some dispute in the kitchen about who is supposed to go to Cane Cave today.'

Marcus made a sound of derision. 'I suppose I'll have to settle it.'

'You won't be very popular,' Justine said.

'What's Cane Cave?' Stefan asked.

Clearly annoyed, Marcus proceeded to tell him. Cane Cave lay a half mile northeast of the house, cut deep into the cliff by centuries of eroding waves. At first, it was used to hoard salvage from vessels that had been wrecked on the rocks, but when Cristobel began producing sugar, the cave became a storehouse for giant kegs of molasses and rum, rolled from the old sugar house down a long underground ramp to wait for transport to England.

The sugar house had long since fallen into ruin but the underground passageway remained, still used as an access to the cave, where in the twentieth century Cristobel's vast collection of wine and its great kegs of priceless Barbadian run were stored. Although the cave was cool even in the hottest weather, Caroline's family had installed an elaborate temperature and humidity control system that kept the air at a perfect sixty-two degrees the year around.

'The servants say the cave is haunted,' Justine said, pouring herself a cup of coffee. 'You ought to see them scramble out of sight when Marcus tells them it's time to draw off some rum. Or when the wine cellar in the house needs restocking. Nobody wants to go.' She passed a plate of pastries to Stefan.

'No, thanks.'

'Actually I can't say I blame them,' she said, a small frown creasing her forehead. 'I've only been there once and I have no desire to go back.'

'Why is that?' Stefan asked.

She smiled a weak smile. 'Marcus says I have too

vivid an imagination.' She glanced over at her husband but he wasn't looking at her. She turned back to Stefan. 'Right after I arrived here at Cristobel, Marcus took me on a tour and we ended up in the cave.' She shivered. 'I felt . . . ? I felt something . . .' She stopped mid-sentence and gave a self-deprecating laugh. 'Who cares what I felt. Anyway, I can understand why the servants think the place is haunted.'

'Typical native mumbo jumbo,' Marcus said, coldly. He got up from the table and crossed to the edge of the pool where he stood silently staring into the crystal-clear water for a minute. Then he turned and said, 'I have some appointments in Bridgetown this morning, so why don't you two talk while I'm gone? The sooner we get to the bottom of this business, the sooner Stefan can get back to New York.'

Good old Marcus, Stefan thought, wryly. Wouldn't want me to stay a moment longer than necessary. Certainly wouldn't want me to think that he's enjoying my company. He turned to Justine. 'Whenever you feel ready . . .'

She reached over and grabbed his hand, squeezing with such force that her knuckles turned white. 'As soon as possible,' she said, then seeing him wince, she let go. 'Oh, Stefan,' she laughed, trying to cover her embarrassment, 'I'm so sorry.'

'I'll survive,' he said. 'Let's get to it.' He ignored the red half-moon marks her nails had made on the back of his hand.

If someone asked J.C. what part of Cristobel he liked the best, he would have had one answer – Cane Cave. Whether you went down the dark sloping passage from the old sugar house or climbed up over the rocks at low tide, risking life and limb, once inside its myriad tunnels, wading in its clear sea pools, it was a world of magic.

The largest cavern, a vast high-ceilinged grotto, was the one where the wine was stored, but that was of little interest to J.C. anymore. He and August used to play Barbarians there, pretending that the giant kegs of rum were their horses. They would shinny up on top and ride them for hours on end. But no more. They were far too grown-up for that now. And once they stole a bottle of wine from one of the racks and drank it. J.C. threw up so much that he thought his stomach was going to come out of his mouth, but Amalie saved him with some secret potion.

Leading away from the main grotto were several tunnels, some of them dead ends, others leading to smaller chambers, and those were the places J.C. and August loved to explore. There wasn't any light in the deepest recesses, so they had a whole stash of kindling and matches and flashlights hidden in their very own most hidden cave of all, a place so secret that not even Marcus knew it was there. The only other person in the world who knew about it was Amalie. The boys never told her where it was but she knew all the same.

The fact that the servants were afraid to go near Cane Cave didn't really bother J.C., mainly because he never went there alone. August was always with him. Besides, he wasn't even sure he believed in spirits. At least not during the day, he didn't.

And now there was another reason to go there. The best, most secret reason of all. Now there was Strike.

'Hurry up,' August called over his shoulder.

'I am.' He picked up speed.

August moved through the mahogany grove at a fast pace and headed up the slope towards the old sugar house. He was in a hurry, and when he was in a hurry they always went by way of the underground passage. To get up to the mouth of the cave over the rocks took much longer, and today they had no time to waste. Amalie had warned them to be back by eleven.

'Did you remember the key?' J.C. asked, catching up with his brother. Years ago, even before their mother had gone away, they had stolen a key from a hook in the pantry. They had kept it hidden ever since for their own private use.

August patted his pocket. 'Right here.'

The most direct path to the underground passage led through the middle of the ruined sugar house, and it had been cleared of debris in order to make the transfer of wine easier. Usually the boys took a more hazardous route, preferring to climb over the crumbled walls and through the rubble that was now half covered by invading vegetation, but not today. Today they went directly through the sugar house to the hatchlike door, set into the side of the hill just behind the old foundation. A heavy padlock held it in place.

August took the key from his pocket and slipped it into the lock. It turned easily but it took both of them, pulling with all their might to lift the massive wooden door. 'Get the light,' August said.

J.C. scurried through the opening and down the stone ramp about five feet and flicked on the switch his great-grandfather had installed years ago to illuminate the passageway.

The light shone dimly bluish against the damp walls of the tunnel, and the boys followed the way, moving slowly downwards until they reached the main grotto. Above the constant hum of the giant air conditioners, they could hear the sound of the waves crashing on the rocks far below the cave entrance.

One of their favourite occupations on days when the sea was calm was to make their way from the mouth of the cave down the side of the cliff and onto the rocks without getting washed away. During one hurricane when J.C. was only three years old, he was told that the waves got so monstrous they actually flooded the cave. He wished he could have been there to see it.

All around the perimeter of the main chamber were smaller recesses, carved in the stone by years of erosion, some leading to other caverns, others simply dead ends. Without a sideways glance the two boys passed by, under the shadows of the huge wooden kegs that lined the back wall, and made their way through the labyrinth of wine racks until they reached the far side of the cave.

There the light was dimmer, and only someone who knew it was there would have paid any attention to the small narrow fissure in the limestone, so like all the others. August dropped his backpack to the cave floor and took out a flashlight and a heavy leather glove. Then single file, they wedged themselves through the opening and into a low, dark passage, so low in fact that even J.C. had to stoop to make it through. August had started to whistle, a low staccato rhythm, and ahead, J.C. heard the answering flutter of wings and the tinkling of Strike's bells.

Within minutes they were inside a small oval chamber, one that was in total darkness except for the light from August's flashlight. J.C. knelt and opened a large tin box that lay just to one side of the entrance. 'Shall I light the candles?'

'No. We haven't got time to screw around.' August had crossed to the middle of the floor, his gloved arm extended. 'Come, Strike,' he said quietly. 'Wait till you see what I brought you.'

The huge peregrine falcon responded instantly, jumping from the screen perch where she was resting onto his clenched fist. The small copper bells on her legs made a soft tinkling sound.

August unhooked the leash from the perch and whistling low to keep her attention, he carried her to the passageway.

'Did she puke yet?' J.C. asked, hurrying after.

'Cast, you jerk, cast. Falcons don't puke, they cast.'

'Well, did she?'

'Yes. And don't forget to grab my backpack.'

'Aren't you going to hood her before we get outside?' J.C. asked. August always slipped the hood over Strike's head before he took her out in the open.

'No. She's not scared. I think she's used to it.' With the bird firmly attached to his hand, August made his way back to the main grotto, J.C. right behind.

They were just past the last row of kegs when suddenly Strike began to bob her head up and down rapidly, panting as if she were exhausted, sure signs that she was agitated.

'What is it?' August said softly. He turned back to J.C. 'I'd better hood her.'

J.C. reached into the backpack, took out the small leather hood and handed it to his brother.

With one smooth motion August slipped it over the bird's beak and up onto her head. Using his

57

teeth and his free hand, he pulled the straps tight, closing the hood.

Normally, once hooded, Strike calmed right down, but now she seemed even more frightened, bobbing her head and flapping her wings.

'Someone's here,' J.C. whispered, dropping back into the shadow.

August did the same.

They listened.

Except for the hum of the machinery and the crashing of the waves they heard nothing. 'There's no one here,' August said.

'Yes, there is.'

'How do you know?'

'Because I do,' J.C. said, suddenly filled with terrible dread. A dread even worse than he felt at the Place of the Monkeys. 'We have to get out of here.' Without waiting for August to answer, he darted out of the shadow and ran up the ramp to the open door. Once outside he didn't stop running until he reached the very edge of the cliff, almost a quarter of a mile north of the sugar house.

Five minutes later August caught up with him. 'What the heck is the matter with you?'

J.C. dropped to his knees, breathless. 'There was someone down there, August' he panted. 'Someone or *something* bad. I never knew it before but I do now.'

His brother snickered. He was always snickering at J.C. 'You really are a jerk,' he said, kneeling on the ground, still holding the leash firmly in his grasp. 'Now, can you stop quaking long enough to get me the lure?'

In the face of his brother's scorn, J.C. forced himself to calm down. He opened the backpack and pulled out a red, felt covered object made out of chicken bones with birds' wings tied on to it. He handed it to August.

August placed it on the ground, reached into his pocket and to J.C.'s shock pulled out the body of a large Barbary dove, setting it on top of the lure. He slipped the hood from Strike's head and the leash off her leg strap.

At once she jumped from his fist and began to pluck the feathers from the dead bird.

'See, Strike?' August said softly. 'I told you I had something special. And after you fly I have another treat.'

'Jeez, August where did you get it?' J.C. whispered. 'You didn't kill it, did you?'

August didn't look up. 'I found it.'

'Where?'

'In the aviary.'

'Is that where you went last night?'

'Strike was getting sick of beef. Besides, it's not good for her never to eat a bird. Birds are her natural food.'

J.C. felt a queer chill. He had seen Strike kill birds before. When they were at school. She could snatch one right out of the air and kill it. And even though he felt sorry for the victims, he knew it was the only way Strike could feed herself. But whenever the boys fed her, they always gave her beef, stolen from the school kitchen when they could manage it, bought at the village butcher shop when they couldn't. And sometimes they would find a dead squirrel in the road and give it to her.

But since they brought Strike home to Cristobel, they'd had no food problems. Amalie made sure they had enough meat to feed her: lean stew beef or chuck or sometimes even round steak. August would add some string or feathers from time to time to help clean out her stomach. So she could cast, which was the same as puke as far as J.C. was concerned.

'Was it dead, August?' he asked. 'When you found it was it dead?'

August looked defensive. 'It was dead, okay? And so what, anyway? So what if it wasn't?'

'What if Marcus caught you?' J.C. didn't want to think that August had actually killed the bird, but worse, he couldn't imagine what Marcus would do if he found out. 'He'd kill you. And then he'd kill Strike.'

'He's not going to catch me.' August snickered. 'And even if he did, he wouldn't kill me.'

'Well, he'd make you get rid of her. Just like he got rid of Gossy.' Gossy had been their mother's falcon. A beautiful blue-black bird with barred wings. Not as beautiful as Strike but bigger. And so fast. Their mother used to take her out on the cliff and send up pigeons for her to catch. J.C. had hated that part of it, but Marcus had hated Gossy because sometimes she would fly high over his aviary and set his birds into a real frenzy. So he got rid of her. Sold her to a man in Canada. At least that's what he said.

August reached out and moved the remains of the dove a few feet.

Unruffled, Strike hopped over and resumed feeding.

'I'd never let him get rid of Strike,' he said, his voice deadly cold.

'Oh yeah? Well, how could you stop him, Mr Big Deal?' August really made J.C. mad sometimes when he acted like such a know-it-all.

August shrugged. 'I don't know.' He looked up at his

brother and he had that weird, mean look on his face that J.C. hated. 'But I'd fix him good.' He reached out and gently eased the lure of what little remained of the dove away from Strike and into a pouch he had taken from his pocket. 'Come on, Strike,' he said. 'Fly time.' He whistled and the huge bird jumped to his arm. He made a quick upward movement and the falcon was off, within minutes soaring to a great height, then making a wide loop out over the open ocean.

The two boys watched the aerial display in awed silence. 'Don't you think she's gone far enough?' J.C. said, finally.

August nodded and began to whistle, a series of short shrill notes, at the same time swinging the lure high above his head.

The peregrine responded at once, circling back, gaining speed as she flew. When she was almost directly overhead, August swung the lure as high as he could. 'Stoop, Strike,' he shouted. 'Stoop.' And tucking her wings close to her sides, the bird dropped straight out of the sky like a meteor falling, striking the lure with talons open, then settling a few yards from where the boys stood.

'Good girl,' August smiled. He reached into his pocket and took something out that J.C. couldn't see. He crossed to where the bird waited, and laid the offering at her feet. At once she began to feed again, first tearing the finch's head off, then stabbing with her beak, plucking the feathers, tossing bits of flesh into the air.

'I suppose you found that one, too,' J.C. said, feeling a sick lump in his stomach.

August didn't answer.

All at once J.C. couldn't wait to get out of there.

He stood up. 'We gotta go. Amalie will freak if we're late.'

'You go ahead and stall her,' August said. 'I want to fly Strike one more time. Then I'll take her back to the cave.'

Normally J.C. would have protested but today he didn't open his mouth. For once, making excuses to Amalie seemed preferable to being with August. Not only because he didn't like what his brother had done to the birds, but for the first time in his life, J.C. did not want to go back to Cane Cave. His favourite place in the world had suddenly become the most dreadful. He wondered how it could have happened. Maybe my friends are right, he thought, shivering. Maybe it really is the place of the living dead. Or maybe something even worse.

7

Stefan knew what he was looking for. Signs of depression. Symptoms of neurosis. Any pre-existing anxiety that might have developed into a full-blown emotional storm.

They decided to work in the small sitting room that adjoined Justine's studio on the second floor. 'It's the repository for some of the bits and pieces of my old life. What little I was able to bring here.' She led the way up the wide staircase, her sandals tapping sharply on the marble floor. 'When I moved to Cristobel,' she said, 'there were some things I couldn't bear to leave behind. My grandmother's writing desk, a chair I bought in a tag sale when I was only seventeen years old.' She opened the door.

The room was small but airy, with tall doors that opened out onto the upper gallery, and it was furnished, as she said, with bits and pieces, but all meshing together somehow to create an atmosphere where Stefan felt very much more comfortable than he had downstairs.

'Let me tell you what little I know about you,' Stefan said. 'Then you can take it from there.' He sat down across from her so he could see her expression as they talked. 'First, you've had a brilliant if somewhat abbreviated career, and you're planning a return to the ballet in September. You married my brother a few months ago, after which you came to live here at Cristobel.' He paused, considering. 'Why?'

'Why what?'

'Why did you two come to live at Cristobel? Didn't it bother you that it was Marcus's ex-wife's family estate?'

'I suppose,' she said, slipping her sandals off, drawing her legs up under her in the chair. 'I know it's a peculiar situation and one I'm not totally comfortable with. Ex-wife's or not, I don't like the place. For all its elegance, it's a very – ' She paused, searching for the right word. ' – a very unfriendly kind of house. But we're here only until Marcus can arrange a sale. Then we'll have enough money to buy a place of our own in New York.'

That piece of information took Stefan completely by surprise. He had assumed that in the interest of his sons, Marcus would never sell Cristobel. Apparently he was wrong. 'Do you have a buyer?'

'Yes. In fact Marcus is meeting with the attorneys in Bridgetown this morning to work out the details.'

Something else she said puzzled him, something that indicated that they didn't have much money, and that didn't make sense. How could his brother possibly be maintaining this place without a massive surplus of cash?

Before he could ask the question, Justine answered it. 'Marcus and I have little income but he is not responsible for taking care of Cristobel. The local courts put all of Caroline's money – at least what they could lay their hands on – into a trust account, to be used solely for the boys' education and for the preservation of this estate. Marcus can't use any of it for his own personal needs.' She smiled. 'But when the place is sold, Marcus says we'll be home free.'

So much for the possibility that Cristobel itself was a problem for Justine. But maybe there was something else. An irrational fear that might indicate an underlying neurosis. 'You said this morning that Cane Cave frightened you.'

She made a face. 'I knew you'd pick up on that. But it really isn't worth discussing.'

'Let me be the judge.'

She threw up her hands in a gesture of surrender. 'You're the boss. What do you want to know?'

'Why were you frightened?'

'I don't know. I was jittery.' She tipped her head to one side, considering. 'I felt – I felt like something was *stirring*.' She wrinkled her nose. Odd choice of a word, stirring. 'That's the only way I can describe it. As if I had just waked the dead.'

He nodded. 'I guess we've all had that experience once or twice in our lives.' He could see nothing abnormal about her uneasiness. Caves were not his favourite places either. Besides, she wasn't faced with living at Cristobel much longer. He changed direction. 'How do you get along with August and J.C.?'

She smiled. 'Have you met them?'

He shook his head.

'Well, let me set your mind at ease. The boys are no trouble to me at all. They've only been home from school for a few weeks, and I really haven't seen much of them. But as far as I can tell they are perfect little gentlemen.' She laughed softly. 'J.C. has his moments. He doesn't know how to walk. He runs. Everywhere. But August is a very well-mannered, well-behaved youngster.' She looked thoughtful. 'Though

65

to tell the truth, I'm amazed that they are both so well-adjusted, having been left to their own devices so early in their lives.'

He waited.

'To have your real father die, to be abandoned by your mother . . .' She stopped mid-sentence and frowned. 'This isn't going to work. I can tell by the look on your face.'

'What isn't?'

Her body stiffened and she stood up, suddenly angry. 'I can see that you're looking for something that isn't there. Poor woman, you're thinking. Stuck here in this steambath of a place, living in the ex-wife's house with the ex-wife's sons. No wonder she's suicidal.' A lock of hair had fallen over her forehead and with an impatient gesture she brushed it away. 'Let me tell you straight out so you don't waste any more of your time. Or mine. Cristobel isn't making me crazy and neither are the boys and neither is my work. I love my husband. I love to dance. I hate the heat. I don't like Amalie. I don't like Cane Cave, but then I didn't like the cellar in my old house either. I'm not unusually nervous. I don't bite my nails or pluck out my hair. I had a happy, normal childhood. I had a dog and two cats. My parents loved me. I never wanted to sleep with my father. When they died, I cried out loud. Now I go and put flowers on their graves whenever I can. Just in case they're watching. I loved them; I like myself. Except . . .' She took a sharp breath and put her hands over her face. '. . . except when I act like an asshole. Which is what I'm doing right now. In fact I've been doing it a lot lately.' She dropped her hands and sank into the chair like a stone. She was breathing hard and all the colour had gone from her face, but

66

in spite of her distress she met his gaze directly. 'Now you know,' she said. 'I *am* nuts.'

Stefan leaned back and whistled softly through his teeth. 'Well,' he said quietly, 'at least we got that much settled.'

'Oh, shit,' she said. All the anger was gone. 'I'm sorry. It's just that . . . it's just that I'm so goddamned scared. I'm desperately trying to convince both of us that I'm normal. But the problem is, I'm not. Normal people don't hear voices that aren't there. Normal people don't try to jump off cliffs.'

He reached over and touched her lightly on the arm. 'No one ever thought that this was going to be easy. It's not. But if it helps to get us on the right track, let me tell you a couple of things. First, I don't believe that every problem is the result of some terrible childhood repression. And second, there are a lot of steps in between what you're calling normal and what you're calling insane. Now, would you like to start all over again?'

She still looked desperate. 'Do you really think you can help me?'

'I do. But first I have to teach you to help yourself. You have to try to let the fear go and concentrate on the facts. Why don't you tell me what happened the night you tried to kill yourself?'

She winced, hearing him say it so matter-of-factly. She narrowed her eyes and looked at him hard, scrutinizing, seeing him really for the first time. He wasn't a terribly handsome man. Not like Marcus. Still there was a strong resemblance. Except around the eyes. Unlike her husband's, Stefan's were a dark, intense blue with tiny lines at the corners that deepened when he smiled. There was a quiet strength in his face, an honesty, and looking at him now, Justine felt an unexpected spark of hope. 'I like you,' she said, surprising herself as much as she surprised him.

'It sounds as if you were expecting not to,' he said, with an easy smile.

'I don't think I really gave it much thought. When you have a toothache, you go to a dentist for relief. You don't really think about whether or not you're going to like him.'

'Have you ever been to a psychiatrist?'

'No.'

'Ever thought you needed one?'

'No more than anyone else. You know. The I-ought-to-see-a-shrink thing when you can't remember where you parked your car.' She frowned. 'But that was before. Trying to kill yourself is a little more serious than forgetting where you parked your car.'

He took out a small notebook and a pen. 'Tell me what happened two nights ago. Step by step.'

She settled back into the chair, speaking easily, tracing her movements from the time she left her bedroom, through the house, and out into the garden.

'Were you afraid?'

She shook her head. 'Not at first. I thought it was my mother's voice I heard.'

'When did you first feel frightened?'

She paused, remembering. 'I think it was when I realized that it wasn't my mother at all. Then I wanted to turn back. But I couldn't.'

'Why not?'

'Because I – ' He saw her tense up. ' – because I couldn't.'

'Do you mean that someone physically kept you from going back to the house?'

68

'No. My legs wouldn't move.'

He nodded, then jotted something down in his notebook. 'Before that, had you been feeling sad? Depressed?'

She shook her head emphatically. 'No, no, that's not it at all.'

He waited.

Still tense, she leaned forward. 'I wasn't depressed. I was terrified.'

'Of what?'

'Of the woman who called to me.'

'Did she threaten you?'

'No.'

'But you were afraid of her.'

She spread her hands in a gesture of helplessness. 'How can I explain it to you when I don't understand it myself? I just knew that I was in the worst trouble of my life.'

Stefan shifted slightly in his chair. What Justine was describing had all the earmarks of a severe anxiety reaction: the fear without reason, deterioration of judgement, panic, loss of physical control. But there seemed to be no pre-existing neurosis. 'Have you ever felt you were in danger before? Ever been badly frightened?'

Small beads of perspiration broke out on her forehead. 'No. Never anything like this. It was – it was sheer unutterable terror.'

'And you remember the entire episode clearly?'

She opened her eyes wide and stared at him. Her gaze was unflinching, her voice firm. 'As clearly as anything that has ever happened to me. Ever.'

Stefan made some more notes. 'Then what?'

'I tried to jump off the cliff.'

'Did you want to die?' Softly.

'No!'

He tapped the end of the pen on the arm of the chair a few times, then said, 'Are you on medication of any kind?'

'No.'

'Ever experimented with drugs?'

'I know where this is going. You think I might have been on some kind of a psychedelic trip.'

'At this point, Justine, I don't think anything,' he said quietly. 'I'm simply asking.'

'Well, I wish it were as easy as that. I wish I could stop all this by flushing some pills down the toilet.' She took a breath. 'Anyway, I don't use drugs. When I was young and far more frivolous than I am now I experimented with marijuana. But that's all.'

'Not even a sleeping pill?'

She shook her head. 'I've always slept like a rock.' She shivered. 'Until recently, that is.'

A sudden flicker of movement just outside diverted his attention. Someone was out on the upper veranda, listening. He stood up and walked to the open door.

'What is it?' Justine asked, frowning.

He stepped out. In both directions the long gallery was deserted. 'That's odd,' he said. 'I was sure that someone was out here.' He turned to find an ashen, trembling Justine standing just behind him.

'Someone was,' she said, staring past him.

'Who was it?'

She shook her head. 'I don't know. I didn't see.'

Stefan took her by the arm and led her back inside. Under his hand he could feel her shivering. Her skin was cold and damp. 'Again I have to ask. Have you any idea why you are so frightened?' he asked.

'It makes no sense,' she whispered, collapsing into the chair.

'Easy, Justine,' he said gently. 'I told you before. You have to try to let the fear go and concentrate on the facts.'

She reached out and grabbed his arm. 'What is happening to me?' She was close to hysteria, half-laughing, half-sobbing. 'I'm so afraid. I didn't see anyone but I know she was there. I know it was the same woman. Oh please, please, tell me what's happening.'

'Someone was outside just now,' Stefan said quietly. 'Someone who frightens you. And if the two of us work together, maybe we can figure out why.'

She was suddenly deadly calm. 'Now can you still say I'm not insane?' And as if she already knew the answer, she squeezed her eyes shut.

Stefan chose his words carefully. 'I think you're suffering. I *know* you're suffering. The question is why.'

Slowly she exhaled and opened her eyes. 'Thank you for that much at least.'

'Why do you dislike Amalie?' The question came out of the blue. He hadn't planned to ask it. At least not now.

'I did say that, didn't I?' Her voice was weary.

'Forget I asked. We can take it up later. Right now I think we ought to take a short break.' He patted her hand. 'You relax. Do whatever you do when you need to unwind. I'm going to take a walk. Get the feel of the place.'

'You're going out to the cliff?'

He nodded.

'Do you want me to come with you?' She made the

71

offer but he knew she was praying that he would say no.

Stefan shook his head. 'Sometime I'll ask you to. But not just yet.' He looked down at his watch. 'We'll meet back here at eleven.'

'I'll be in the studio.'

'You're not supposed to work.'

'Dancing isn't work,' she said with a weak smile. Again the child, whistling in the dark. 'Besides, you told me to do whatever I do to relax.'

He left her then, wondering why he felt so uneasy. Not about Justine. It was far too early in the game for him to make any judgments about her. It was something else. Something about Cristobel itself that unnerved him. Justine had been right. It wasn't a very friendly house. A pricking of my thumbs, he said to himself, then laughed out loud. Next thing you know you'll be the one seeing things.

He went out past the pool and through the gardens. How strange, he thought, that everything seemed so wild, so untouched, and yet in fact had been so deliberately planned. The night flowers were tightly closed, shaded from the sun by a thick, leafy canopy, but there were drifts and drifts of brilliant day blooms filling every inch of space with colour.

The stone walkway ended where the trees began, and he was well on his way up the path towards the ocean when all at once he stopped. So certain was he that Justine had followed him that he turned, smiling. 'I thought I told you you didn't have to come with me.'

His words echoed down the deserted path behind him.

'Justine?' he said.

No reply.

He waited a moment, frowning, then turned and continued up the path, occasionally glancing behind to see if she was following, aware now that he was walking faster, cursing himself for the eerie chill that had begun to spread across his back. As if someone was going to jump him from behind. Maybe you're the one who's nuts, he thought. Still he couldn't shake the feeling that someone was behind him. Ahead he could see the open sky and he knew he was almost to the ocean. He quickened his pace, anxious to be out of the trees and into the sunlight.

And then he was there, standing at the very edge of the cliff. So abruptly did the scene change that it almost made him dizzy. As far as the eye could see, the grey Atlantic stretched, restless, hostile, bearing no resemblance to the calm, turquoise Caribbean that bathed the western side of the island. Not a very inviting prospect, he thought grimly, to jump into that. I could certainly think of better ways to kill myself.

So absorbed was he in his thoughts that he didn't notice the bird until it was almost over his head. It was flying at a fantastic rate of speed, a magnificent hawklike creature with long tapered wings and sharp, curved talons, and it came in so low that for one mind-numbing moment he thought it was going to attack him.

He dropped to his knees and threw his arms up to protect himself.

The falcon swooped down, talons open, feet thrust forward. Just as it was about to strike, it pulled up sharply and flew off to the north, leaving Stefan gasping for breath. The bird had passed so close to his head that Stefan had felt the rush of air from its wings. 'Jesus!' he exclaimed, and watched as the bird flew high along the cliff, then disappeared from view.

'She didn't hit you, did she?'

Stefan turned to see a young boy standing only a few yards away. 'No. But I sure thought she was going to.'

The boy breathed a sigh of relief. 'She does that sometimes. She likes to scare people.' That said, he turned and ran off down the path towards Cristobel.

8

It was nearly ten after eleven, and J.C. ran down the path without looking back. Not only was he already late and Amalie would be in a terrible mood, but he still had to make excuses for August. He would have liked to stop and talk to the man back there, find out who he was. J.C. prayed he was just a dumb old tourist who had found his way to Cristobel by accident. Tourists were always doing that and Marcus was always threatening to get guard dogs.

But what if he wasn't just a dumb old tourist? What if he was someone who knew Marcus? What if he told about Strike? That she almost attacked him up on the cliff?

No problem, J.C. said to himself as he sped along. We can just say it's a wild falcon. That we don't know anything more about it.

But what if he noticed the jesses and bells on her legs? Then he'd know it wasn't a wild falcon.

Then Marcus will hunt her down and kill her.

But he can't kill her if he can't find her.

J.C. was so lost in thought that he never saw Remus until it was almost too late. He froze in the middle of the path, certain he had been seen. Then he clamped his hand over his mouth, and jumped to one side to hide behind a thick clump of lantanas. From there he could see Remus clearly. Just like a mongrel, the black boy was going to the bathroom against the trunk of a wild orange tree.

J.C. hated Remus. He didn't belong at Cristobel. In fact as far as J.C. was concerned, he didn't even belong on the earth. Remus lived over in Christ Church parish, but he came to Cristobel sometimes when his father made deliveries. He was old, at least fifteen, and big. He had the wide shoulders and muscles of a full-grown man, but his head was small and his eyes were glinty black like two pieces of coal.

Remus didn't like J.C. or August any better than they liked him. 'White maggots,' he called them, and J.C. knew that he would have loved to beat them up, or worse. Except for one thing, like a lot of other people, Remus was afraid of Amalie.

J.C. held his breath until Remus finished his business. Then the black boy lowered his head like an old hound dog and loped away through the underbrush. As soon as he was out of sight, J.C. took off. He had almost reached the terrace when he heard someone call from behind. 'Hey! Wait!'

J.C. skidded to a stop, heart in his mouth. For one desperate minute he thought it was Remus. But it wasn't. It was the man on the cliff. He couldn't believe it. The dumb old tourist had actually followed him. His first instinct was to ignore the man and run for cover inside the house, but concern for Strike stopped him. What was more important here? Being a little late, or trying to save their falcon?

In the time it took him to make a decision, the man had come out of the trees and was walking purposefully up towards the terrace.

J.C. narrowed his eyes. The guy didn't seem the least

76

bit hesitant. It was as if he knew exactly where he was going. J.C.'s heart began to beat faster. This man wasn't a tourist at all.

The man came right up to him and held out his hand. 'You must be one of Marcus's boys,' he said, smiling.

J.C. groaned silently. All was lost. He took the hand and shook it. 'I'm Jean-Claude,' he said. 'But most everyone calls me J.C.'

'Hi, J.C., I'm your Uncle Stefan.'

J.C. couldn't believe the rotten luck. Not only wasn't the man a tourist, he was their goddamn uncle.

'You seem to be in quite a hurry.'

J.C. nodded. 'We were supposed to be back for our French lesson at eleven.'

'Looks like you're late.'

Nod.

'Are you going to be in trouble?'

'Yes, sir.'

At that moment Amalie appeared on the corner of the veranda. 'Jean-Claude.' Her face was smooth, unsmiling, her voice level, and J.C. knew that she was very, very angry. 'What time is it?'

'After eleven,' he said, looking down at his feet.

'It isn't his fault, Amalie,' Stefan said. 'I got into a bit of trouble up on the cliff and he stopped to help.'

J.C.'s eyes opened wide and he looked over at Stefan with a spark of hope. If this uncle of theirs was willing to try to help him out of a jam with Amalie, maybe things weren't so bad after all. Maybe if they had a chance to talk to him before he told Marcus about Strike . . .

'Jean-Claude,' Amalie said very quietly. 'Where is your brother?'

'He's . . . he's . . .' The story he was supposed to tell

77

was that Strike had flown off and wouldn't come back and August had to go and look for her. But with his uncle standing right there he couldn't say a thing.

'Never mind,' she said. 'Please get washed and go to the reading room.'

J.C. ran into the house without looking back, grateful to escape, at least for the moment. He prayed that by the time he was cleaned up and ready for his lesson, August would be back. Then August could deal with Amalie. He was so much better at lying than J.C. was. Besides Amalie was never as hard on August because he had The Gift.

On the way up the stairs, J.C. suddenly remembered something that Amalie had said that awful day at the Place of the Monkeys. Something about asking God or whoever to keep them safe from the strangers who had come to Cristobel. Their father's new wife. And his brother. J.C. felt the sick lump come back into his stomach. Maybe their uncle wasn't to be trusted after all. Maybe before they did anything they should talk it over with Amalie, even if she was mad at them.

It was cool in the studio and Justine lowered herself to the floor and began her warm-ups, going through the motions effortlessly, her body responding automatically. Normally her exercises relaxed her, but not this morning. After only a few minutes, she stopped. She stood up and looked at herself in the mirror. What she saw was an average-looking young woman with brown hair and freckles that made her look too young and circles under her eyes that made her look too old. How odd, she thought, that I still look like me when I feel so different. She reached up and touched the purple smudges under her eyes, gently at first, then hard, as if with enough pressure she could erase them. 'That's what I want to do. I want to erase everything.' She felt the prickles of fear begin to creep up the back of her neck. She remembered Stefan's words. 'You have to try to let the fear go and concentrate on the facts.'

'Okay, okay,' she said to her reflection. She crossed to the record player and pushed a button, then changed her mind and pushed another. Prokofiev was her favourite. Prokofiev calmed her, encouraged her to do what she loved most.

For the first half hour she warmed up, then she began to trace the dance patterns on the floor, patterns she had long ago committed to memory. Now and then she paused, not satisfied with herself, and began again. But for the most part she flowed with the music, pushing back her fear, concentrating on every movement, watching herself in the mirror to catch the slightest flaw.

After one particularly difficult passage she stopped. 'Good work,' she said, then stepped across the room and began again.

Her sense of time and place began to fade. She was happy. She felt safe. And she imagined herself far away from Cristobel. She was on stage, performing with the entire company. She had made her comeback and she had been brilliant.

So real was the fantasy that when she first saw the figure in the mirror, dancing right behind her, she was only faintly surprised. But within the instant, surprise became disbelief and disbelief became terror.

She whirled around and saw . . .

Nothing.

The room behind her was empty.

She had never experienced anything before to prepare her for the terror that gripped her now. Deep in her throat she felt the scream begin. Her mouth opened, but the only sound that came out was a kind of sick whimper. Stefan's words echoed again in her brain. 'Let the fear go and concentrate on the facts.'

Gathering every ounce of strength, slowly she turned back towards the mirror. She knew that the room behind her was empty, but in the depths of the glass, the woman in white danced on.

'Help me,' Justine whispered, sinking to her knees. 'Dear God, someone please help me.'

It was eleven-fifteen and Stefan climbed the stairs to the second floor, aware that J.C. wasn't the only one who was late. He had told Justine eleven, but he was sure she wouldn't mind having time for the extra practice. He had left Amalie outside on the veranda, and yet for some weird reason he felt as if she were still watching him from somewhere, her eyes cold, forbidding.

After J.C. had fled into the house, Stefan had talked to the woman for only a minute, hoping to help get the boy off the hook. She had listened politely but without interest, as if she knew that he was lying, as if she knew that he had nothing whatever to do with J.C. being late.

Strange lady, he thought as he headed down the hallway. Mighty strange. He decided that his first task was to find out why Justine didn't like Amalie.

He stopped outside the studio door and hesitated for a minute, listening. He could hear music. He knocked lightly, then opened the door.

Justine was huddled in the middle of the floor, her knees drawn up to her chest, her arms tight around them, hugging herself. She was whispering the same thing over and over. 'I'm crazy. I'm crazy. I'm crazy.'

Stefan crossed the room and knelt beside her.

She lifted her head and looked at him, her expression one of absolute hopelessness. 'It's no use,' she said dully. 'I am insane.' In the same vacant tone she told him that she had seen a woman in the mirror. A woman who wasn't in the room.

He didn't question her. This was clearly not the time. He lifted her to her feet, took her to her bedroom and gave her a mild sedative. Just before she fell asleep he heard her whisper, 'Now I know what happened to Leah.'

Stefan stood watching her for a moment, thinking how young she looked, how defenceless, and a curious sadness tightened his throat. Here she was, ready to try a comeback after many months of gruelling labour, and now it might all be for nothing. Recovery from severe emotional trauma could take years. In the worst scenario, Justine might never be able to dance professionally again. No. The worst scenario was even more tragic than that.

He didn't know exactly what he expected to find, but he decided to take another look in her studio. The room was empty, the doors and windows to the upper gallery all closed tight against the midday heat, the blinds only partially open. The air was cool, the light soft, diffused. The farthest thing from a threatening environment, Stefan thought.

He walked along one side and ran his hand along the *barre*. He checked the record player. He looked in all the mirrors but the only thing he saw reflected was his own image. Exactly what he had expected. Still, he couldn't help feeling uneasy. He could well imagine Justine's terror. There was something about the mirrors that was unnerving. As if someone really might be there. Behind the glass. Watching. Waiting. He felt a faint tingling at the base of his spine. You ass, he said to himself, giving himself a mental kick.

He wondered how Marcus was going to react to all of this. Not well, he imagined. He walked to the window to see if his brother's car was back and it was then that he saw it. On the parquet floor, something shiny wet, dark amber. A streak of liquid, almost as if someone had dragged a mop in front of the doors leading out to the gallery. He bent down and touched the liquid with his finger. He sniffed. The odour was unmistakable. It was the pungent smell of rum.

9

J.C. sat on the edge of a chair in the reading room, inspecting a blister on the sole of his foot. It hadn't broken yet and he wondered if he had time to stick it with a pin before Amalie came in.

'Psst. Jean-Claude.'

He jerked his head up, and through the open door he saw Clyde, one of the gardener's sons. J.C. liked Clyde. He and Best and Clyde used to go fishing together, at least they did before Best got scared away from Cristobel.

'Want to see a python?' Clyde whispered, stepping up onto the edge of the veranda.

'No such thing as pythons on Barbados,' J.C. said, chuckling. He walked to the door, and it was then that he saw Remus, leaning against the trunk of a palm tree. His mouth went dry.

'Is too,' Clyde said. 'Remus found one. And he's going to kill it and plant an Angel's Trumpet seed in its head and bury it in the swamp and when it grows big, he's going to make a belt out of it.' He dropped his voice to a whisper. 'And that's going to give him the power to kill the *bocor*.'

'What's a *bocor*?'

'A witch.'

J.C. kept one eye on Remus. 'No such thing as

witches either,' he said with a bravado he didn't feel.

Clyde looked around nervously. 'Yes, there is, Jean-Claude. Yes, there is.'

'You want to see my snake, little puss, or are you too 'fraid?' Remus taunted, showing a whole mouthful of white teeth. Shark teeth, J.C. thought.

J.C. shook his head. 'Even if I believed you, which I don't, I'm not afraid of any old stupid python.' He knew he was lying. He knew that if he ever encountered such a creature, a serpent so big it could swallow a whole cow, he would run as fast as his legs would carry him – that is, if he could move at all. He wasn't sure which terrified him more. Ghosts, Amalie's *loa* or huge slithering snakes.

In slow motion Remus straightened up. 'You'll surely be 'fraid when my Angel's Trumpet grows tall and I come to get the *bocor*.'

'You can't scare me, you big jerk,' J.C. said. 'You don't know anything about anything.'

'Maybe little Jean-Claude will change his mind,' Remus said. 'Maybe very soon.' The tone was soft but there was something menacing in it. Still smiling, Remus took a few steps towards the veranda, then stopped abruptly, his small eyes narrowing. He reminded J.C. of Gravel, the dog that guarded Papa Daynell's lumberyard. Gravel was mean to the bone, not afraid of anything. Except when the old man came around the corner with a rope in his hand. Then Gravel looked just like Remus did now. Still mean enough to chew glass, but not certain he dared to.

And then from behind, J.C. heard a voice. Deadly quiet. Glacier cold. 'Perhaps you didn't take me seriously on your last visit to Cristobel, Monsieur Remus.'

J.C. turned to see Amalie standing just inside the doorway, her face cool, expressionless, and J.C. couldn't help but shiver. He had heard Amalie use that tone before, with the servants and sometimes even with Marcus. It wasn't loud or even angry but for some reason it scared the hell out of J.C. And he knew that it scared Remus too, because the older boy had stopped moving towards the veranda. He threw Amalie a vicious look, and for one breathless minute J.C. thought he was actually going to challenge her. Then, eyes narrowed to slits, he hunched his shoulders and backed away into the shadow of the trees.

As for Clyde, when he heard Amalie's voice, his eyes went round as saucers and he looked as if Remus' python was right there in front of him.

'Clyde,' she said, 'I believe your mother is looking for you. To shell the peas for dinner.'

Clyde didn't waste a minute. Without a backward glance he disappeared around the corner of the house, almost knocking August over as he went.

August came up onto the veranda and through the open door into the reading room, throwing his brother a sour look as he passed. 'I'm sorry, Amalie,' he said, breathing hard, 'but something spooked Strike and she wouldn't come when I called.'

Half truth, half lie, J.C. thought. He's so cool. He doesn't even look guilty or shuffle his feet.

Amalie touched August lightly on the shoulder. 'There is much to be learned, August,' she said quietly. 'And very little time. Certainly no time for lying.'

J.C. couldn't see his brother's face but he knew the expression by heart: the blank, innocent stare that said he couldn't imagine what she meant, and the slight flush of resentment across his cheekbones that she should dare lecture him. And something suddenly occurred to J.C. that he had never really thought of before. August was the only person he knew – besides their mother, of course – who wasn't afraid of Amalie.

'Well now,' she said, picking up her lesson book. 'Shall we begin?'

'Tomorrow, *mon petit*,' Amalie said, closing her book, 'you may have the afternoon off. August and I have some things we must do. We must go to the Place of the Monkeys.'

J.C. couldn't believe his ears. They had never left him behind before, and in spite of his fear of the place, his sense of relief was smothered by a sudden feeling of abandonment.

'We're going to the Place of the Monkeys,' August said, putting his books back on the shelf, 'and you can't come.'

Amalie crossed to J.C.'s side and lifted his chin with one long tapered finger. 'I know it frightens you,' she said gently.

'It does not,' he said, feeling the hot tears sting his eyes.

Amalie turned away. 'Too much is happening at Cristobel,' she said almost to herself. 'And there is no time left. Something must be done.'

J.C. wiped his nose on his sleeve. 'Is it because Uncle Stefan came here? Is he bad?'

'He is an annoyance. Nothing more.'

'He saw Strike.'

August glared. 'He did not.'

'Did so.'

'Did not. I would have seen him.'

'Well, he did all the same.'

Amalie raised a hand to silence them. 'Where did Doctor Leyland see the falcon?'

'On the cliff,' J.C. said. 'Strike tried to dive-bomb him.'

August's anger changed to amusement, but Amalie frowned. 'That means you will have to take the bird away from Cristobel if you want to save her.'

'I won't take her away,' August said, his face tight.

'Do you think he'll tell Marcus?' J.C. asked.

'He has no reason not to,' Amalie said.

J.C. jumped up from his chair, knocking his books to the floor. 'Maybe if I ask him . . .'

'You'll ask him nothing,' Amalie said sharply. 'He is not part of us.' She folded her arms across her chest. 'We belong here. This was your grandfather's home. And your mother's. And now it is yours and there is only one way that it can remain so. Your mother must come home.'

August looked sullen. 'She won't. You know she won't.'

'She will,' Amalie said quietly.

'Next time she calls, you talk to her, Amalie,' J.C. said. 'She'll come if you tell her to.'

'Bull,' August said under his breath.

Amalie reached up and touched her pendant. 'It won't be necessary for me to tell our Caroline anything. The *loa* will do it for me. In the meantime, we'll take the bird to Bathsheba. Lebon will take care of her.'

J.C. knew that Lebon was the only person on the island who Amalie trusted. He was a very old black man who the natives said had come from Haiti hundreds of years ago. But strangely enough, he was still alive.

August narrowed his eyes and his face stiffened the way it did whenever he was really upset. 'I'm not taking Strike anywhere.'

'Marcus or no Marcus, the bird cannot stay in Cane Cave, August,' Amalie said calmly. It always amazed J.C. that she was so tolerant of his brother's moods. 'It's too damp. You know that.'

'I know,' he muttered. 'So I'll move her. But don't think I'm doing it because I'm afraid of Marcus.'

'Then it's settled. We'll go to Bathsheba tomorrow. The Place of the Monkeys will have to wait.' She turned to J.C. 'And you, *mon petit*, can come to see Lebon with us.'

For a minute J.C. felt happy. Then he remembered he'd have to go to the cave first. 'Is it haunted? The cave, I mean? Are there spirits there? Or . . . or ghosts?' He fastened his eyes on Amalie's face.

Her expression never changed. 'Why do you speak such nonsense?'

'Because all the natives say so. And besides,' he added reluctantly, 'someone was in there this morning. Someone bad.'

'You're such a jerk,' August said.

Amalie ignored him. 'The people on this island are full of superstitions,' she said to J.C., her voice tinged with scorn. 'They know nothing. They are *nigauds*.'

J.C. knew what *nigauds* meant. He had looked it up in a French dictionary once. It meant simpleton. But he didn't think that's what Amalie meant when she used it. 'Well, I know one thing for sure. Remus is a *nigaud*,' he said. 'He told Clyde that he caught a python, and he's going to use it to kill a *bocor*.'

August convulsed into laughter. 'A *bocor*? That cretin doesn't even know how to spell the word.'

J.C.'s eyes widened. He had thought Remus had made the word up. 'Do you know what it means?'

'Of course. It means witch.'

'Well anyway,' J.C. continued, 'he said he's going to plant an Angel's Trumpet seed in the python's head. And when it grows big, somehow he'll have the power to kill the *bocor*.'

'Monsieur Remus is courting disaster,' Amalie said quietly. 'He had better be careful or he might wake one day to find that he cannot open his mouth wide enough to eat, let alone ramble on about pythons and *bocors*.' She crossed to the door. 'You boys are to join Marcus for lunch in the conservatory at one o'clock. He's going to introduce you to his brother.'

'What should I say if he asks about Strike?' J.C. said.

'Nothing. As far as you are concerned, the falcon does not exist.'

'But – '

She silenced him with a look.

J.C. was the first to arrive at the conservatory. August was taking his own sweet time getting cleaned up, but J.C. knew that even though Marcus wasn't back from Bridgetown yet, there would be hell to pay if either of them were late for lunch. He made his way through the maze of potted plants to the far end of the room where the table had been set for lunch. Next to eating by the pool, J.C. liked eating here in this green paradise the best.

He walked around the table, trying each of the chairs, finally picking the one nearest the terrace. Farthest away from where he knew Marcus would be sitting.

'Guess we're the only ones who are hungry.'

J.C. looked around to see his uncle standing in the doorway.

'Guess so.'

Stefan came and sat next to him. 'How'd you make out with Amalie?'

'Okay, I guess.'

'She wasn't mad?'

J.C. shook his head.

'That's good.'

Silence.

'So. Is it your bird?' Stefan asked.

J.C. looked down and pretended to inspect a bug bite on his leg. Amalie's words echoed in his head. *As far as you are concerned, the falcon does not exist.* But how could he deny knowing about it when he saw Strike dive-bomb? When like a dummy he stopped and asked if his uncle was all right?

'Does it belong to someone around here? Because if it does, I, for one, want to be prepared if I see it again.'

J.C. shrugged. He didn't know what else to do. He wished August would hurry up. Why the hell wasn't he ever around when he was needed? He racked his brain to think of something to talk about besides Strike. 'So,' he said, straightening up in his chair, 'how long are you here for? At Cristobel, I mean.'

'Not long. Just a few days.'

J.C. suddenly realized what an odd situation this was. 'I didn't know until a couple of days ago that my father even *had* a brother.'

Stefan smiled. 'I'm not surprised.'

'He has never talked about you.'

'I'm sure not.'

J.C. glanced at Stefan out of the corner of his eye. 'How come? Doesn't he like you?'

'Let's just say our lives have taken us in different directions.'

He said it pleasantly enough but there was something in his tone that gave J.C. an idea. Maybe his uncle and his father really didn't like each other very much. Maybe, in spite of what Amalie said, he should level with his uncle. After all, what was there to lose? He took a breath. 'My father doesn't like you, does he?' he said straight out.

Stefan folded his hands on the table. 'No. I don't suppose he does.'

'Then why are you here?'

'Because Justine isn't well and I'm a doctor.'

J.C. raised his eyebrows. 'What's wrong with her?'

'I'm not sure.'

'Well, I hope it's not serious. Justine's okay, and my father is much nicer when she's around.' He leaned his chin on his hand. 'What do you think about secrets?'

'Good secrets or bad?'

'I guess it depends. Some people might think it was bad. But other people think it's good.'

'Who thinks it's good?'

'Me. And August.'

'And who thinks it's bad? Amalie?'

J.C. broke into a grin. 'Oh, no. Not Amalie.'

'Does she know about it?'

J.C. nodded.

'And you trust her not to tell anyone?'

J.C.'s eyes widened. 'Of course we do. Amalie is our nurse.' He paused. 'Well, at least she used to be when we were young. Now I guess she's more like a governess or something. But she's really part of our family.'

91

'And she knows your secret?'

J.C. nodded. 'Do you want to know it?'

'If you want to tell me.'

J.C. dropped his voice to a conspiratorial level. 'Marcus would kill us if he knew.' He met his uncle's steady gaze, had a momentary second thought, then took a deep breath and plunged on. 'Strike – that's her name. The bird on the cliff – she's our falcon. Well, actually she's August's. But Marcus doesn't know we have her. He hates falcons because they spook his birds, but we don't let her go near the aviary so he doesn't have anything to worry about, even if he knew. But he doesn't.'

Stefan nodded. 'I see. So you'd rather I didn't mention seeing her.'

'That's it exactly.' J.C. waited for the reaction.

'What's it worth to you?' Stefan said finally.

J.C.'s head jerked up, then seeing his uncle's expression, he laughed. 'I've got seven dollars saved and August has sixteen. You can have it all.'

'I'll think about it. But at least for now, your secret is safe with me.'

At that moment August came through the door. J.C. shot him a triumphant look, a look that was ignored by his brother. He crossed the tiled floor to Stefan's side and held out his hand. 'I'm August,' he said in the phony, grown-up voice that J.C. hated. 'You must be Doctor Leyland. Marcus said to tell you that he won't be joining us for lunch so we're to go ahead.' He sat down. 'Or would you prefer to eat alone?'

'Not at all,' Stefan said, smiling. 'This will give me a chance to get to know you a little. And since your father isn't available, perhaps after lunch you'll show me around.'

'Have you seen the aviary?' J.C. asked.

'No.'

'It's neat. We'll go there first.'

One of the servants appeared with a tray of fruit and sandwiches, and J.C. helped himself to a slice of melon and some cherries. His favourite. He popped one into his mouth, and had just spit the pit into his spoon the way Amalie had taught him, when a slight movement just outside the open door caught his attention. Someone was standing there.

J.C. stared. His first horrified thought was that it was his father, that he had been there all along, listening. He glanced first at August, then at his uncle, but neither of them seemed aware.

Still sure that someone was hiding there, J.C. turned slightly to one side, so he could see more of the terrace outside the conservatory. He shivered as another thought occurred to him. Maybe it wasn't Marcus at all. Maybe it was Remus, sneaking back to beat him up. Or worse, maybe it was the thing from Cane Cave.

A cooling breeze moved through the room, stirring the leaves on the plants, and suddenly J.C. caught a flash of white. His eyes widened. Whoever it was, was wearing a dress. Was it Amalie? And if it was, what the heck was she doing?

No longer frightened, he slipped from his chair and crossed the room to stand near the door just behind a huge ficus tree.

'What are you doing, J.C.?' August asked sharply. 'Did you ask to be excused?'

J.C. ignored him. He still couldn't see who it was. He inched closer.

Close enough almost to see.

And suddenly he froze, filled with the most terrible

certainty that if he *did* see, the sight would be so horrible that he would surely die. His teeth began to chatter, and losing all control, he felt the warm trickle of urine run down his leg. He began to cry, but was still unable to stop himself from moving forward.

At the last moment, at the very brink of death, he felt his uncle grab him by the shoulders, pull him back, keep him from seeing what stood outside the door.

'Must have eaten a bad cherry,' August snickered.

J.C. was so filled with terror that he didn't even hear.

10

Amalie was in the room almost before Stefan got J.C.
back into his chair, and in spite of the uneasiness he
felt when she was around, he couldn't help but admire
the way she handled the boy.

She sat beside J.C. and wiped his tears, soothing
him in a soft, hypnotic tone. 'It's all right, *mon petit*.
I'm here.'

'Oh, Amalie, make her go away,' he babbled. 'The
lady in the white dress. Make her go away.'

Gently she took his face between her hands and
stared at him as if she could see into his mind, see
what had frightened him so. 'You have nothing to fear,
Jean-Claude. Do you understand? Nothing.'

J.C. stared back, hiccoughed a few times, then
grew calm.

After several more minutes of reassurance, she pulled
him to his feet. 'Come,' she said. 'We will have lunch,
just you and I, by the pool. And we will reason together
so there will be no more of this nonsense.' She turned to
August. 'You will please entertain Dr Leyland. I'm sure
you are more than able.' Without another word, she led
J.C. from the conservatory, out onto the terrace.

Stefan watched them go, the tall, intimidating black
woman and the small, thin boy, holding tight to her
hand.

'My brother spooks easily,' August said, clearly unconcerned. 'He takes things too seriously.'

Stefan sat back down. 'Like what?'

The boy shrugged. 'Oh, I don't know. Just things.'

'So I take it this has happened before?'

August looked blank. 'I'm not sure what you mean.'

Stefan repeated the question. 'Has this ever happened to J.C. before? Where he's seen something that has frightened him for no apparent reason?' Stefan had just witnessed all the symptoms of a classic panic attack: the perspiring, the trembling, the loss of muscular control, and the irrational, overwhelming terror. But what had induced it? He frowned. Twice now in the same day he had seen two people suffering almost identical symptoms: Justine and Jean-Claude. He found it impossible to believe that there was no connection.

'My brother likes to imagine things,' August said, then smiled. 'Although I must admit, I've never seen him so freaked out. I don't know what he saw but he really put on quite a show. I'd better get someone in here to clean up the mess.' He pointed to the puddle J.C. had made on the floor by the door. He reached over and rang the small silver bell on the sideboard, then helped himself to a croissant. 'Anyway, it's probably because of what Remus said about killing a *bocor*.'

'What?'

August regarded him with an amused look. 'Remus told J.C. that he knows where there's a *bocor*. That's like a sorcerer or a witch. Anyway, he's going to do some mumbo jumbo so he can kill it.' He snickered. 'As if he knew anything at all about *vodoun*. Or ever could, for that matter.' He was about to say

96

something more but just then one of the servants appeared in response to the summons. 'J.C. had an accident, Marie,' August said, very much the master of the house. 'It needs to be cleaned up.' He turned back to Stefan.

'Who's Remus?' Stefan asked.

'He's a Neanderthal who comes around here from time to time with his father.' His voice was full of derision. 'He's so stupid I don't know why anyone would pay attention to anything he said.'

'But J.C. does?'

August nodded.

'Why? Does J.C. like him?'

'Of course not,' August snorted. 'J.C.'s scared stiff of him.'

'And you?' Stefan asked quietly. 'Are you scared stiff of him?'

'No,' the boy replied just as quietly. 'I hate him. Actually I'd like to kill him.' Then slowly, thoughtfully, he picked up his croissant and took a bite.

Stefan was taken aback, not by what August had just said but by the cool, calculating way he said it. He made it sound as if such a thing as killing Remus might actually be in the realm of possibility. He leaned back and looked at the boy with new perspective.

'You ought to try one with mushroom and cheese,' August said, offering the platter of sandwiches. 'They really are quite good.'

Stefan helped himself and they finished the rest of the lunch in semi-silence, he asking questions, August answering in monosyllables. It wasn't until he mentioned the falcon that August showed any animation.

'So J.C. was telling the truth. You did see her.' His flat grey eyes scrutinized Stefan.

'I did. I thought she was going to attack me.'

'Are you going to tell Marcus?'

'No. J.C. already told me about your problem. I don't see any reason to get involved one way or another.'

If he had expected an expression of gratitude from the boy, he didn't get one. August simply shrugged. 'It doesn't make any difference anyway. I still have to take Strike to Lebon tomorrow. It's too damp to keep her where she is.'

'Where's Lebon?'

'It's who.' August wiped his mouth with a napkin and dropped it on the table beside his plate, a clear signal that as far as he was concerned, the luncheon had ended and so had the conversation. He stood up. 'Would you like to see the aviary now?'

'I'd enjoy it very much,' Stefan said. He glanced out across the terrace to the edge of the pool where Amalie and J.C. had been sitting, but they were no longer in sight.

'Follow me then.' August stepped briskly through the open door.

Once outside in the full sun, the heat was suffocating. It amazed Stefan that it could stay so cool inside.

August was already across the terrace, heading around the corner of the house, and Stefan was about to follow when something on the white stone edging the flower beds caught his eye. It was a large splash of something dark amber and sticky looking.

'Are you coming?' August called.

'I'm right behind you,' Stefan answered, then took out his handkerchief and wiped up some of the liquid. He didn't have to smell it to know it was rum.

'Dr Leyland?' August made no attempt to hide his impatience.

Stefan stuck the handkerchief back in his pocket and hurried after his nephew.

August led the way along a winding stone walkway, bordered on both sides by rows of flowering shrubs in huge terracotta pots. They had gone about two hundred yards when the path ended abruptly, and Stefan found himself standing in front of a solid wall of vegetation. Gigantic vines of bougainvillea and trumpet flowers twisted together with other exotic species to form a barrier that was at least thirty feet high.

'It hides the mesh fence,' August said, opening a small gate almost hidden by the lush growth. 'The fence goes all the way around the aviary and across the top. Nothing can get in. Except insects, of course. And nothing can get out.'

Stefan stepped through the bower of vines and found himself standing in a rain forest that could best be described as primeval. Overhead, the sun barely penetrated the thick canopy of leaves, but he could see that the understorey was full of birds. Birds of every colour and description, none of which he could identify. Below, pale clouds of steam rose from a crystal clear pool where more birds splashed, and the surrounding shrubs were alive with them. But the thing that struck him most forcefully was the sound. A fluttering, chirping, twittering, whirring, cawing sound that was so intense it was almost dizzying.

'The pool is only two inches deep at the most, with drains to keep it from ever getting too full,' August said. 'It was made just for the birds. In fact, everything in here was made just for the birds.'

Stefan stood where he was, transfixed. Never had

he seen such a sight. Awesome, and yet at the same time disturbingly nightmarish, surreal.

August gestured for Stefan to follow and they make their way along a gravel path that led to a long, low oriental structure that reminded Stefan of a teahouse. Along one side was an open, flat-tiled pavilion. 'That's to catch the rainwater,' August said. 'It's piped to all the other bird pools in the aviary.'

Stefan looked around. He hadn't noticed before, but now he could see feeders and water containers, some in the trees, some on the ground, all carefully designed to be inconspicuous.

'Come on,' August said.

Inside the building, one wall was lined with huge stainless steel bins filled with seed, and along another stood dozens of covered aquariums, some filled with crickets, others with spiders. In the middle of the floor were several plastic tubs with ventilated lids.

'That's where he cultures the live food,' August said. 'You know. Whiteworms and fruit flies and grindalworms.' He continued across the room and stopped beside a long low refrigerator unit. 'And that's where he keeps the salad.' August pointed.

'The salad?'

'Lettuce, chickweed, fruit. Some birds need it to survive.'

'I didn't know that.'

The boy grinned. 'Neither did Marcus. At first. He learned the hard way. A lot of the birds used to die.'

They crossed to the opposite side of the building and stepped out into a shaded atrium where several smaller cages were hanging. 'This is where the new shipments are kept. The birds have to be quarantined for a while before they can be let out with the others.'

August stopped and peered into one cage with sudden interest. 'Well, well, well,' he said, 'I see he finally got his finches. I wonder how long they'll last this time?' He turned to Stefan. 'Did you ever see a Gouldian finch? These two have yellow heads, which makes them quite unusual.'

Stefan stepped closer. Inside the cage were two magnificent multi-coloured birds with lilac breasts, green wings and yellow bodies.

'The last pair he had lived only about two weeks before they succumbed, so Marcus is experimenting again,' August said, openly amused. 'You should have been here when he brought the first birds in.' He waved an arm. 'Every morning, dead bodies all over the ground. The groundskeepers would gather them up in bags, and Marcus would get furious and call them nasty names. And then he'd send off for a whole new batch of birds. He blamed everyone else, but it was really his own ignorance that was killing them.' He stuck his finger between the bars of one cage, and the startled birds beat their wings frantically. He smiled and pulled his finger out. 'But then he got smart and hired an aviculturist. He learned which species get along together and what kinds of food to feed them. And how to prevent disease. Since then the mortality rate has dropped a lot.'

'I can see why your falcon might make Marcus nervous,' Stefan said, watching a small, silvery dove feeding on the ground nearby.

August's face stiffened. 'She can't get in here.' He shrugged. 'Anyway it doesn't matter because I never let her fly anywhere near the aviary.' He looked at Stefan out of the corner of his eye. 'You haven't changed your mind, have you? About telling Marcus?'

'No.'

The boy shrugged. 'Not that it matters. I still have to take her to Lebon. I just wish I could keep her here.'

'Maybe if you discussed it with your father . . .'

August threw him a withering look. 'You don't know him at all, do you?'

Stefan smiled wryly. 'I know him well enough to realize I never should have even suggested it.'

August shrugged and was about to leave when he noticed a new cage at the far end of the atrium. 'I'll be damned,' he said, and gave a low whistle. 'He finally got the Maximilians.'

Stefan followed him. Inside the cage was a pair of parrots, and as the sun struck their plumage, Stefan was stunned by the seemingly endless variation of dark greens and blues. 'Wow,' he said.

'Wow is hardly the word,' August said. 'Marcus has been waiting for these birds for almost a year.' He looked suddenly on edge. 'Do you want to hang around here by yourself for a while? I have to go.'

'I can find my way back.'

The boy nodded. 'Just be sure you close the gate securely when you leave or there'll be hell to pay.' With that he turned and disappeared up the path.

Stefan watched until he was gone, then turned his attention to a pair of beautiful plum-coloured birds that looked like some kind of parakeet, feeding at a hopper just outside the atrium. No sooner had they flown off when several other birds flew in, equally exotic, equally unidentifiable. Marcus had truly created a fascinating world here, a monumental effort in terms of both time and money. And if what Justine had said was true – that Marcus was in the process

102

of selling Cristobel – Stefan wondered what would become of it all.

He walked down the path and across a small bridge just behind the storage building, and found himself in a small tropical garden where large cages filled with pairs of parrots and cockatoos were hanging. He sat down on a stone bench beside a shallow pool. He needed to think, to try to make some sense of the bizarre things that had been happening here.

First of all, Justine and J.C. had both suffered paralysing panic attacks after seeing a woman in a white dress. Stefan had no doubt that this woman existed. To imagine that they had each conjured up an identical hallucination strained credulity. But why had each of their reactions been so violent? What was the common link? Justine had denied using any kind of drugs and he believed her. She was too bewildered, too terrified about what was happening to her to be deliberately inducing this madness. But that didn't rule out the possibility that some toxic substance could still be responsible. It would explain why J.C. and Justine had freaked out over this woman, whoever she was. He decided to make some phone calls to a few colleagues back in the States, people who were experts in biochemistry. But first he'd run this all by Marcus.

Two small budgerigars in a cage nearby distracted him for a minute with a series of high-pitched whistles. Then all was quiet.

Stefan stretched his legs out in front of him and turned his mind to thoughts of August. The boy was a puzzle, with his cynical smile and his secretive air, as much of an enigma as his brother J.C. was an open book. He found himself wondering how August liked his stepmother.

And that brought him to the final player in the piece – Amalie. Stefan shivered in spite of himself. If ever there was a person who could provoke an anxiety attack just by her presence, it was that lady. He frowned. What, if anything, had she to do with all of this? She's Haitian, he thought, so maybe that's where all the talk about *bocors* and *vodoun* comes from. Maybe she's some kind of voodoo high priestess. And he was unnerved to find that in spite of the absurdity of the notion, he didn't feel like laughing. He decided that it might not be a bad idea to find out all he could about Queen Amalie.

How long he sat and tried to sort it out he wasn't sure, but all at once he realized that most of the birds had left the garden and it had grown strangely quiet. Even the ones in the cages were still. He looked up through the trees. The sun had disappeared behind a huge, threatening cloud, and a strong breeze had come up. He decided to head back before he was caught in a downpour.

He stood up and began to follow the path back to the gate, but after several minutes of brisk walking he realized that he had taken a wrong turn. Yet he didn't remember ever having had a choice.

He continued on. Above the whistle of the wind the crunching of his own footsteps was the only sound. Once or twice he glanced back over his shoulder, half expecting to see someone coming up from behind. It was the same eerie feeling he'd had earlier on the cliff path. 'Ridiculous,' he said. He stopped to take a breath and consider his options. There was no way he could be lost. The aviary couldn't be *that* big. Surely if he just continued in the same direction, eventually he would have to run into the fence.

He listened.

And suddenly, just above the rushing of the wind he thought he heard a whisper. And then the faintest echo of laughter.

He frowned, a vague suspicion forming. Was August playing games? Had the boy run off knowing that Stefan would have a hard time following? Was there something tricky about the way the aviary had been laid out? Like some medieval labyrinth? Had Marcus planned it so that the unsuspecting visitor would become hopelessly lost? It would be exactly the kind of thing that Marcus would find amusing, Stefan thought.

He turned back, and feeling the first heavy drops of rain, he began to run. He'd head back to the storage building and wait for the shower to pass, then try to find his way out. He stopped when he reached the pavilion and stood for a minute, breathless, trying to get his bearings. And all at once he felt a slow, creeping chill steal up his back and across his shoulders, a chill that had nothing to do with the weather. Someone was watching him. He knew it now with absolute certainty.

'All right, August, you've had your fun,' he shouted. 'Now get me the hell out of here.'

The only answer was the steady sound of the rain, pelting down through the trees.

And then beyond – he heard it clearly this time – a woman's laughter.

Already drenched by the downpour, he left the pavilion, forcing his way through a tangle of vines, trying to follow the sound but it was like trying to follow an echo. Elusive. Sometimes to the right, sometimes to the left, and just when he thought he had caught up with her, the sound changed direction, coming from where he had just been.

And all at once he could go no further.

He wiped the rainwater out of his eyes and opened them to find that he was smack up against the mesh fence. He leaned against it, took a deep breath, and listened.

All was quiet.

He began to inch his way along the fence, and after going only a few yards he found himself at the gate. Without a backward glance he opened it and stepped through. Somehow he knew that whoever had been in the aviary with him was gone, and for some reason he felt a strong sense of relief.

The rain had stopped, and just as he reached the edge of the terrace, the sun came out, sending pale clouds of steam into the air.

And then he saw her. A woman dressed in white, hurrying through the trees on the far side of the garden.

'Hey, you!' he shouted, breaking into a run. 'Wait!'

And to his astonishment, she did. Instead of trying to escape, she whirled around and began to run toward him. 'Jesus Christ,' she said, breathless, wiping the rain off her face. 'Is this place in the boondocks or what?'

Stefan stared in disbelief. Before him stood a narrow-hipped, blonde-haired gamine in a white smock, drenched to the skin, carrying a beat-up duffel bag. It was his former sister-in-law. 'Caitlin!' he exclaimed. 'What the hell are you doing here?'

Her eyes widened and she gave a huge sigh of relief. 'Well, I'll be damned. If it isn't the doc. Hi, Doc. Am I glad to see you!'

11

Remembering, she lay still, not daring to move, not daring to open her eyes. She had come awake slowly, at first thinking it was morning, at first thinking everything was fine. But then she remembered the mirror and the reflection she had seen. She began to shudder. She tried to stop herself, to shut off her mind before it was too late. 'You're safe in your own bed,' she whispered. 'You're safe in your own bed.' Oh God, oh God, if only she could make herself believe it.

Desperate to escape the throbbing fear, she sat up. She remembered once when she was very young, sliding fast down Oak Hill on her sled when the crossbar came off in her hands. That was how she felt right now. Out of control with no way to steer. Only now it was worse. Eighty million times worse.

'What time is it?' she said aloud, not really caring to know, but needing to see if she could still speak.

'It's almost four o'clock,' Marcus said, coming into the room. 'I was getting ready to wake you.' He bent down, tipped her chin up with his finger and kissed her softly on the lips. 'You've been asleep for hours.'

She looked up at him and tried to smile but it was a futile effort.

'Jus?' His green eyes were full of concern. 'What's wrong? Has something else happened?'

She didn't want to tell him, didn't want him to know how crazy she really was. She looked down at her hands, pathetic creatures twisting under the sheets. 'Have you seen Stefan?'

He sat down beside her. 'No. I've been busy all afternoon, and I have no idea where he went.' His voice drifted off and for some strange reason he seemed to forget she was there.

'Marcus?'

He didn't answer and suddenly she couldn't bear his closeness. She stood up and began to pace, all at once desperate to see Stefan, feeling that if she didn't, she would lose all control. She tried to keep her voice calm but she only succeeded in sounding angry. 'Where is Stefan? Why isn't he here?'

'Justine, for God's sake,' Marcus said, back with her again, 'what is it?'

The tears came in a flood. 'I saw her again, Marcus. Jesus help me, I saw her.'

'The woman?' He sounded tired.

She nodded.

'Where?'

The horror of it overwhelmed her. 'In the studio,' she whispered. 'She . . . she was in the mirror.'

'In the mirror.' Toneless.

She fought for control. How could she describe this madness to her husband? How could she explain to him that the woman she saw was in the mirror, *but not in the room*. 'I've lost my mind,' she said quietly. 'It's true. I've lost my mind.'

Marcus stood up, his face turned to stone. 'And where, may I ask, is my brother, the brilliant psychiatrist? I brought him here to help you, and instead you're getting worse. And it's all his doing. I always knew he was a fool.'

His anger was cathartic. To her astonishment, watching him, Justine felt a sudden urge to laugh. How could Marcus be so ridiculous? How could he possibly blame Stefan for any of this? 'Marcus, for heaven's sake, surely you don't mean what you're saying.'

He didn't answer. He crossed to the door and threw it open.

Stefan stood just outside, arm raised, about to knock.

'Where the hell have you been?' Marcus demanded.

Startled, Stefan drew back. 'In the aviary. Why? What's wrong?' He threw a quick look at Justine over Marcus's shoulder. 'Nothing else has happened, has it?'

She shook her head.

'What do you mean, nothing else?' Marcus's voice was edged with sarcasm. 'Isn't seeing an imaginary someone in a mirror enough for you?'

Stefan stepped past him into the room. 'Your wife had an anxiety attack,' he said levelly. 'I still don't know why.'

'Do you think you ever will, or did I make a stupid mistake in bringing you here?'

Before Stefan could respond, Justine stood up. 'I trust Stefan,' she said quietly. 'I know he'll help me. I think it's important that we all stay calm.'

For a moment there was absolute silence, and then she began to laugh. 'Now *there's* a joke. Let's all stay calm.'

'Jus . . .' Marcus was beside her in an instant, taking her hands. 'You're shaking.'

'I know,' she said. 'But it's all right. I'm feeling much better. Really.'

Marcus seemed to have forgotten all about Stefan.

He was staring at her with an intensity she had never seen before. 'I love you, Justine. You are the only thing in the world I care about. I know how much you hate it here, but you don't have to put up with it much longer. We're going to leave Cristobel. And then everything will be all right.'

Stefan cleared his throat. 'Excuse me, Marcus. I wonder if I could talk to you for a minute.'

Marcus ignored him.

'I think there's something you should know.'

He didn't turn. 'Well?'

'It's about Caitlin.'

Marcus stiffened, then dropped Justine's hands and looked around at his brother. 'Caitlin? What about Caitlin?'

Stefan cleared his throat again. 'She's here.'

Silence.

'She's here,' Stefan repeated. 'Downstairs.'

'Impossible.'

Stefan shook his head. 'She just arrived.'

Marcus didn't say another word, not to Stefan nor to Justine. He turned abruptly and left the room.

'Caitlin is here?' Justine asked, incredulous. 'At Cristobel?'

'She arrived this afternoon.'

Justine frowned. 'Did Marcus call her, I wonder? Because of me?'

'No. Caitlin told me she had a premonition that Marcus was in trouble, and when she got this assignment in Brazil she decided to stop by on her way.' He smiled. 'Typical Caitlin. When she wants to do something, she does it. Right now she wants to check things out at Cristobel. So here she is.'

'So here she is,' Justine echoed. She felt his eyes on

her but she didn't look at him.

'Does it upset you? Having her here?'

She tipped her head to one side and thought about it. She knew Caitlin and Marcus shared a unique kind of affection for each other in spite of the divorce, but she had never felt threatened. Even while they were married, Justine knew that they had never shared any burning passion. Not like she had with Marcus. Rather their relationship was based on a peculiar kind of trust. A no-questions-asked camaraderie. A mutual understanding. And when they finally divorced, it wasn't for the usual reasons. It was simply because it was time to go their separate ways. There was no cutting, no animosity. They parted best friends, without rancour, without hostility, each agreeing that the institution of marriage had brought nothing to their lives that hadn't been there before. Or after. They didn't need it.

Justine felt a momentary twinge of envy, wondering what it might be like to have that kind of friendship, and she suddenly remembered that Stefan was standing there. 'I'm sorry,' she said softly, 'What did you say?'

'I asked if Caitlin's being here upset you?'

'No,' she said quietly. 'I envy them their friendship, that's all. And maybe she can help him. He's worrying about me. He needs someone he can talk to. He certainly doesn't talk to me.'

Stefan came across the room to sit beside her. He didn't touch her, but for the first time in what seemed to her forever, she felt comforted. 'Are you okay?' he asked.

'I'm okay.'

'Good.'

'It was amazing,' she said, shaking her head. 'Do

you know that when I saw how angry Marcus was with you, I had a terrible urge to laugh?'

Stefan smiled. 'That's a very good sign.'

'It is?'

'You can still see some humour in life.'

'Very little, if you want the truth.' She stood up and crossed to the window. 'And even if I am crazy, I'll be so happy to be away from this place.' She pointed. 'That's where I saw her. Right under that tree.'

Stefan came to stand beside her. 'I want you to try to remember something. Had you had anything to eat or drink just before that?'

She turned and stared at him. 'What are you thinking?'

He didn't mince words. 'That maybe your problems have been chemically induced.'

Her breath came out in a rush. 'But I told you I don't take drugs.'

'I know. But it may have nothing to do with you.'

Her mind felt coated with mud. What was he saying? She shook her head, trying to clear it. 'Oh damn,' she said, 'I don't understand anything any more.' She turned. 'I have to sit down before I fall down.' She went to a chair by the bed and sat down hard. 'Please.' She spread her hands in a helpless gesture of appeal. 'Try to explain this to me in terms that even a moron could understand. Because that's what I feel like.'

Stefan sat down across from her, facing her squarely. 'Is there any way anyone could have heard about what happened to you on the cliff? Or the woman you saw? Did Amalie know? Or either of the boys?'

She shook her head. 'Marcus has been obsessive about keeping it a secret.'

'The woman. Did you see what she was wearing?'

She shivered. 'Some sort of a dress. A white dress.'

'You saw it clearly?'

She nodded. 'Both times.'

He never took his eyes off her face. 'This afternoon in the conservatory, J.C. was badly frightened. No. More than frightened. He was terrified. By someone he said was hiding just outside the door.'

Justine grew pale. She leaned forward, listening now with a sort of desperate attention, as if missing one word would spell disaster.

'He said it was a lady in a white dress.'

Before she could react, he held up a restraining hand. 'Let me explain what this may mean.' He spoke slowly, choosing his words carefully. 'J.C. has had an episode that so closely parallels yours as to be unbelievable. You have both seen what I assume to be an ordinary woman, and yet your reactions to her have been anything but. So I ask myself why. Could you both be suffering from the same psychosis at the same time in the same way? Hardly. And that gives me a legitimate reason to suppose that the cause is not psychological.' He took a breath, then continued. 'Having witnessed J.C.'s episode first hand, I think it might have been chemically induced.'

She was appalled. 'You mean someone has poisoned us?'

He shook his head. 'Not necessarily someone. There could be a toxic element in the environment that both of you have come in contact with. I'm not a biochemist, so I don't know what it might be. An alkaloid of some kind, perhaps. Maybe something atopical. Or something you've both eaten.' He paused, suddenly remembering. 'This morning in your studio. Did you spill anything on the floor?'

'No. Why?'

'Just a thought.' He felt in his pocket. The handkerchief was still there. He knew what he was going to do with it.

She let out a long, tentative breath. 'What you're saying is that there may be some hope I'm not crazy.'

'Right.'

'So. Where do we go from here?'

'We'll have to talk this over with Marcus first. See if he has any objections. Then I want to talk to J.C., find out exactly what happened to him this afternoon. Then we go into Bridgetown for blood tests.'

She felt dazed. The mere thought that someone else might have experienced what she had was overwhelming. 'Can I talk to him? J.C., I mean.'

'Not yet. But after I've spoken to him, perhaps. It all depends on what he tells me. As far as I know, Amalie is the only one who's talked to him since it happened.'

She nodded.

'And while I'm thinking of it, you said this morning that you didn't like Amalie. Why?'

She shrugged. 'I don't know.' She hesitated for a minute. 'Yes, I do. She scares me even more than Cristobel does.' She spread her hands in a helpless gesture. 'But then what doesn't these days?'

'Have you and Marcus ever discussed her?'

'As a matter of fact, Marcus and I had a long talk only a few weeks ago.' She looked wistful, as if she were remembering an ancient pleasure. 'About how happy I'd be if we had a place of our own. And about what to do with Amalie when Cristobel is sold.'

'And?'

'I know the boys count on her for everything, and

114

it's going to be very hard on them when we move.' She made a face. 'But to be perfectly honest, neither Marcus nor I could imagine bringing her with us to New York.'

'I can understand that.'

'To tell the truth, I think Marcus dislikes her even more than I do. But he tolerates her. Mainly because Cristobel is so spacious that he doesn't have much contact with her. She does her job and, to be fair, she does it well. As far as he's concerned, that's reason enough to keep her here.' She frowned. 'But New York is a different story. I can't imagine buying a place of our own only to find Amalie gliding through the halls like some voodoo high priestess.'

Interesting, he thought, how closely her impressions echoed his own, but he said nothing.

She flushed. 'I'm sorry. I have no right to criticize her. She's never done anything to offend me.' She smiled an impish smile. 'Unless, of course, you consider scaring me to death offensive.'

Stefan smiled back. 'I'd say it's fair cause for grievance.'

She leaned back and studied his face, liking more and more what she saw. Stefan made her feel almost normal. For the first time since it all began, she had actually engaged in a conversation without thinking about her fears. And as fragile as it was, he had given her a ray of hope. Maybe, she thought, just maybe, the sled will come to a stop without killing me, even if I can't steer.

Dinner began pleasantly enough. Caitlin joined them and the four ate in the small supper room, a more intimate, far less formidable place than the main dining room.

Justine seemed relaxed, but every once in a while Stefan caught her watching him, the way a small child watches a parent he fears is about to leave for the evening. He wasn't surprised. It was normal for someone dealing with extreme emotional stress to view their doctor as a sort of human security blanket. He smiled at her and she smiled back, and suddenly, for one disturbing moment he found himself wishing that they had met in another time, another place. That he wasn't her doctor, and that she wasn't his brother's wife. He shoved the thought aside almost before it had formed.

As for Caitlin, she was her usual chatterbox self, detailing every minute of the last two weeks of her life, from the moment she decided to come to Barbados right up to the present. Stefan still wasn't sure just why she happened to come to Cristobel. She had babbled something earlier about having had a premonition. But then Caitlin was always having a premonition of one kind or another. One of her many eccentricities was that she considered herself a clairvoyant of sorts.

Marcus, on the other hand, seemed remote, distracted, his mind clearly on other things, which Stefan found odd, considering the fact that the only two women in the world he cared about were sitting at either side of him.

'So, Doc.' Caitlin turned to Stefan, passing a tray of bread as she spoke, 'What brings you to this steamy paradise? Has your brother finally realized what a jewel you are?' She didn't wait for an answer. 'I have to hand it to you, Marc,' she said. 'This is really a palace. An absolute palace. Your descriptions hardly do it justice.' She laughed, a low infectious sound. 'Do you know what he told me? He said it was a cottage. Can you imagine? A cottage.'

'It's all relative, Caitlin,' Marcus said. 'To Baron de Rothschild it *is* a cottage.'

'I suppose so.' She took a sip of wine.

'You never did finish telling me why you're here.' Stefan said. 'The last I heard you were trekking around somewhere in Asia.'

'Oh, that was ages ago. Since then I've been all over the place selling medical equipment. Unlike some people, I do need to work from time to time. Anyway, there I was, having lunch in Cozumel when suddenly I had the strongest premonition that Marcus was in deep trouble. I mean really in the weeds. And you know me. No matter how far away I go, I still worry about him. So I jumped on a plane and here I am.' She looked at Justine. 'But I can see I was wrong. He doesn't need help. He's doing just fine.' She paused. 'Isn't he?'

'I'm doing just fine, Caitlin,' Marcus said. 'I don't know what would make you think otherwise. Except that sometimes you don't think rationally.'

Caitlin was indignant. 'I told you, Marcus. I had a premonition. And you know very well that sometimes my premonitions turn out to have a great deal of merit. Anyway, I can't see that any harm's been done. I'm glad I came. Aren't you?'

Marcus didn't respond.

Caitlin laughed. 'Well, you don't have to say anything. I know you're glad.' She tipped her head back and drained her glass. 'By the way,' she said lightly, 'speaking of caring people, where is the Lady Caroline?'

Marcus didn't look at her. 'You know where she is, Caitlin. She's gone. Hopefully never to return.'

117

Caitlin looked surprised. 'That's odd. I could have sworn I saw her.'

Slowly Marcus looked up.

Stefan glanced over at Justine. She, too, was staring at Caitlin.

'On the way to the house.' Caitlin was aware that she had said something upsetting. She turned to Stefan, looking for help. 'Didn't you see her? Just before I saw you, I thought I saw Caroline drifting through the trees. I did think it was strange at the time because it was pouring with rain. Oh, well,' she said with a shrug, 'it must have been someone else.'

There was a long heavy silence. Then, in a barely audible voice, Justine spoke. 'I know this sounds weird, but what – what was she wearing, the woman you saw?'

Caitlin was clearly aware of the tension. She cleared her throat and looked from Justine to Stefan to Marcus and back. 'What was she wearing?' she repeated. 'Why on earth would anyone care about that?'

'Answer the question, Caitlin,' Stefan said quietly.

'Well, I'm not sure,' she said, frowning. 'Some kind of white dress or something.'

So it's true, Stefan thought to himself. She *is* real.

Marcus put his fork down with a sharp click. 'I'll be damned if I know what all this is about. I'm sure she is some local miscreant who delights in spying on us. To see how the good life is lived. So let's forget about it. Now, who would like more wine? It's a bottle of Cristobel's finest. Just brought down from Cane Cave.'

Cane Cave. Just the words made Justine shiver. What poor devil drew the short straw and ended up fetching the wine from that hellhole? she wondered.

118

12

It was the dream that woke J.C. His mother was holding him in her arms, comforting him because he was so frightened. But it wasn't the fear that made him wake up. It was the surprise, because in his whole life he never remembered his mother doing such a thing.

He rolled over in bed and put the pillow over his head. Amalie had told him not to think about what happened to him today, and he had promised he wouldn't. But it was hard, because he knew that no matter what Amalie said, something bad had come to Cristobel. Something awful, but he couldn't imagine what it might be. Earlier, in the conservatory, it had been right outside the door, waiting. In broad daylight his world had turned into a dark and fearful place. And now, lying helpless in his bed in the middle of the night, he was afraid to move.

He held his breath, listening; he wasn't sure for what. And in spite of what Amalie had said, he couldn't help remembering. Not so much what he saw, but what he *didn't* see.

And all at once he couldn't stand it anymore. He shot out of bed and raced for the door, not caring how much noise he made, knowing only that he had to get to August's room before . . .

Before what he didn't know. Heart thudding, he

pounded down the hall and slammed into his brother's room, closing the door tight behind him. He sagged against it, breathless.

He squinted. Even in the dark he could see that August's bed was empty.

'August?' he whispered, taking a few steps forward. He was feeling much calmer now that he was safe in his brother's room, and it didn't occur to him to be concerned about August's absence. He probably just went to the bathroom. J.C. crossed to the bed and got under the covers, for the first time wondering what he was going to say when August found him there. What excuse could he give? He knew what August's reaction would be. He'd dump all over him. Maybe before he came back, J.C. ought to scram.

But the prospect of going back to his own room was unthinkable. No matter what August said, it couldn't be as bad as that.

How long he waited he wasn't sure. He dozed on and off, in between times wondering where the heck August was.

And then he heard it, and it brought him crashing awake. It was the birds. In the middle of the deep night there was a sudden terrible shrieking of birds. Then silence.

He sat straight up. From his own room he never would have heard the death cries because his room faced the ocean. But August's was on the other side of the house, overlooking the pool. And beyond the pool, the aviary.

August is in the aviary, he thought, horror-stricken. He's killing more birds.

He jumped out of bed and slipped out onto the upper veranda. He sprinted across the wide, open gallery to the stairs. In the face of this new horror he forgot his old fear. How could August do such a thing? He had plenty of food for Strike. There was no excuse. Marcus's birds were helpless, and worse, they had no fear of humans.

The velvet night sky was cloudless and in the moonlight he could see clearly. Ignoring the sharp sting of the gravel on the soles of his feet, he flew down the path to the aviary, opened the gate and slipped through.

Inside it was much blacker. The heavy cover of leaves kept most of the moonlight from filtering through. But it didn't matter. J.C. could find his way through the aviary blindfolded.

He stopped to listen.

Silence.

He left the path and made his way as quietly as he could toward the atrium. If August were going to kill a bird, that would be the obvious place to go, since the birds there were caged. But he changed his mind almost at once. August wouldn't be that stupid. The last thing he would want would be for Marcus to notice that one was missing. He felt a sudden sick lump in his stomach. I'll bet he's after the doves again, he thought. They're so tame they jump right into his hands.

He made a wide circle around the storage building and was almost to the dovecote terraces when he heard a soft rustling in the bushes just ahead. He froze. Was it August?

Silence.

And suddenly he knew he had made a terrible mistake. Why had he come here? What good would it do? Even if he did find August his brother would pay no attention to him.

And then something occurred to him that made the hair stand straight up on the back of his neck. What if August wasn't out here at all? What if it was just a trick by *her* to get J.C. alone? And that thought filled him with such terror that his legs almost gave out.

Holding the tears back, J.C. turned around, heading back through the tangled growth that had now turned hostile, threatening. Growth so thick that *anything* might be hiding there. Don't let her get me, he prayed. Oh, please. Don't let her get me.

And then, to his eternal horror, from behind he heard a whisper. 'Jean-Claude.'

And a hand was on his shoulder.

He shrieked, and with all his strength he jerked away, falling backward into the bushes.

'Oh, shut up, for Christ's sake,' August said.

Trembling, J.C. opened his eyes to see his brother's legs, then his stomach, finally his face.

August was grinning.

'You son of a bitchin' bastard!' J.C. said, scrambling to his feet. 'You dirty son of a bitchin' bastard!'

'Scared you, didn't I? Well, it serves you right, sneaking around here, spying on me.'

J.C. caught his breath. 'I wasn't spying.'

'Well then, what the hell are you doing out here in the middle of the night? Looking for ghosts?' He snickered, then turned away and began to make his way back to the gate.

In spite of his outrage, J.C. followed, staying as close to his brother as he could. 'Well, how 'bout you, August? Why are you out here?'

August didn't stop to answer but he didn't have to. J.C. already knew. And in spite of his relief at being rescued from the dark, he felt sick. Deep-down shivering sick that his brother could be so rotten.

Like two shadows the boys slipped up the stairs and back into August's room.

But J.C. didn't stay. As afraid as he was to be alone, he didn't want to be in the same room with his brother. Or – wherever he had hidden them – the poor dead birds.

Amalie was shaking him. 'Wake up, Jean-Claude. We've much to do today.' She crossed the room and cranked open the shutters. 'It's so close in here. Why were they shut?'

J.C. rolled over and rubbed his eyes. He didn't answer, but he knew who had done it. He had. After he had come back from August's room. To keep *her* out.

'Get dressed and come down to the summer kitchen for breakfast as soon as you're ready. Then we'll be on our way.'

For a minute J.C. was tempted to tell Amalie that he was sick and couldn't go with them, but the thought of staying here alone was even more frightening than the prospect of going to Cane Cave. He sat up on the edge of the bed. 'Are we going to see Lebon?'

'We are. And it's a long walk so wear your sturdy shoes.'

He was left alone then to wash and get dressed. He was just tying his shoes when August appeared in the doorway. 'Done any spying lately?'

J.C. scowled and didn't answer.

August came in. He had the snotty expression on

123

his face that J.C. hated. 'You aren't going to tell Marcus about me being in the aviary, are you?'

J.C. shot him a disgusted look. 'Of course not. But I should. At least I should tell Amalie.'

August smiled his secret smile. 'She already knows.'

J.C. stared. 'You liar. She doesn't know. If she did, you'd really be in trouble.'

'But she does. She's the one who taught me.'

J.C.'s mouth dropped open. 'Taught you? Taught you what?'

'How to kill them. When Amalie does it, they don't even have a chance to squawk. She just reaches out and – ' He made a quick snap with his fingers. ' – *sssssk*. She breaks their necks in half.'

J.C. was speechless. August was a lying pig. It wasn't possible. 'Amalie wouldn't do that,' he finally managed to whisper. 'Why would she do something like that?'

August considered for a minute. Then he said, 'You know the black box?'

J.C. nodded. The black box that looked like a little coffin that Amalie always brought to the Place of the Monkeys.

'She needs to bring a sacrifice. For the *loa*. So she brings one of Marcus's birds. In the box.' He leaned over close to J.C.'s face. 'Sometimes she bites the head off first.'

That was too much for J.C. Outraged, he shoved his brother away. More than anything, he wanted to slap the smile off his stinking face. 'You liar! Amalie would never do that! Never!'

August drew back, and the smile turned to a smirk. 'Oh, really? Well, why don't you just ask her? Then we'll see who's lying.'

J.C. ran to the door and threw it open. 'Boy, August, you really *are* in trouble now, because I'm going to tell what you said, and then Amalie is going to whip your fat ass.' He didn't wait for his brother to answer.

By the time J.C. got to the summer kitchen he had lost some of his nerve but none of his anger. If August was counting on him to chicken out he was badly mistaken. J.C. was still determined to tell Amalie what that shitty brother of his had said. *And* what he had done to the birds.

But one look at Amalie drove all thoughts of telling out of his mind. Amalie was angry. So angry that her eyes were glowing. Like they were on fire. J.C. hadn't seen that look since their mother left.

'Sit,' she said. 'Eat.'

J.C. obeyed instantly, daring to look up from his food only when August came into the room.

'What do you know of this?' Amalie said, taking August by the arm. She opened a cardboard box on the floor by the door.

All colour drained from August's face. 'I . . . I . . .'

She took his face in her hands, her eyes impaling him with such a look that J.C. shivered. 'Well, if not you, August,' she said softly, but oh, so full of menace, 'then who?'

For the first time in years August looked really scared. 'I don't know,' he whispered. 'I would never do anything so stupid. I swear. It wasn't me.' He looked back down into the box. 'Where . . . where did you find them?'

'On my doorstep. Someone left them this morning. After I went upstairs. And that's not all. Come with

125

me.' Ignoring J.C., she and August left the kitchen.

J.C. sat like a stone, the only thing moving, his heart in his chest. He knew what was in the box. He was sure of it. He didn't want to look. But he had to.

He slipped off the chair. *Oh August, how could you? Why?* But with each step he took he became more and more confused. Why would August do something like this? To Amalie of all people. He couldn't believe it. But as Amalie had said, if it wasn't August, then who?

The top of the box had fallen closed. With a shaking hand J.C. leaned over and lifted it.

He looked in, but as prepared as he thought he was, he wasn't ready for what he saw.

Inside the box were Marcus's two prize Maximilians, or rather what was left of them. Their heads were gone, their bodies mutilated, their guts hanging out. Their beautiful blue-green feathers were dull, blood-soaked.

A huge wave of nausea hit J.C. and he felt his breakfast coming back into his throat. He clamped his hand tightly over his mouth. *Oh August. What have you done? Holy shit. August.*

13

On his way down to breakfast Stefan met Caitlin on the stairs. She look tired. For the first time, he could see age in her face, she who had never looked a day older than eighteen.

Just outside the dining room she turned. 'I want to talk to you,' she said in an agitated tone. 'Alone. Before Marcus and Justine come down.'

'What about?'

'As if you didn't know. About Marcus, of course.'

The room was deserted so they went in and sat down at the table. 'What about Marcus?' Stefan said, pouring himself a cup of coffee.

'Something weird is going on with him and you know it. And I want to know what it is.'

'Did you ask him?'

'I did.'

'And what did he say?'

'He said he was under a lot of pressure because of Cristobel.'

Stefan raised an eyebrow. 'Because of Cristobel?'

'Oh, come on, Doc. Don't play dumb with me. I know that you and Marcus are hardly devoted siblings. So if you don't know what's wrong, then why the hell are you here? Paying a social call perhaps? Just happened to be passing Barbados and thought you'd drop in for a chat?'

Stefan took a sip of coffee. 'I know that Marcus is under a lot of strain. I think it's up to him to tell you why. I certainly can't.'

Caitlin's eyes flashed. 'Well, he won't. And that's one reason I know he's in deep shit. Marcus has always told me everything.' She picked up her cup and handed it to him. 'Pour me some of that poison, will you?'

Stefan filled her cup, then handed it back. 'What did Marcus tell you about Cristobel?'

'He said he wanted to sell it. But now he can't. Something about not being able to do anything with it legally as long as the boys are underage. And as usual, Marcus is broke, so without a sale, he can't move to New York.' She frowned. 'I know he's desperate to leave this place. Not for himself, but for her. For Justine. He knows she hates it here. He really loves her, you know. And she's good for him. Not like Caroline.' She made a face. 'Now there's a real bitch. Anyway, he told me Justine hates it here. Not that I blame her. Kind of a nutty situation, living in the ex-wife's ancestral home. I can't say I'd like it much myself.' She threw a nervous glance over her shoulder. 'Besides, for such a gorgeous house it's not very inviting. In fact, now that I think about it, the whole place really gives me the creeps. Ever since I got here, I've had this shivery feeling that someone was watching me.' She looked nervously over her shoulder again. 'Well, anyway,' she said, not waiting for a response, 'Marcus hasn't been himself for a long time. I know that better than anyone. So last night after you went to bed I tried to talk to him. It was like talking to a tree.' She frowned. 'Marcus is more than just preoccupied with some real estate venture gone sour.

He's . . . he's obsessed. It's like he's having some kind of a nervous breakdown.' She had been talking along as if to herself, not expecting any answers from him, but all at once she stopped and raised her eyebrows. 'Is that it? Is that why you're here? Is Marcus sick?'

Stefan reached over and took her hand. 'Relax, Caitlin. That is not why I'm here.'

'Well, why then? Is it Justine? Has this something to do with her? She isn't leaving Marcus over this Cristobel business, is she? Oh God, that *would* kill him.'

Stefan shook his head, hoping she wouldn't pursue that line of questioning, hoping she wouldn't ask any more about Justine. If Marcus wanted her to know, it was his business to tell her. Or Justine's. But certainly not Stefan's.

'Well?' Caitlin pressed.

At that moment, much to his relief, Marcus came into the room, and Stefan didn't have to answer, didn't have to decide what or what not to tell her.

Later, he couldn't help but wonder if it might have made a difference.

Stefan caught Marcus just as he was about to leave for town. 'We have to talk.'

'I haven't the time right now. Can't it wait?'

'No, Marcus, it can't.'

Displeasure showed in his brother's face. He seemed unusually anxious about something. 'My car is waiting.'

'This is important.'

'Then walk along with me. Surely you can talk and walk at the same time.'

Stefan ignored the remark, and together they went

129

along the stone walk and into the shadow of the trees, following the path that led down to the main road. 'J.C. had a panic attack yesterday,' Stefan said. 'In the conservatory while we were having lunch.'

'And?'

'It was almost a replica of Justine's. The same symptoms, the same hysteria, all apparently triggered by the appearance of a woman in a white dress.'

Marcus stopped and turned his feline eyes on his brother. 'I'm perfectly aware of that. I've notified the groundskeepers to be on the lookout for her. If she appears again, she'll be arrested.'

'That's not a solution, Marcus. What we need to know is why Justine and J.C. are so frightened by her.'

There was a moment's silence. 'Do you have a reasonable explanation?'

'Maybe. There may be some chemical intoxication involved here that's causing their distress. An alkaloid perhaps. I don't know.'

Marcus stared. 'Are you saying that someone is poisoning my wife?'

'Not necessarily someone. But it is a possibility. In any case, if some mind-altering substance, some psychoactive agent has been applied to either of them, it would answer a lot of questions.'

'And create a lot of others, don't you think?'

'It might, depending on the kind of intoxicant. It could be entirely accidental. Maybe something they've eaten, or it could be atopical. Something absorbed through the skin.'

Marcus shifted his briefcase from one hand to the other. 'I guess it would be better than insanity,' he said.

'It would. So I'd like to talk to J.C., and then I'd like to take some blood samples from both of them. Justine has already agreed, but I need your okay for J.C. I'd suggest we do it as soon as possible. This afternoon if I can arrange it.'

Marcus's face defrosted a little. 'By all means, take the tests. Can you do it here at Cristobel?'

'I'd rather take the two of them into the hospital in Bridgetown. And then we'll see. The samples will probably have to be flown to New York. Or maybe Johns Hopkins, depending upon what type of testing facility we need. This kind of analysis might require considerable sophistication.'

'Do whatever you have to do. I just want her well again.'

'So do I.'

Marcus gave Stefan a long chilling look. 'My wife, as I'm sure you've noticed, is a very lovely but vulnerable woman. I'm sure I don't need to remind you that your interest should remain strictly professional.'

Stefan was startled. Had that momentary thought last night somehow shown on his face? But then he realized that Marcus was just being his usual horse's ass self. He kept his voice calm, impersonal. 'I like Justine, Marcus. I'd like to help her if I can. You can make whatever you like out of that. And then you can either accept my help, or ask me to leave. It's all the same to me.' He took a step backward, but before he turned away he couldn't help but add, 'I don't think I need to remind *you* that it was you who asked me to come here. Not the other way around.'

Something dark moved beneath the surface of Marcus's pale green eyes, but he said nothing.

'I'll phone the hospital and make the arrangements

131

for the tests,' Stefan said. 'Hopefully they can do them this afternoon. Will you be back in time to go along?'

'I'm not sure. But if not, Jonas will take care of seeing that you have transportation.' Marcus paused. 'Is that all?'

Stefan hesitated. 'One more thing. Have you told Justine that you aren't going to be able to sell Cristobel?'

Marcus's jaw tightened. 'Who told you that?'

'Caitlin.'

'Damn Caitlin.'

'Then I can assume that you haven't told Justine?'

'I saw no reason to upset her.' He stared past Stefan and was silent for a moment. Then he said, 'After all, nothing is certain.'

'Then you have an alternate plan?'

Marcus didn't answer. He simply turned away, and Stefan got the clear impression that he had been dismissed and forgotten. He frowned. Caitlin was right. There was something odd about Marcus. Not that he had ever been very open. But last night and again this morning he had seemed preoccupied, unusually secretive. And for the first time it occurred to Stefan that maybe he had something more on his mind than just Justine.

Marcus was almost out of sight when Stefan suddenly remembered about Amalie. 'Marcus. Wait,' he called. 'There's something else.'

Marcus stopped but he didn't turn. 'For God's sake, Stefan, can't it wait?'

'No, it can't.'

Marcus turned abruptly to face his brother. 'Then get on with it,' he snapped.

'You said that Amalie came from Haiti.'

132

Marcus's voice was light and dry. 'That's right. A gift to Caroline's mother.'

'Do you know that Justine is afraid of her?'

'I do.'

'Is there any justification?'

He smiled. 'Perhaps Justine listens too much to the servants. Besides, everyone is a little afraid of Amalie.'

'Why?'

Stefan had expected Marcus to respond in his usual derisive fashion, but when he answered, there was not a trace of mockery in his voice. 'They say she can change a man into a toad. And that she can turn herself into a fireball. And kill without leaving a trace. And that she can bring people back from the dead.'

Stefan narrowed his eyes. There was something in Marcus's tone that was decidedly disquieting. Almost as if he believed what he had just said.

'Is that what you wanted to know?' Marcus said quietly.

'I'm not sure.'

'There are a lot of things about Amalie that remain a mystery. No one really knows what ancient skills she brought with her when she came to Barbados.' Marcus raised his eyebrows. 'Don't tell me that you are suggesting that she might have had something to do with all of this mess.'

'I'm not suggesting. I'm merely inquiring. At this point I still don't know whether there's any cause for question. We won't know that until we have the blood tests completed.'

'Well, let me tell you something. I don't know much about what goes on in Queen Amalie's private world, but I do know one thing. She would never harm Jean-Claude. Never.'

'Perhaps it was accidental.'

Marcus smiled. 'My dear brother, Amalie never does anything accidentally. If you spend much more time at Cristobel, you'll soon realize that.' He glanced at his watch. 'Now, if you're finished, my car is waiting.'

'Forgive me if I've inconvenienced you,' Stefan said, bowing deep from the waist. Then he turned and headed back up the path toward the house. Marcus hadn't told him much, but he had confirmed one thing. Amalie was probably very knowledgeable about the use of intoxicating alkaloids. But whether she would ever apply them was another question. Marcus said no, but Stefan wasn't so sure. He decided to reserve judgement until he saw the results of the blood tests.

He suddenly remembered the package in his pocket. The one that contained the stained handkerchief. He turned and caught Marcus just as he was getting in the car. 'I need to have you mail something,' Stefan said. He handed him the package.

Marcus took it. 'What is it?'

'Something I found that needs to be analysed.'

Marcus frowned. 'I hope it's worth my trouble.'

'We'll soon find out.'

Stefan was almost back to the house when he saw Amalie crossing the terrace, heading up the path towards the cliff. Several paces behind were the two boys, shuffling along, heads down, as if the weight of the world were on their shoulders. Stefan raised an arm to wave, but they never looked up.

14

J.C. had to hurry to keep up with Amalie. She was taking long, man-sized strides, moving swiftly and in silence.

August wasn't speaking either, but J.C. didn't care. There was nothing he had to say to his brother. Nothing that could possibly describe the sick feeling in his stomach. Ever since he had seen the remains of his father's parrots he'd been in real danger of puking his guts out.

They left the path and headed west until they came to the open cane fields, but half-way up the hill Amalie stopped and lifted her head as if testing the air, the way an animal does when it senses an intruder. Then she pulled her shawl tight across her shoulders and continued on.

August cast a sidelong glance at J.C. 'What's the matter with you?' he growled.

J.C. didn't answer. He just kept stumbling along through the tall grass, not looking to the right or the left, but straight ahead at Amalie's stiff back.

'I suppose you think I did it,' August whispered.

'Well, didn't you?'

'No,' August snarled. 'Why would I do such a stupid thing?'

'I don't know. Maybe because you're just rotten mean.'

'Well, I didn't do it and anyway I don't really care what you think, you dumb shit.'

J.C. looked over at his brother. 'Well, if you didn't do it, who did?'

'I don't know. But whoever did it stole some of Amalie's things.'

'What things?'

For the first time August looked nervous. 'Some of her *gris-gris*.'

J.C. was shocked. Amalie's *gris-gris* were the magic bags that held her herbs and powders. She even kept locks of hair and pieces of bone in them. J.C. knew that the *gris-gris* were very powerful. 'Does Amalie think you stole them?'

'No.'

'How come?'

'Because she doesn't, that's all.'

'I bet you didn't tell her you were in the aviary last night,' J.C. whispered.

'Why should I?'

J.C. didn't answer. They were almost to the old orange grove and he could see the ruins of the sugar house just ahead. He still hadn't decided how to tell Amalie that he didn't want to go down into Cane Cave.

'Amalie found something else in her room,' August said. His scowl was gone but the nervousness in his voice wasn't.

'What?'

'Why should I tell you? You don't believe anything I say.' He lengthened his stride, leaving his brother several paces behind.

J.C. ran to catch up. 'What did she find?' He was asking but he wasn't really sure he wanted to know.

August flashed a nasty look over his shoulder. 'Now

wouldn't you like to know.'

'Never mind, shithead. I don't even care.' J.C. slowed down and let August move ahead. He didn't know why he let his brother bug him. After all, it was August who was in trouble, not him. But if what August had said was true – that Amalie believed him – then he wasn't in trouble either. No one was. At least not until their father found out about the mutilated birds.

J.C. had no more time to consider because they had reached the sugar house, and within seconds Amalie had unlocked the heavy door in the side of the hill and had pulled it open. She turned. 'August, do you have the gear?'

He nodded.

'Then let us waste no time.'

'I'll . . . I'll wait here,' J.C. stammered.

August snickered. 'What's the matter, sissy face? Afraid you'll see a ghost?'

'Silence!' Amalie said sharply. 'We are here to do you a favour, August. I don't want to hear another word from you unless it is to thank us.' She turned to J.C. 'If you wish, *mon petit*, you may stay outside. I believe you could benefit from the fresh air. We won't be long.'

J.C. breathed a sigh of relief. His stomach still ached real bad, but at least he didn't have to go into the cave. He watched as they disappeared down the ramp. Then he sat down cross-legged beside the door to wait.

Nearby, a butterfly hovered over a clump of hibiscus and he watched it flutter from flower to flower. He decided it would be very boring to be a butterfly. And very dangerous. Butterflies had lots of enemies. But then he guessed so did people.

Time passed and his eyelids grew heavy. He was tired. He hadn't slept much last night, and after the horror of seeing what had happened to his father's birds he really felt exhausted. He wondered if August was telling the truth. And if he was, then who had killed the parrots? And what about the other things August had said, about someone stealing some of Amalie's *gris-gris*? And about her finding something else in her room? With all these questions racing around in his head, he lay back in the grass and closed his eyes.

He wasn't sure what made him open them. It wasn't a sound. It was a feeling. A feeling that someone or *something* was watching him. He sat up with a jerk and stared.

Beyond the ruins of the sugarhouse was a huge tulip tree. Amalie called it the Flame of the Forest, and around its trunk lots of small, stunted shrubs struggled to survive. But they were big enough to provide screening so he couldn't see beyond.

He squinted. There seemed to be no movement, but J.C. had a sudden horrible feeling that someone was hiding. Breathing silently. Watching him.

Slowly he got to his feet and backed towards the door in the side of the hill, never taking his eyes off the tulip tree and whatever hid in its shadow. He knew without a doubt that he had to get to Amalie and August if he was to be saved. He had no more fear of the cave. Whatever had frightened him yesterday wasn't in there anymore. It was out here. Watching him.

He took three short steps backwards, then whirled around and was about to bolt through the door when all at once a hand came out of nowhere and closed

138

around his arm. He felt the scream come up in his throat, but it stuck there. He jerked around to find himself staring up into the grinning black face of Remus. 'Let me go!' he gasped, wrenching away, almost falling down.

'You aren't happy to see your good friend Remus?'

'What . . . what're you doing here? You aren't supposed to be here. This is private property.'

The mocking expression in Remus' eyes matched his smile. 'What man strong enough to drive me off? Answer that.'

J.C. drew himself up to his full height. 'My father will.'

Remus laughed out loud, a deep rumbling sound. 'He don't belong here no more than me.'

'Well then, my mother will.'

'Your mother?' Remus' expression changed, became lewd. 'Your mother is a whore. I seen her without any clothes.'

J.C. felt his face burn. 'Liar!'

Remus laughed again. 'She like to swim without her clothes.'

J.C. wanted to hit Remus in the face as hard as he could, but he didn't dare.

'Aren't going to cry, are you, little puss?' Remus stepped closer.

J.C. held his ground. 'You better get out of here. This land belongs to Cristobel.' The black boy was so close to him now that J.C. could smell him. A sour, unpleasant odour. He could feel the tears but he blinked them back hard. No way was he going to cry in front of Remus. He gathered what little was left of his courage. 'If Amalie sees you, you'll really be in trouble.'

The smile faded, but this time the mention of Amalie's name didn't seem to frighten Remus. It only made him look more dangerous. His small black eyes glinted. 'I'm not afraid of no white man's nigger,' he snarled. 'Not no more.'

J.C. gasped. He had never heard anyone call Amalie that word before. Not ever. And the way Remus said he wasn't afraid of her sent shivers up J.C.'s spine. It sounded as if he really meant it. 'You're going to get in big trouble, Remus,' J.C. said, backing away.

Remus smiled, an evil smile and oh, so confident. 'After today, ain't no one going to give Remus Hastings no trouble. And you know why? Because I got the mightiest power of them all. I don't have to wait for the trumpet seed to grow.' He reached into the sack he had tied around his waist.

J.C. stared in horror and disbelief. Held reverently in the black boy's outstretched hands was Amalie's serpent god, the fearsome Lord Damballah, its hideous jaws half-opened, its obsidian eyes glittering in the sunlight.

J.C. shrank back, his heart exploding in his chest. Every nerve in his body told him to run, to get Amalie, but Remus stood between him and the door. And suddenly J.C. felt the burning in his throat and he knew without a doubt that he was going to throw up.

Taking his time, enjoying every minute, the black boy advanced, making small circular movements in the air with the snake's head. 'Think your nigger can save you from this?' Leering, he thrust it forward almost into J.C.'s face.

At that, J.C. lost all control. His breakfast came into his mouth so fast that he didn't have time to choke it back, and in the next instant it shot out of

140

his mouth and with a disgusting splat landed on the ground between the two boys.

Remus stopped in his tracks, his expression one of complete surprise. Then he looked down at his feet and let out a long low howl. 'Fuckin' white pig! You got some on me!'

J.C. saw his chance. Remus was big, but J.C. was quicker. Before Remus could move, he darted past him and through the open door. Without a pause he shot down the ramp into the cave. He could hear Remus' feet pounding behind.

Amalie was standing near the entrance with her back to him, staring out at the ocean, and J.C. flew across the floor of the cave and grabbed her around the legs, almost knocking her over. 'Save me, Amalie!' he gasped.

She turned around. 'Whatever is it, *mon petit*?' But before he could tell her, he felt her stiffen.

Remus had entered the cave. He stopped on the far side of the massive rum kegs, rocking slowly back and forth on the balls of his feet, Damballah's head still cradled in his hands, and for one wild, terrifying moment J.C. thought he was going to attack them. '*Bocor*,' Remus rasped. 'Black witch. I know what you are, and I used to be afraid, like some weak old woman.' He smiled a grotesque smile. 'But now *I* got the power. Your power. And I ain't afraid no more.' His voice grew dark, like a wild animal growling. 'Soon I will know how to use it. Then I will be master, and *you* will be the one who is afraid. You and the two puny white maggots.' Then he turned and disappeared up the ramp.

J.C.'s stomach was throbbing and his mouth tasted awful and now the tears came in a flood. 'He did it,

141

Amalie,' he sobbed. 'Remus killed the birds. And he stole the Lord Damballah. And now he's got your magic *gris-gris*, and he's going to kill us too.'

She bent down and put her arms around him. 'Hush, Jean-Claude. Monsieur Remus is going to do nothing of the kind. This time he has indeed gone too far.'

'But you saw,' he stammered. 'And you heard what he said.'

August stepped out of the shadow, Strike on his arm. 'What's the matter?'

'It wasn't you, August,' J.C. blubbered. 'It was Remus.'

August's face stiffened. 'How do you know?'

'He . . . he has Damballah.' He shuddered.

Amalie took a deep breath and straightened up to her full height. 'I think it is time for Monsieur Remus to learn respect,' she said quietly.

J.C. looked up at her, and all fear left him. He couldn't imagine ever having been afraid of Remus. Amalie was all-powerful. She didn't need her serpent god or her pouches full of herbs and stuff. It was nothing but powder and dust. The real magic was inside Amalie, the indestructible giantess who would protect him forever.

Coming out into the sunlight, J.C. blinked, his eyes adjusting quickly. He knew Remus was gone, but that wasn't who he was looking for. He squinted. The fields and the forest beyond seemed deserted now. Unthreatening. Like Remus, whoever or *whatever* had been there before was gone.

August was right behind him making low whistling noises to Strike.

'Aren't you going to hood her?' J.C. asked.

'Not yet.' He turned to Amalie who had just come through the door and had stopped to slip the padlock on. 'Can I fly her, Amalie? Just once before we take her to Lebon?'

She shook her head. 'We have no time.' She looked up at the sun. 'It is at least a two hour walk.'

August frowned. 'But you know as well as I do that she'll take the trip much better if she's been flown first. And anyway, I have to feed her.'

J.C. shivered, wondering what his brother had in his bag, wondering what Amalie was going to say about it.

'Very well,' she said. 'Go along the bluff. J.C. and I will follow you.'

August started off at a brisk pace through the waist high grass, up across the low hills to the edge of the cliff. J.C. followed closely but Amalie lingered behind, as if checking to make certain no one was following. Once or twice she stopped to make strange marks in the dirt, and J.C. smiled to himself, feeling much better. Amalie was already working her magic. And very soon, Remus Hastings would be sorry he ever heard of the Leylands or Cristobel.

15

Justine paused just outside the studio and wondered if she would be able to go into an empty room ever again without worrying about what might be waiting for her on the other side of the door. No longer did she accept the idea of 'impossible'. For her now, anything might happen. She shuddered. Anything.

Ever since yesterday afternoon when Stefan suggested she might be suffering from some kind of poisoning, she had thought about everything she had eaten, touched, worn, even the soap she had bathed with. She supposed it could even be in the air she was breathing. But the only thing she accomplished was to make herself feel crazier. And now she wanted more than ever to leave this place. To get away from Cristobel. She hoped the sale would be quick but it was only a hope. She hadn't heard any of the details. Last night Marcus hadn't mentioned his meeting at all, and it made her wonder about him. Had he always been so self-absorbed, so tight-lipped? Or had she simply never looked closely enough?

She took a quick breath. In any case the most important thing right now was to have her blood tested, and until then she was determined to keep busy, to practice until she dropped, so that maybe she would forget the terror. At least for a while.

She opened the door and stepped into the studio. The air was cool and she could hear the quiet hum of the air conditioner. She crossed the room – without looking in the mirror – and took out her ballet slippers. 'Come on, Justine,' she muttered out loud. 'Time to stop feeling sorry for yourself. There'll be plenty of time for that later, after you find out whether or not you've been poisoned.'

A voice from behind asked, 'What do you mean "poisoned"?'

Justine whirled around to see Caitlin standing at the window. 'My God, Caitlin,' she said, her heart pounding. She was shocked to find herself so close to the edge for such little cause. 'You startled me.' Wrong, she thought. You scared the shit out of me.

'Sorry. I came up earlier because Marcus said you were going to practise this morning, and I wanted to talk to you. It was so deliciously cool I decided to wait for you.' She threw up her hands apologetically. 'I should have made myself known. Are you okay?'

Justine forced a laugh, trying to recover as quickly as she could. 'I'm just jumpy, that's all.'

'I know what you mean,' Caitlin said, sitting down on the long low bench in front of the windows. 'This place gives me the creeps.'

Justine wasn't sure how to respond so she said nothing.

Caitlin continued. 'I can't help it. Maybe it's because I'm sensitive to things like this, but I feel as if there's someone watching all the time.' She wrinkled her nose. 'To be truthful, I think it's a perfectly dreadful house. I can understand why you'd want to get away from the place as soon as you can.'

'You've been talking to Marcus.' Justine looked

down at the hands in her lap that still held tight to her slippers. For a minute she felt betrayed, wondering just how much her husband had told Caitlin.

'That's why I wanted to talk to you.'

Justine tried to keep her tone light. 'What about?'

'Why, about Marcus, of course.' Justine could feel her eyes, probing, puzzled.

'What has he told you?'

Caitlin sighed. 'Not much. Not much at all.' She paused. 'But I know that Marcus has changed. It's like he's gone away somewhere and I can't find him. And I'd like to know why.'

Slowly Justine put her slippers down on the bench beside her. She turned and looked at Caitlin. In the other woman's eyes, Justine could see nothing but concern. And a deep sadness. As if she had lost something that she feared she would never recover. Justine felt a terrible wave of guilt wash over her. She knew that regardless of whether anything else was bothering Marcus, she was causing him a lot of pain. And Caitlin had a right to know. 'Marcus is worried about me,' she said quietly.

Caitlin nodded. 'I knew it. It's because of Cristobel, isn't it?'

Justine's face went blank. 'Cristobel?'

Caitlin looked away. 'I know how much Marcus wants you to be happy because he told me. And I know how much you hate this place because he told me that too. So naturally this business about not being able to sell it is bugging him.'

Justine forgot everything else. 'What do you mean, he can't sell it?'

'Oh, hell. Didn't he tell you?' Caitlin stood up and began to pace back and forth. 'Why didn't he? My

146

God, he's even worse off than I thought. And now I've really put my foot in it.'

'Caitlin. Sit down.' Justine didn't mean to sound angry but she did. 'Tell me what you're talking about.'

Caitlin sat back down hard. 'His solicitor told Marcus that he can't sell Cristobel while the boys are underage. So since he has no money, you and he can't leave.'

'I see.' Her own words echoed in her ears. *I see.* What the hell did that mean, *I see*? She didn't *see* anything. She didn't understand anything and she felt a sudden desperation out of all proportion to what Caitlin had just told her. They weren't going to leave Cristobel. So what? She felt sick. So everything.

Caitlin put a timid hand on Justine's arm. 'Justine, I'm sorry I blabbed. It's just that I was sure Marcus had told you. Are you okay?'

Justine nodded.

'I'm sure he'll work things out,' Caitlin said brightly. 'He always does, you know. When Marcus wants something, there's nothing he won't do to get it. And in the meantime, pay no attention to me. It really is a beautiful house. I'm weird. Ask anyone. I have a reputation for imagining things. Like my premonitions.' She gave a nervous little laugh. 'Nobody should ever pay any attention to me.'

Justine took a deep breath. 'Don't worry, Caitlin. It doesn't really matter.' And she supposed that in the long run it didn't. What mattered was Stefan wanting her to get her blood tested. And praying that he was right about the poisoning. That there was something she and J.C. had come in contact with that was causing this insanity. Cristobel was the least of her worries. But even as she thought it, she had the most horrible

147

feeling that it wasn't so. That staying at Cristobel was the worst part of all.

'Marcus is going to kill me for telling you,' Caitlin said. 'And so is Stefan.'

'Why are we going to do that?' Stefan asked, coming into the studio.

Caitlin didn't answer. She just made a face.

He crossed the room and stood in front of Justine. 'I thought I'd find you here. We have to talk.'

Caitlin stood up. 'You might just as well know. As usual, I've made a perfect mess of things.'

'No, you haven't,' Justine said. 'I would have found out sooner or later.'

'Found out what?' Stefan asked, knowing already. Marcus had been right. Damn Caitlin.

'Marcus isn't going to be able to sell Cristobel until the boys come of age. So I guess that means we aren't leaving.' Justine's tone was matter of fact, but Stefan knew that underneath the calm exterior, she was badly shaken.

'You don't know that for sure,' he said.

'Yes, I do,' she said flatly. 'If Marcus told Caitlin, it must be so.'

'He'll find a way out,' Caitlin said brightly. 'He's a cat. He always lands on his feet. Right, Doc?'

'He always has before.'

Justine stood up and with that extraordinary fluidity of movement she crossed to the mirror. There she stood, staring silently at her own reflection. Then she turned to Stefan. 'What did you want to talk to me about?'

Caitlin saw her chance to escape and headed for the door. 'I know I made a mess,' she said as she went, 'and Marcus is going to be furious.' At the door, she stopped. 'But I know that something weird is going on here, and I still wish that someone would tell me what it is. If either of you are looking for me, I'll be at the pool.'

After she left, Justine walked back to the bench and sat down. 'Poor Caitlin. I almost told her, you know. She really cares about Marcus. She deserves to know as much as I do.'

'But you didn't tell her about what happened to you?'

She sat rigid. 'No. We got sidetracked when she told me about Cristobel.' He could see she was struggling for control. 'I know my problem has nothing to do with this place. But with every day that passes, I feel more and more frightened here. And I can't help but wonder if it would be the same in New York.' She twisted her hands in her lap. 'But it would be, wouldn't it? I'm only kidding myself to think it would be different. The problem is right here.' She tapped her temple with one long tapered finger. 'It has nothing to do with Cristobel.'

He took her hands. 'It might very well be different away from here, Justine. That's what we're going to find out. We have an appointment in Bridgetown this afternoon at two. For you and J.C. And then we'll know.'

Her smile came slowly, like a child's. It began at her mouth, then spread to her eyes, then lit up her whole face. 'And Marcus has agreed?'

'He has.'

The smile faded. 'I'm setting myself up. The whole idea of poisoning is too bizarre.'

'And the alternative isn't?' he asked quietly.

She was silent for a minute. Then she said, 'What about J.C.? Have you talked to him?'

'No. He's not here. I saw him leave earlier with Amalie and August. But as soon as they get back, I'm going to find out exactly what happened to him yesterday. And then we'll all go into Bridgetown.'

'If I can stand to wait that long,' she said, almost to herself. She took a deep breath, bent over and picked up her slippers. 'So now I'm going to work out. And I'm not going to think about anything else until two o'clock.' And although she didn't know how, somehow she managed to smile.

J.C. couldn't look when August fed Strike. He didn't want to watch. Instead he walked up along the bluff to the point where he could see well past the mouth of Cane Cave. He waited there until he finally saw the falcon flying high out over the ocean. Then he turned and trotted back to the spot where Amalie and August stood watching Strike.

'Will Lebon fly her on days when I can't be there?' August asked.

Amalie shook her head. 'Lebon knows nothing about falconry. But he will give her food and shelter, and you may go to Bathsheba whenever you wish. At least you may once Monsieur Remus has been taken care of. Until then neither of you are to go anywhere alone.'

'I'm not afraid of Remus,' August said.

'Me neither,' J.C. echoed.

'Bull,' August snorted. 'You are too. I saw you holding on to Amalie like a bawling baby.'

'Hush, August,' Amalie said. 'After what the Hastings boy did, J.C. has good cause to be cautious. And if you had an ounce of sense, you would be as well. You are far too intelligent to be speaking as if you were an imbecile.'

August's grey eyes clouded over. 'If you'd let me, I'd fix him for good.' It wasn't a threat. It was a simple statement of fact.

Amalie's expression was impassive, but her black eyes never left August's face. 'You will do nothing. Nothing. Do you understand?'

August started to turn away but she reached out and took his chin firmly in her hand, forcing him to look at her. 'Is it understood, August?'

For a minute the two were locked in some kind of silent battle, and J.C. could feel his brother's anger. Then August pulled away. 'I understand.'

'Very well,' Amalie said. 'Now call the bird. It is time we were on our way.'

August picked up the lure and walked to the edge of the cliff. He threw it high into the air at the same time whistling sharply.

J.C. watched, fascinated as always. He never could figure out whether Strike heard the sound first or saw the lure, but it didn't seem to matter. Within minutes she always came, flying at full speed, sometimes seeming to fall right out of the sky. Today was no different.

The three watched as the falcon responded, at first only a small black speck on the horizon, then clearly recognizable as she swept in high above the tops of the waves.

. August threw the lure again. 'Stoop, Strike!' he yelled.

The falcon was directly over their heads, and about to dive for the lure when all at once she pulled up in mid-air and wheeled off sharply to the north, so

sharply that it was as if she had been jerked by a chain.
She flew rapidly away from the ocean and within seconds she had vanished over the tops of the trees.

August was so astonished that for a minute he just stood motionless, mouth open, staring. Then he grabbed the lure and threw it up again, whistling loudly. Again and again he repeated the ritual but there was no sign of the peregrine.

'What happened?' J.C. said when he finally found his voice. 'Where did she go?'

August was frantic. His face had gone as pale and as grey as his eyes. He turned to Amalie, pleading. 'Why did she go? Why doesn't she come back?' Desperate, he threw the lure into the air as high as he could.

Amalie reached out and took him firmly by the arm. 'Be calm, child,' she said sternly. 'We will have to go to look for her.'

August pulled away. 'She can't survive alone.' His face grew even paler. 'And what if Marcus sees her?' That thought was too much for him. He grabbed his backpack and without another word he ran off through the high grass, back down towards the house.

J.C. touched Amalie lightly on the hand. 'Why did Strike fly off like that? She's never done anything like that before.'

Amalie's voice sounded strange, like she was far away. 'I don't know, *petit*. It was as if someone else called her.'

J.C. frowned. 'But who would do that? Who even knows she's here? Only my uncle, and he doesn't know anything about falcons. You're the only one besides August who knows how to call them.'

Her face was expressionless. 'Time will tell,' she

said. 'Now I am going to take you back to the house. You are to stay there until I return.'

'And where are you going?' J.C. asked, hurrying to keep up with her.

'I must go and help your brother.'

J.C. surely hoped she could.

A shadow passed across the face of the sun. The air turned suddenly chill and the wind picked up, turning the tops of the waves to foam. The shadow that was the falcon moved on, and yet oddly enough it seemed as if there was no return of warmth to the earth.

The peregrine flew above the highest branches of the trees, ignoring the screams of smaller birds below, driven to flight by her passing. Far off in the distance she could still hear the sound of the boy's shrill whistle, but she ignored it, drawn by a force far more powerful. Something that spoke to her most primitive instincts.

She flew at incredible speed and within minutes she had cleared the trees and was out into open country. On a rising current of air she soared high above the canefields, her falcon's eye searching for something on the ground, and in the next instant she found it. But she didn't dive. Wings still spread, slowly she began to circle downward.

At the last minute she thrust her feet forward and, like a feather, settled gently on the arm of the woman in white.

16

Stefan shivered as he stepped out onto the terrace. A creeping sense of foreboding had been with him ever since he left the studio, and as much as he told himself it was nonsense, he couldn't shake the feeling that some terrible nightmare was unfolding at Cristobel, something in which Justine was playing only a bit part.

He ran his fingers through his hair, trying to think logically. Somehow all these pieces had to fit together. But how? What was he missing? The more he thought, the more convinced he was that the blood tests would tell the story.

He looked across the mirrored sapphire of the pool and saw Caitlin asleep on a chaise in the sun. He felt a strong wave of affection wash over him. Caitlin could be such a royal pain in the ass, but there was an honesty about her that made it impossible to stay mad at her for long. He suddenly realized how happy he was that she was here. He decided to wake her, to lay it all out for her review, everything that had happened, and see what she could make of it.

He was halfway around the pool when all at once he saw Amalie. As usual she was dressed in regal crimson, and as she stepped from the shadow of the trees, the gold pendant around her neck glittered in the sun. J.C. followed a few steps behind.

She greeted Stefan in her impeccably polite but unnerving fashion, then turned to J.C. 'You stay here with your uncle until I return,' she said.

Stefan watched as she moved away, her back straight, her head held high on the long slender neck. Every inch the queen, Stefan thought. But queen of what? 'Queen of spooks,' he answered under his breath.

J.C. sat down on the slate and took off his shoes and socks. Then he crawled to the edge of the pool and dangled his feet in the water.

'Looks like a great idea,' Stefan said. 'Mind if I join you?'

J.C. shook his head.

The water was cold, but it felt good on his bare feet. 'Been out for a walk?' he asked.

'We went to get Strike. To take her to Lebon.'

Stefan nodded, remembering that August had told him about it yesterday. 'So now she's safe?'

J.C. was clearly upset. 'She flew away. And now August is really scared that something will happen to her.'

'Has she ever done that before?'

'No. She always comes when August whistles. Always.'

'Maybe something scared her.'

J.C. looked over, startled. He hadn't thought of that before. Maybe his uncle had stumbled onto something without even knowing. Maybe *she* scared Strike. He shivered. If that were true, then Strike was gone forever. The falcon would never come back if she had been as scared as J.C. was.

'You were pretty scared yesterday,' Stefan said, seeming to read his thoughts.

J.C. looked down into the water. He really didn't want to talk about yesterday. He was trying hard to forget.

'Can you tell me what happened? Maybe I can help.'

J.C. felt uneasy. He wished his uncle would go away. 'It was just my imagination,' he said. 'Amalie said so.'

'Do you think that was all it was?'

J.C. looked at Stefan out of the corner of his eye. 'How come you're asking? Amalie said I should forget about it.'

His uncle's voice was very quiet and very serious. 'But you're still scared.'

Miserable, unable to deny it, J.C. nodded.

Stefan pulled his feet out of the water. 'J.C., I'd like you to come upstairs with me. To see Justine.'

J.C. was thrown off balance by the sudden change in direction. 'Justine? How come Justine?'

Stefan put his hand on the boy's shoulder. 'Because Justine has seen her too. The lady in the white dress.'

J.C. jerked his head around and stared at Stefan.

'That's why I came to Cristobel. I'm a psychiatrist and my job is to help people who are troubled. Something or someone scared Justine so much that it made her sick. And I'm trying to help her get better.'

'Then it's true,' J.C. whispered, his face as pale as ash. 'I didn't imagine. *She* really is here.'

'This is going to be hard for you to understand, J.C., but I know you're a real smart boy so I'm going to try to explain.'

J.C. never took his eyes off Stefan's face.

'You and Justine have both been frightened. Badly

frightened. By a lady in a white dress. And it's my job
to find out why you were both so afraid of her.'

'I know why.' J.C. could barely get the words
out. 'It's because ... it's because *she's* dead. The
lady is dead.'

Stefan saw the boy shudder. 'She isn't dead, J.C.,'
he said gently.

'Yes, *she* is.' J.C.'s head bobbed up and down.
'Yes, *she* is.'

'I don't think so. I think that maybe you and Justine
ate something, or touched something, or breathed
something that made it seem like you were in a nightmare. So that when you saw the lady, you thought that
somehow she was going to hurt you.'

'A nightmare,' J.C. echoed. It *had* been like a nightmare. Except that he hadn't been asleep. He had been
wide awake.

'I think if you talk to Justine about it, maybe you'll
both feel a little better. Maybe you can help each other
figure out why you were so afraid. And then we're all
going into Bridgetown to the hospital, so the doctors
there can take some blood tests to find out what it was
that got you two into so much trouble.'

J.C. pulled his feet out of the water. He wasn't sure
whether he felt better or worse. But it didn't take him
long to decide. He felt worse, because deep down
inside he already knew why he had been so frightened.
It didn't matter what his uncle said. Deep down, J.C.
knew the truth. Even though he never saw her face,
he knew that the lady in the white dress was dead.

Stefan opened the door and let J.C. go past him into
the studio. Music was playing softly. Justine was

standing at the *barre*, moving slowly from one dance position to the next. She really is pretty, J.C. thought. She really is.

The two stood watching quietly until she stopped, but still she hadn't seen them. She stood looking down at her feet, adjusting them slightly, concentrating on something about their placement that she obviously found imperfect. There was a faint frown on her face, but when she finally looked up to see them there her eyes widened in surprise and she smiled. She took two quick steps forward, then stopped.

'I think you and J.C. may be able to help each other out,' Stefan said. 'So why don't we go into your sitting room and talk.'

Justine nodded, her excitement evident, and without a moment's hesitation she led the way. Once inside the room she sat down and held out her hand. J.C. could see it shaking. 'Come,' she said to him. 'Sit here beside me.'

For a minute J.C. thought about making a run for it. Getting out before it was too late. But it was already too late. The door was closed. So he sat down next to Justine, folded his arms across his chest, and stared down into his lap. He didn't want to be here. He didn't want to talk about *her*. He just wanted to do like Amalie said and forget it. But how could he? Now his uncle wanted him to go to the hospital because maybe J.C. had eaten something or touched something that made him scared. Sort of like when eating too many pastries made you throw up, J.C. supposed. But it didn't make any sense. Mainly because no matter what anyone said, J.C. knew that *she* was dead.

'Your uncle told me that you saw a lady in a white dress,' Justine said quietly.

J.C. didn't look up. 'I didn't see her exactly. I only saw her dress.'

'Where was she?'

'Standing outside the conservatory door.'

Justine looked over at Stefan and he nodded. 'Go ahead. Talk to him. Ask him whatever comes into your head,' he said. 'I'll stop you if I think there's a problem.'

She took a deep breath, and J.C. could feel her staring at him. 'Do you know why you were so frightened?'

He nodded. 'But nobody believes me.'

'I know. Nobody believes me either. They . . . they think maybe I'm crazy.' She stopped. 'Except your uncle, that is. He's not sure what I am.'

J.C. was surprised at that. 'Why do they think you're crazy? They don't think I am.'

She managed a weak smile. 'I know. But I'm a grown-up.'

He felt a sudden rush of sympathy for his step-mother. And a real sense of the unfairness of it all. Being grown-up should have nothing to do with it. He lowered his voice. 'What did *she* do to scare you?' he asked.

She looked right at him. 'I think you know. She didn't do anything. She just was there.'

He nodded, frowning. 'So I don't understand why they don't believe you. You aren't a little kid. You don't imagine things.'

She shrugged. 'I didn't used to think so.'

J.C. glanced over at his uncle, then turned back, his tone hushed, conspiratorial. 'Do *you* think you're imagining?'

She didn't answer.

159

He leaned over until his lips were almost touching her ear. 'You're not imagining, Justine,' he whispered. 'Because I know *she's* here at Cristobel. All the time.' He paused. 'I don't know what *she* wants. But I do know why *she's* so scary.'

His stepmother waited, barely breathing, concentrating on his every word as if he were just as old as she.

'It's because *she's* dead. And dead people are scary. They don't have to *do* anything. They just have to be there.'

She didn't say anything nor did his uncle. They just sat there. Then Justine reached over and squeezed his arm really tight, and all of a sudden J.C. knew that she understood. That she would be his friend. That if it happened again, he could tell her and she would believe him.

Justine sat beside J.C. and waited for the nurse to finish drawing her blood.

'Don't look,' J.C. whispered. 'Then it won't hurt so much.'

She closed her eyes. She had always hated needles, but this kind was the worst because it wasn't quick, in-out. It made her think of a leech. She gritted her teeth.

'There you are, Mrs Leyland,' the nurse said. 'All done.'

J.C. looked up at her, grinning. 'See? I told you it wouldn't hurt much.'

'Let's get out of here,' she said, taking him by the hand. 'I think your uncle needs to get us something to eat to help us get our strength back.'

160

Stefan was outside talking to one of the technicians, and when he saw them he smiled. 'Nothing to it, right?'

She made a sour face.

'So. I guess it's back to the old homestead,' he said.

She realized all at once that she couldn't bear the thought. Ever since they had left Cristobel for the hospital she had felt almost normal. Such a wonderful word, normal. 'Do we have to go back right now?'

Stefan seemed to know what she was feeling. He shook his head. 'Not if you don't want to. Let's get a snack or something. How about it, J.C.? Know a good spot?'

'Let's go to Hogarth's,' J.C. said, and as if he were the adult, he took Justine by the hand.

Later, on the way back up the narrow road to Cristobel, the boy turned to her, his face unsmiling, almost comic in its seriousness. He kept his voice low, confidential so that Stefan couldn't hear. 'Don't worry, Justine,' he said. 'I know you're not crazy. And I'm not either.'

She didn't know why but it made her feel like laughing and crying at the same time.

17

Trouble, Stefan thought. As soon as he stepped into the living room and saw Marcus's face, he knew there was trouble. Big trouble.

Caitlin was sitting beside him, fanning herself with a magazine, her face pale, drawn.

Justine stopped just inside the door, equally aware that something was wrong. She turned to J.C. who had come in right behind her. 'I think you'd better find Amalie and let her know you're back safe and sound.'

'Okay,' he said, 'but don't forget what I said.'

'I won't.'

Stefan watched J.C. slip out into the hall. He wasn't sure how much good the talk with Justine had done the boy, but he knew it had been great therapy for Justine. He had never seen her so relaxed. At least she had been until they caught the first glimpse of Cristobel through the trees. Now, standing next to her in the living room, he could feel her tension.

'God, I hate this place.'

Stefan heard the words and, startled, looked over at Justine. Then he realized it was Caitlin who had spoken. 'I think I have a terminal case of goose bumps,' she said. Beside her Marcus sat motionless, made of stone. He didn't even seem to realize that Justine and Stefan had come in.

'Marcus,' Justine said, taking a few steps towards him, then stopping. 'What is it? What's wrong?'

Slowly he lifted his head. 'How long have you been home?' he asked. 'I didn't hear you come in.' He stood up. 'How did it go?'

'Very well,' she said. 'I hardly felt it.'

'I expected you back sooner.' Marcus glanced over at Stefan.

'We went over to Broad Street and had a snack.'

'Well, you didn't miss anything,' Caitlin said, and Stefan noticed that her hand was shaking.

'Something happened while we were gone,' Justine said, staring at her husband.

'It's nothing for you to be concerned with. Amalie is going to take care of it.' His tone lightened. 'Would anyone care for a drink? It's a little early but – '

'I'll have a double gin on the rocks,' Caitlin said quickly.

Stefan crossed the room and sat beside her. 'Strong poison for someone whose favourite drink is weak tea,' he said. 'Is that your usual fare these days, or has something happened to warrant a change?'

'I'll say it has, but Marcus will have to tell you,' she said, fanning herself with renewed vigour.

'Tell us what?' Justine asked.

'Let me fix you a drink, darling,' he said softly. 'Then I'll tell you about it.' He crossed to the sideboard. 'Your usual?'

'That'll be fine,' Justine said.

'I'll have a vodka martini,' Stefan said.

'Better make it a double,' Caitlin muttered. 'You'll need it when you hear the latest.'

No one spoke until after Marcus had finished serving the drinks. Then Caitlin swallowed nervously and said, 'Do you want me to tell them?'

'I think you're making too much of it,' Marcus said, running one finger around the rim of his glass.

'Too much of it? Jesus Christ, Marcus, I never saw anything so barbaric in my life. And I never want to again.'

'Don't worry, Caitlin,' he said coldly. 'The price will be paid.'

Stefan glanced over at Justine who was watching her husband intently. He cleared his throat. 'Why don't you tell us what happened?'

'Someone slipped into Amalie's quarters this morning and stole a number of her personal possessions. Then he went into the aviary and killed a number of my birds.'

Caitlin made a gagging sound. 'Killed is a rather mild term for it, don't you think? Shredded would be more like it.'

Marcus gave her a sharp look. 'I don't see that there is any profit to be gained from indulging in lurid details.'

'You seem rather calm under the circumstances,' Stefan said. And it was true. Normally he would have expected his brother to be out with a lynch party by now.

'As I just told Caitlin,' Marcus said quietly, 'the price will be paid.'

'Do you know who's responsible?'

'I do. I'm just not sure of the motive.' His voice was flat, unemotional.

'Who was it?' Justine sounded numb, as if she was having a hard time recognizing the fact that for once she was not in the centre of the maelstrom.

'Remus Hastings.'

The name lingered in the air, but no one reacted. Even Justine looked blank.

'He's one of the local black boys from over in Christ Church parish,' Marcus continued. 'We've had trouble with him before.'

'How do you know it was he?' Justine asked.

Marcus seemed surprised that she had to ask. 'Amalie told me.'

'How stupid of me,' she said softly. 'I should have known that nothing happens at Cristobel that Amalie doesn't know about.'

'How did Amalie find out?' Stefan asked, taking a sip of his drink.

'The boy destroyed my prize Maximilians last night and after he ransacked Amalie's quarters this morning, he left them as a gift on her doorstep.' He paused. 'He left something else as well – a doll.'

'A doll?' Stefan said.

'A hex doll. You've seen them, I'm sure.'

'You mean the kind they stick pins into?'

'In Hollywood they do. Remus used thorns.'

'This is all too sick,' Caitlin said. 'Who is the doll supposed to be?'

Marcus shrugged. 'Amalie, I suppose.'

'But I didn't think voodoo was practised in Barbados.'

'It's not. But it seems that somehow Remus Hastings has acquired a small amount of knowledge about the religion.' His face went hard. 'And as we all know, a little knowledge can be a dangerous thing. A very dangerous thing indeed.'

'And that's not all,' Caitlin said. 'Amalie said this Remus character threatened to harm the boys, and I'll tell you one thing for sure. After what I saw in the aviary, I wouldn't want Remus Hastings within a

165

hundred miles of my children, never mind my birds.'

'Amalie is going to take care of it,' Marcus repeated.

'You mean you didn't call the police?' Justine asked, incredulous.

'That's the last thing we need at Cristobel right now,' he said. 'Besides, whenever we have trouble here with the locals, Amalie always takes care of it.'

'How?' Stefan asked, watching his brother's expression. He found this whole discourse unbelievable. Marcus didn't like Amalie, in fact seemed to be eager to be rid of her. And yet here he was allowing her to play judge and jury in what was clearly a personal attack on him. Why?

'What's Amalie going to do?' Caitlin asked. 'Bury him up to his neck and let the ants eat him?'

Marcus looked down into his glass. 'She has her ways. Amalie has always been very effective in dealing with the blacks on the island. I see no reason to interfere this time.'

An uncomfortable silence followed. Clearly everyone found Marcus's reaction odd to say the least. Finally Caitlin spoke. 'God, it's hot.'

'I think I'll shower and get ready for dinner,' Justine said shakily, setting her glass on the end table.

'Are you okay?' Stefan asked.

'From the looks, I'd say I'm about as okay as anyone else is in this house.'

Another silence. Then Caitlin said, 'Well, I'm going for a quick swim. I'm so hot I could die. Anyone care to join me?'

Marcus shook his head. He swirled the rest of his drink around in his glass, then drank it.

'How about you, Doc?'

'Sounds like a spectacular idea,' he said. Maybe

a swim would rid him of the nagging feeling of uneasiness he'd had all day. 'I'll change and meet you in the pool.'

Justine dressed slowly, wondering why she felt so . . . so relieved. As if getting through this single day without an episode was a landmark of sorts. A measure of some kind of success. Even though this morning she had learned that Marcus could not sell Cristobel she had still kept her balance. Somehow she would survive. She hadn't mentioned it to him and she wasn't going to. She knew that when he was ready, he'd tell her. He'd have to.

She passed the mirror. 'Congratulations. You're still alive,' she said softly, and felt a sudden spark of hope at seeing herself looking so normal. Even the circles under her eyes had begun to fade. You can't be crazy, she thought, suddenly angry. I won't allow it. J.C. is right. I'm not crazy and neither is he.

But if you aren't, said a voice in the back of her head, *then what are you?*

She turned away and sat down on the edge of the bed, trying to ignore the voice, thinking instead about the boy. With his youthful assurances, he had given her more comfort than she had thought possible. And hope. Because she was certain that J.C. wasn't crazy, and if he wasn't, then maybe she wasn't either. After all, he had felt the same irrational terror that she had.

But he's only a child, the voice said. *Children are sometimes frightened without cause.*

'I don't care,' she said aloud. 'He knows she's real, and I believe him.' And hearing her own words, she shuddered. What was she saying? If the woman was

a real live human being, then why was she so terrified of her?

*And what about the mirror, Justine? What about the
mirror?*

She put her hands over her ears but she couldn't
block out the next question. *And how could she make
you try to kill yourself?*

Stefan's words echoed in her head. *I think it might
have been chemically induced.*

But J.C.'s words echoed even louder. 'Because *she's*
dead.'

'If you believe that, you really are crazy,' she said
out loud.

Then why didn't you laugh when he said it?

'Because I didn't want him to think I didn't believe
him.'

Oh? Is that really why?

'Shut up,' she said, shivering. She was feeling frightened again. She stood up and was about to leave the
room when all at once she thought she heard Caitlin
call. She crossed to the open window.

In the past hour the wind had changed direction,
blowing once again from the ocean, and the air outside
was cool, refreshing. She felt it touch her brow and she
realized that she had been perspiring.

She looked out across the lawn. It was deserted.
From her vantage point she couldn't see the pool.
Only the dark velvet squares of lawn, and the patches
of bromeliads and ginger and ferns in between. In the
dimming light everything had taken on a watercolour
mistiness. It was impossible not to see the beauty.

She sighed at the same time that a timid knock came
at the door. 'Come in,' she said and turned to see J.C.
standing in the doorway. 'J.C.,' she said, surprised at

how happy she was to see him. And oddly, how much less afraid. 'What's up?'

He stepped into the room and stood with his hands in his pockets, shifting from one foot to the other, clearly uncomfortable. 'I . . . I just wanted to tell you something I forgot.'

'Come and sit,' she said, pointing to one of the chairs by the window.

He eased himself down gingerly, sitting on the very edge. 'I can only stay a minute. Amalie is waiting for me. And she'd be real mad if she knew I was here.'

'Why?'

'Because she doesn't want me to talk about what happened. About the woman, I mean. You see, Amalie says I'm special. I wasn't born to behave like one of the ignorant native boys. And she's really angry because my father let me have my blood tested.'

Justine frowned. 'Does she know why we did it?'

'I told her what my uncle said, and she said it was all nonsense. That if there was something poisonous around here she would know it.'

Justine leaned forward and smiled reassuringly. 'Well, maybe she's right. But it didn't hurt anything, did it? Except our arms. Besides, we got to go to Hogarth's for treats.'

J.C. relaxed a little. 'Anyway, what I wanted to tell you . . .' He lowered his voice. 'I . . . I know where *she* lives. And I just wanted to warn you not to go there.'

Justine felt something tingle at the back of her neck. She made herself ask, even though somehow she already knew the answer. 'Where?'

'Cane Cave.'

'How do you know?'

'You know how,' he said quietly. 'I felt her.' He

169

tipped his head to one side, considering. 'It's really strange, you know? Cane Cave used to be my favourite place in the whole world. Before *she* came there, that is. But then maybe *she's* always been there and I just never felt her before.' He paused. 'You know what I think?'

'What?'

'I think something happened to wake her up. You know, like ghosts who come back when someone disturbs their graves? Or werewolves who come out when the moon is full?'

The two sat looking at each other for a long moment, the young woman and the boy. Then Justine reached out her hand and J.C. took it and held on tight.

From somewhere far away they heard the sound of a clock striking six. J.C. jumped up and headed for the door. 'I have to go. Amalie will be waiting.'

'Thanks, J.C.,' she said softly. 'Thanks very, very much.'

He turned. 'It's okay. I just thought you ought to know.'

She nodded.

Justine finished with her make-up and was about to go down to dinner when she heard it. The high, screeching sound of a bird. Almost like a baby crying. She crossed to the window and looked out. It was nearly dark, but against the silver grey backdrop of the fast moving clouds she could see a huge hawklike creature, circling high above the trees. She watched, fascinated. She had never seen a hawk around Cristobel before. She wondered if Marcus knew about it. There would be hell to pay if it ever got into the aviary.

170

As she watched, the bird seemed to be taking aim at something on the ground. It began to circle lower and lower until finally it dropped from the sky to land on the arm of a woman who had just stepped out from the dark shadow of the giant mahogany tree. *It was the woman in white.*

She's waiting for you, Justine thought as waves of terror washed over her. She's still waiting. Then, just as before, she heard the woman speak in a low quiet voice, as if she were right beside her, murmuring into Justine's ear.

'Tonight,' the woman whispered. 'Tonight.'

Justine threw her hands up and covered her ears. Frantic, with eyes shut tight, she began to pray. Dear God, make her go away! Please, please, this time let it be my imagination.

When she finally dared to look again, the grounds were deserted.

J.C. was halfway up the back stairs when he heard it. A soft, far-away whisper that turned his blood to ice. 'Tonight,' it echoed. 'Tonight.' Terror-stricken, he turned around and ran back downstairs to find Amalie.

Stefan closed his bedroom door firmly behind him and headed down the hall. He was almost to the top of the stairs when all at once he stopped, held motionless by the most incredible sense of absolute helplessness, as if no matter what, nothing could be changed.

Tonight. The word came unbidden into his head. *Tonight.*

He frowned and looked behind him. As he had known he would be, he was alone. Then as quickly as it had come, the feeling passed, leaving him shaking his head in disgust. 'You lunatic,' he said and continued down the stairs to dinner.

18

In spite of the heat, Justine shuttered the windows and closed the louvres tight. She didn't care how hot it got during the night. At least she knew nothing could get in. Then, leaving the lights on, she crawled into bed.

She lay on her back, staring up at the ceiling fan turning slowly, soundlessly above, the single word echoing over and over in her head. *Tonight*. She wished that she might have been able to talk to Stefan. Maybe he could have reassured her, helped explain away what she had seen. You should have told him, she thought. She just knew it would have helped. Somehow with his cool reason Stefan always managed to make things seem less terrifying.

She had tried to find a minute alone with him, but there had been other people at Cristobel that evening. Marcus had invited Jack Thomas and his wife to dinner so he could deliver the final set of photographs, but he spoke very little during the course of the evening. He seemed to have lost all interest in his work.

In a way, Justine had been grateful for the Thomas's company. It had forced her to behave normally. They were an interesting couple, pleasant to talk to and vastly impressed with Marcus's work. She found herself clinging to every word they uttered, no matter how trivial. They seemed so calm, so completely removed from the nightmarish quality of life at Cristobel. At one point she found herself wondering what their reaction would be if she suddenly blurted out that she had tried to kill herself only three nights ago.

The other person who helped her through the evening was Caitlin. Justine was beginning to understand why Marcus cared for her so much. Caitlin was a truly ingenuous creature, so happily unconventional but so utterly sincere in her convictions, however bizarre. It was impossible not to like her. Listening to her talk about life as she saw it was like going on a trip to another planet. Over coffee, when Caitlin was describing her experiences in Mozambique, Justine actually heard herself laugh out loud.

With the Thomas's departure, the evening ended abruptly. Lost again in his own thoughts, Marcus disappeared into his darkroom, Caitlin challenged Stefan to a game of chess, and all at once Justine found herself alone in her room, wondering how in hell she was going to get through the night.

Now, lying here in her bed, closed up in a room that should have been open to the cooling breeze, she felt the all too familiar chill of fear at the base of her spine. It came like the beginning of a sneeze, when you think that if you reach up quickly enough to touch your nose, you can stop it. But she couldn't.

'No!' Suddenly furious with herself, she sat bolt upright. 'I'm not going to allow it!' She got out of bed and marched to the shelf on the other side of the room, pulling out the first book that her hand touched. She didn't bother to consider the title. She carried it back to her bed, propped herself up against the pillows and opened it at the first page.

'Emma Woodhouse,' she read, 'handsome, clever,

and rich, with a comfortable home and happy dis-
position seemed to unite some of the best blessings
of existence; and had lived nearly twenty-one years
in the world with very little to distress or vex her.'
Lucky Emma, she thought.

She drifted in and out of sleep, sometimes waking
with a start to find herself bathed in perspiration, other
times coming to consciousness slowly, full of apprehension, surprised to find the book still in her hands.

It was almost two o'clock in the morning when the
book finally slipped to the floor.

The clock struck two, and on the other side of the
house J.C. lay flat in his bed, wide awake. Like Justine,
his lights were on and his windows closed and shuttered, but unlike his stepmother he hadn't slept at all.
He kept hearing that single whispered word. *Tonight*.

The house stirred around him, then seemed to settle
down to wait. And so did the boy. Finally he slept.

At precisely twenty-five minutes after two, J.C. came
crashing awake, his mouth bone dry, his face wet with
tears and sweat. He bolted out of bed and fled from his
room, running through the long dark hallways as fast
as he could. He felt as if Amalie's serpent god were
slithering right behind.

'Justine!' he gasped as he threw himself through her
door.

She was already awake, sitting straight up in bed,
eyes wide with fear, and without a word she held
out her arms. He flew across the room and collapsed against her, sobbing, and like two frightened

175

children they huddled together, neither daring to breathe.

Justine's teeth were chattering so hard she couldn't speak. 'It's all right, J.C.,' she finally managed. 'We're safe. We're safe. Nothing can hurt us.'

'But what's happening?' he whispered, his face still hidden in the curve of her shoulder.

'I don't know.' She shook her head helplessly. 'Dear God, I don't know.'

'*She's* coming,' he said, shuddering. '*She's* coming.'

Justine didn't answer. As insane as it seemed, she knew he was right.

After the chess game was declared a stalemate, Stefan and Caitlin retired for the evening, but he couldn't sleep. For hours he had been sitting at the desk in his bedroom, filling sheet after sheet of paper with notes. Notes on depression, on suicide, on drug intoxication, on auditory and visual hallucinations, on everything he could think of that might help him understand what was happening at Cristobel.

Slowly he began to sift out what was irrelevant, those things that didn't apply, and after all was said and done, he was still left with only one possible explanation. Some kind of hallucinogenic agent was at work. But then where did this woman in white fit in? Who was she? Was she simply a curious interloper, as Marcus had suggested, who had unwittingly triggered some private, psychotic fear in both Justine and J.C.? Or had she come to Cristobel with a more sinister purpose in mind?

He frowned, chewing on the end of the pencil, then began to write again. One thing was clear. Justine

176

and J.C. were both terrified of this woman out of all proportion. Whatever her reason for skulking around, something had to be altering their ability to perceive her in a normal fashion. Something toxic, something that they had stumbled on accidentally.

But what if it hadn't been accidental? What if it had been deliberately and skilfully applied to induce fear and madness?

Who would do such a thing? And why? Was it the woman herself? Had she done it, knowing full well what the results would be?

He decided that he was jumping the gun. He leaned back in the chair, surprised to find that he was breathing hard. He did a mental countdown. First, he had to get the results of the blood tests. And an analysis of the stains on the handkerchief that Marcus had mailed this morning. The blood samples had been expressed to Johns Hopkins, so Jacob VonVost would have the whole batch in the lab by tomorrow. Stefan decided to call his colleague first thing in the morning, prevail upon him to speed things up. Maybe by tomorrow night they would know what they were dealing with.

And if you're right? he asked himself. If someone is poisoning them, what then?

Cross that bridge when you come to it.

Far down some distant corridor he heard a clock strike two and he was astonished. He had been sitting here for hours, and he realized suddenly that he was exhausted. The three days he had spent at Cristobel seemed like three hundred.

He stood up and went through the open doors to the outer gallery, feeling the need to stretch his legs, get some fresh air before collapsing into bed.

The night was eerily bright with brief moments of

darkness when the fast moving clouds blew across the face of the moon. The wind had picked up, filling the trees with mysterious rustlings, and somewhere far away a night bird called, a long mournful sound. Stefan wondered if it was Strike.

He suddenly realized that he was clenching his fists so tightly that the fingernails were digging into his flesh. He flexed his hands and reached up to rub the back of his neck, trying to relieve the sudden throbbing ache of tension. *What was wrong?* And all at once he was overcome by an apprehension so powerful that he actually felt giddy.

He stared across the garden, along the curve of the trees. *And then he saw her.*

For an instant she stood motionless, her long white dress blown by the wind, her silver-blonde hair loose around her shoulders. He couldn't see her face, but even so she seemed confused, uncertain which way to go. She took a few steps, then a cloud covered the moon and she vanished into the darkness.

'Oh, no you don't,' he said grimly. 'Whoever you are, you aren't getting away this time.' He raced to the end of the gallery and down the stairs, sprinting towards the spot where he had seen her disappear.

At the edge of the lawn he stopped, not sure which way she had gone, and then far up ahead on the path leading to the ocean he saw a flicker of white, and something inside screamed at him to hurry. He began to run. He was going to catch this woman in white and at the very least find out who she was, what she was after.

In the full moonlight he could see his way clearly, but when the clouds blew in to cover the moon he was forced to slow down. He cursed himself for not having brought a flashlight, but then he hadn't had time. Even as it was, he was afraid she had escaped.

The clouds passed and he took advantage of the light to move quickly. Beyond the eerie whispering of the wind, and the crunching of his own feet on the gravel, he could hear the low roar of the ocean, deep, sullen. He was almost at the end of the path when all at once he was filled with a premonition that something ungodly was about to happen, that he should never have come out here. *Go back!* He stopped and looked over his shoulder. He knew he was still chasing someone, but now he felt as if someone was chasing him too. It wasn't that he could see anyone. Nor was it a sound. It was a *feeling*. A feeling of whispered laughter. Cruel. Mocking. And it chilled him to the marrow because it made no sense. He was sure that the woman was just ahead. And yet . . .

He managed to make his legs carry him out of the shadow of the trees. And there she was, standing at the edge of the cliff, her back turned toward him, her hair blowing free in the wind, the whiteness of her gown bleached even whiter in the moonlight.

For a moment, he stared in disbelief, and then the truth of what was happening hit him. Filled with horror he opened his mouth to shout, to scream, but nothing came out.

In a last desperate attempt to stop her, to pull her back, to keep her from plunging onto the cruel boulders below, he threw himself forward. He felt his fingers touch the gauze of her nightdress, and in that final instant she looked back, a flash of stunned surprise on her face, as if she couldn't imagine where she was or what she was doing.

And then she was gone.

He crawled to the edge of the cliff and looked down. 'Caitlin,' he whispered. 'Dear God, Caitlin.'

19

It was just dawn and it was raining. The kind of oppressive, all-day rain that comes so rarely to the islands. Justine stood on the edge of the veranda and watched as Marcus and Stefan disappeared down the path that led to the road. The authorities were waiting there to take them to the hospital in Bridgetown. The hospital where Caitlin lay, fighting for her life.

Justine wanted to call them back, beg them not to leave her here alone, but she didn't. She kept herself in tight control because of Marcus. She had never seen her husband so full of rage. But it was an icy rage. He was unapproachable. She would never forget the sound of his voice as he cursed himself for not having left Cristobel sooner. It was as if he thought that somehow Cristobel itself had been responsible for what had happened to Caitlin.

Caitlin.

Remembering, a new wave of horror washed over her. She walked around the corner and sat down shakily in one of the wicker chairs beside the conservatory door. The palms of her hands were wet with perspiration. She felt feverish. Four hours ago Caitlin had jumped off the cliff. It had taken them hours to reach her, and even now, no one knew whether or not she would survive.

She repeated it to herself. *Caitlin jumped off the cliff. Just like you tried to do,* her voice said.

Slowly she put her hands over her ears. It took tremendous effort. Every part of her body seemed to weigh a thousand pounds. A single question haunted her. Why in the name of heaven had Caitlin done it?

Why did you? asked the voice.

She tried to focus on what Stefan had told her. That he was more convinced than ever that somehow they were being poisoned. That blood tests would prove that Caitlin was a victim of the same toxins as Justine and J.C.

So why was her feeling of terror growing instead of diminishing? And why did she feel that she and J.C. and poor Caitlin were the victims of something far worse than poisoning? That maybe J.C. was right and they were all being terrorized by someone who was not alive. 'You're a sick person,' she said out loud. 'A very, very sick person.'

She got to her feet. Unsteady, she stood for a minute looking out across the lawn to the edge of the trees. In the rain they looked almost purple against the heavy grey of the sky. The air smelled thick, sickly sweet, and along the edge of the lawn she could almost see the plants growing, sucking up the rain, making the forest more dense, more impenetrable. 'I hate it here,' she said with a shudder. 'With all my heart I hate it.'

She turned and went through the open doorway into the conservatory, suddenly desperate not to be alone. She decided to look for J.C. , to talk to him, to see how he was dealing with what had happened to Caitlin. If he even knew. Last night the boy had stayed with Justine, huddled beside her until the commotion downstairs erupted. Then Amalie had appeared at the door and had taken him away.

Justine hurried across the tiled floor and through the low-arched doorway that led to the entrance hall, her sandals making sharp staccato clicks on the marble. It was the only sound in the house. And even though she knew it was impossible – at Cristobel there were always servants everywhere – the house seemed empty. Deserted. Rats and a sinking ship, she thought.

She stopped, feeling the way one would in church. Making sound where there should be only silence. She stood still, barely breathing, waiting.

For what?

She let out her breath. 'You jackass. For the men in the white coats, who else?'

She began to walk again, only this time on tiptoe. She was almost to the stairs when a low voice behind her froze her in her tracks. 'Mrs Leyland. Have you a moment?'

Justine didn't turn. She was afraid to, even though what was left of reason told her that it was only Amalie. Only Amalie, she thought, feeling an hysterical urge to laugh. Facing Amalie right now seemed just slightly less terrifying than facing the woman in white.

When Justine didn't move, Amalie spoke again. 'Mrs Leyland, there is something I would like to show you.'

Gathering herself together, Justine turned.

The black woman was standing just inside the front entrance. Behind her, through the open door Justine could see grey swirls of mist and for a minute it seemed as if Amalie was part of it. A spectre drifting in from some primordial past.

'Come,' Amalie said. She didn't wait for Justine to respond. She crossed the hallway and headed towards the back of the house.

Like a robot, Justine followed. It never would have occurred to her to do anything else.

Amalie's quarters were at the far end of the east wing, almost directly below August's, but Justine had never been there before. She stood just inside the door, silent, feeling the beads of perspiration beginning to form on her face.

There was an austerity about the place, a barrenness that reminded Justine of a monastery. There were no signs of personality, no pictures, no knick-knacks, no decorative touches. It might have been a cell in a dungeon for all its comforts. A narrow bed with a plain muslin coverlet stood along one wall, beside it a small table with a solitary candlestick. On the opposite wall was a mahogany chest of drawers and a straight-backed chair. On the wall between were two tall louvred doors leading to the rear courtyard, but they were closed tight, making the room hot and stuffy. It smelled of burnt candles.

Amalie crossed to the chest and opened one drawer. Still without speaking she took something out, then turned. 'Do you know what this is?' She held out her hand.

Justine stared. Amalie was holding a crude doll fashioned from plaited palm leaves. A single thorn had been driven through the centre of the body. Another pierced the head.

'It was left here yesterday morning.' Amalie's voice was controlled, her face devoid of any expression.

Justine was struck dumb but she managed to raise her eyebrows in question.

'It was sent in a primitive attempt to frighten,' Amalie said softly.

'To frighten? To frighten whom?'

The woman's dark eyes never left Justine's face. 'To frighten me.'

'But why?'

'Some use such things to extract a small measure of respect. Others have reasons all their own.'

'Marcus said you knew who left it.'

'I do.'

Justine waited, not sure what to say, wondering why she had been brought here, where this was leading.

'Remus Hastings is a dangerous young man,' Amalie continued. She kept her voice low and steady, almost hypnotic. 'In the same way a fool can often times be dangerous. He has stolen things from me that he believes can give him great power. But he is mistaken, and that makes him even more to be feared.'

Justine's throat ached. 'But what has this to do with me? Remus Hastings should be arrested. It's my husband you should be speaking to. Or the authorities.'

For one awful minute Justine thought Amalie was going to touch her. The black woman reached out, then let her hand drop to her side. She turned away and threw open the doors to the courtyard. She made a sweeping gesture with one arm. 'This is Cristobel. *My* Cristobel. And in spite of all my efforts, disaster has come here.' She turned back to face Justine. 'I have prayed for Caroline to come home, and I know that she will. I feel it in my soul. But when she does, there will be much unpleasantness, much turmoil. It would be better for all of us if you and your husband left Cristobel. Right now. Before my Caroline comes. Before there is any further tragedy.

Because in spite of all that has happened, the worst is yet to come.' The words were spoken simply and with absolute certainty.

Justine stared. So this was what it was all about. Amalie wanted them to leave Cristobel. 'You and I are in perfect accord,' she said.

For once Amalie seemed taken by surprise. 'Do you mean that you are planning to leave Cristobel?'

'Didn't you know? But surely Marcus told you.'

'Told me what?'

'That he wants to sell Cristobel.'

For a moment there was silence. It was as if Justine had suddenly become invisible. Amalie looked right through her. Then she crossed the room and opened the door to the hallway. 'I see. Thank you for coming,' she said. There was still no emotion in her voice but somehow Justine knew that Amalie was truly stunned. The black woman stood to one side and waited for Justine to pass. Then she closed the door with a soft click.

'Why do *you* think she did it?' J.C. asked. He was sitting on the edge of his brother's bed, watching August stuff gear into his backpack.

August shrugged. 'Amalie says she's crazy.'

'Do you believe that?'

'Why not? You'd have to be crazy to jump off a cliff, wouldn't you? Remember the time that smartassed Bajan kid tried to dive over the rocks up near Flower Cave?' He snickered. 'That was some mess.'

J.C. was silent. Ever since Amalie told them what Caitlin had done, he had been filled with terror, because he knew that as sure as he was breathing, *she* had made it happen. This morning he had looked for Justine so he could talk to her about it, but she was busy with his father, so J.C. went to look for August. Not that he wanted to talk to his brother about what he knew. No way. He'd never mention anything about *her* to August. But J.C. was scared. He didn't want to be alone,

'Can't I go with you?' he asked. August was almost ready to leave on his quest to find Strike.

'No. I already told you I don't need any sissies along.'

'But I won't be a sissy. I promise,' J.C. said. 'Besides, maybe I can help find her.'

August snorted. 'Help? How could *you* help? Do you think maybe if you burst out crying Strike will hear you and come flying back?'

J.C. looked down at his sneakers. 'Amalie's going to be really mad at you. She told us not to go anywhere without her.'

'You see?' August said. 'That's what I mean. Sissy talk.'

'You won't be so brave if Remus finds you when you're all alone.'

August shot a dark look at his brother. 'I hope he does. I have a surprise waiting for young Remus.'

J.C. gasped. 'But Amalie told you not to do anything. She made you say you wouldn't.'

August put on his raincoat, then slipped his arms through the straps of his backpack and hoisted it up. 'I have news for you, little brother.' He smiled his cryptic smile. 'Sometimes I lie.'

J.C. followed him out onto the upper veranda, stalling for time, more desperate than ever not to have August leave. 'Where do you think Strike is?'

187

'Somewhere up on the cliff. And I'm bringing something special for her that she won't be able to resist.'

'What?'

That smile again. 'None of your business.'

J.C. felt a lump in his throat but he had to ask anyway. 'You haven't killed another bird?'

'No.' August was still smiling. 'Better than that.'

'What?' J.C.'s curiosity was stronger than his desire not to know.

August was silent for a minute, then he shrugged and smiled more broadly. 'Oh, what the hell. It's too good to keep it a secret.' He lowered his voice. 'Remember how Mother used to attract Gossy?'

J.C. sucked in his breath. He remembered all right. It was one of the things he had hated most in all the world. He could never understand why his mother had forced him to watch. How she could laugh so infectiously while he could only cry.

'Ah ha,' August crowed. 'I see you haven't forgotten. Well, that's what I'm going to do. I have these two plump juicy Barbary doves stashed away, all caged and ready to go. And one at a time I'm going to let them go free. If Strike is anywhere near, you know she won't be able to resist.' He bent over and stuck his face so close to J.C.'s that their noses were almost touching. 'On second thoughts, little brother, why don't you come along? I know how much you'd like to see Strike pluck those beauties right out of the sky and – ssskk – snap their necks in half.'

J.C. jerked back. 'I hope Remus finds you!' he yelled. 'I hope he finds you and beats you to a pulp.' Then he turned and ran back inside.

20

J.C. didn't know what to do with himself. Normally on a gloomy day like today he would have gone exploring to see what strange creatures the rain had brought out, to see what the ocean was doing, to play in Cane Cave with his brother. But today was unlike any day he had ever known. Amalie had forbidden them to go anywhere without her. And even if she hadn't, J.C. was afraid to leave the house alone. He decided he never wanted to go to Cane Cave again. Not ever. No matter what.

He slipped down the back stairs and across the courtyard, heading toward Amalie's rooms. He knew Amalie would ask where August was and he'd have to lie, but it didn't matter. Anything was better than being alone. Maybe she could think of something for him to do where he'd have company. But when he got to her door, it was closed tight, and he knew better than to knock. When Amalie's door was closed it meant she wanted privacy, and in spite of his disappointment, J.C. felt vaguely comforted, because Amalie wanted privacy only when she was meditating, getting ready to do her magic. He wondered what she was planning for good old Remus.

Outside, the rain pounded down on the slate, and he went back across the courtyard quickly, heading for the kitchen area. Maybe Clyde or some of the other children would be there. Maybe he could talk them into playing with him. But when he got there, the only person in the kitchen was Belinda, the cook. 'I got plenty of things for you to do,' she said, wiping her hands on her apron.

J.C. wrinkled his nose. He knew the kind of things Belinda had in mind. Like polishing the copper bottoms on the pots and pans, but for a minute he actually considered helping her, until he remembered that the utility room was kind of dark. And he would definitely be alone in there.

He shook his head and headed back towards the front of the house. He guessed the only thing left was to go upstairs and read comics, try to keep calm.

He was almost to the stairs when she called to him. 'Hi, J.C., what're you doing?'

He turned to see Justine standing just outside the living room door. He smiled a huge smile. 'Nothing. Nothing at all.'

She smiled back and held out her hand. 'Want to come upstairs and help me label my records? Put them all in proper order?'

'You bet,' he said. He crossed the hall and took her hand, feeling as grateful as he ever had in his life, and together they went up the wide staircase to the second floor.

J.C. sat on the floor in Justine's studio, sorting out her music, putting the records in alphabetical order by composer. Justine was busy going through some papers, but every now and then she'd look over and smile at him. He felt safe.

190

Finally he got up the courage to ask. 'Why do you think Caitlin did it?'

Justine left what she had been doing and came across the room to sit down beside him on the floor. 'I don't know,' she said, shaking her head.

'I do.'

She turned to him, a funny, nervous look on her face.

'*She* made it happen,' he said quietly. He watched her closely, saw her wince. 'Does that make you more scared than you already were?'

She made a face. 'Yes, J.C., it sure does. How about you?'

He nodded and looked down at his hands. 'I wonder why she wants to hurt people?'

Justine shivered. 'I don't know. But then I don't guess I know much of anything anymore.'

J.C. lowered his voice even though he knew no one else could hear. 'I heard her last night. That's how I knew something bad was going to happen. That's why I came into your room.'

His stepmother's face went very pale, all except the freckles on her nose. 'What did you hear?'

'I heard her whisper one word – "tonight". That's what she said.'

A little sound came out of Justine's mouth. 'When did this happen?'

'Right after August and I finished dinner. On my way upstairs.'

Justine was quiet for one minute. Then she said, 'I probably shouldn't tell you this, but then I don't see how things can get much worse. I heard her too. And I saw her again.'

J.C.'s eyes opened wide. 'Where – where was she?'

191

'Outside. On the edge of the lawn.'

'What was she doing?'

'Nothing.'

'Did she call to you?'

'She just said one word.'

'Tonight?'

She nodded.

He put his hands over his face. 'I hope I don't ever see her. Not ever.'

Justine put her arm around him, trying to think of something to say that would reassure him. But what could she say that would possibly help when she was more frightened than he was? Then she remembered the bird. 'You know something else? Something really strange? While she was standing there, a huge hawk came out of the trees and landed right on her arm.'

J.C. dropped his hands and stared at his stepmother in disbelief. Could it be possible? 'A hawk? What did it look like?'

As Justine described the bird, J.C. felt his heart lurch. 'That wasn't a hawk,' he said, unable to contain his excitement. 'It was a falcon. That was Strike.'

Justine frowned. 'Strike? Who is Strike?'

'August's falcon. But she flew away yesterday and wouldn't come back.' He jumped up. 'August went to the cliff this morning to look for her, and I have to tell him. I have to tell him that she was right here last night. Right on the lawn.' He ran to the door and opened it, then stopped short. What was he thinking of? Amalie had forbidden him to leave the house alone. That was bad enough. But that wasn't the worst. The worst was that somehow the woman in white had called Strike and the falcon had responded. So now, what if Strike belonged to *her*? What if *she* was out there waiting?

192

He had to warn August. He had no idea what he was going to tell his brother, but that didn't matter. What mattered now was getting August to come home. The trouble was that he was terrified to go to the ocean all by himself.

Slowly he turned back. Justine hadn't moved. She was still sitting on the floor, watching him.

'Would you come with me?' he asked quietly. He didn't need to explain why. Somehow he knew she would understand.

She didn't say anything. She just nodded, and hand in hand they left the house.

It had stopped raining but the sky was still overcast, full of ominous dark clouds. Justine and J.C. skirted the aviary and headed north, not up the cliff path but through the trees and into the open cane fields below the old sugar house.

Justine held tight to the boy's hand, not sure if it was more for his comfort or for hers, and it wasn't until her side began to ache that she realized that she and the boy had been running. She pulled him back and stopped to catch her breath. 'Where are we going?' she asked.

'Up there a little way.' He pointed towards the east. 'August went to look for Strike on the cliff.' He caught the sharp look on Justine's face. 'Don't worry. We aren't going anywhere near where Caitlin fell.' He lowered his voice. 'And we aren't going anywhere near Cane Cave either. It'll take us a little longer to get to the bluff, but if we cut through the old orange grove we should be there real soon.'

Justine stood motionless for a moment, feeling a

sudden shiver of fear. What was she thinking of? They should never have left the house without Marcus or Stefan. It was a stupid, stupid thing to do. She glanced over her shoulder.

J.C. saw her expression. 'Come on, Justine,' he said. 'If we hurry, it'll be okay.'

Together they moved on through the cane fields and into the shadow of the trees. Here there was no path and the undergrowth was thick, but J.C. seemed to know exactly where he was going. Once, Justine wanted to stop and wipe the mist from her face but for some reason she was afraid to. They hurried on, even though her inner voice screamed to turn around, to run back to the safety of the house as fast as she could, even if she had to drag J.C. with her.

Her breath caught in her throat and she clutched his hand, but still she let him lead, not daring to look to the right or to the left for fear of what she might see. Her eyes burned. Don't turn, she said to herself. For God's sake, don't turn around.

She felt J.C. tighten his grip on her hand and all at once they were both running, stumbling over roots and stubble, pushing through the underbrush. 'Don't look back!' J.C. cried, but she barely heard him, aware only that something was coming behind. Something that now was only a breath away.

Ahead, the forest seemed to grow more dense, the long branches dipping down to impede their headlong flight, and incredibly, the faster she tried to run, the slower she seemed to go, as if she were a music box toy that was starting to wind down.

'Justine!' J.C. screamed, yanking hard on her hand. 'Hurry!'

She felt the world around her grow dark. 'I can't,'

194

she whispered. And just as she felt herself spinning, falling into oblivion, suddenly they were out of the trees and onto the grassy slope that led to the crest of the bluff.

And somehow, incredibly, she knew they had escaped.

Justine let go of J.C.'s hand and sank to her knees, feeling a wild rush of relief.

The boy knelt down beside her, breathing hard. '*She* almost caught us,' he choked, his teeth chattering.

Justine nodded. 'I know.'

'I was so scared.'

'Me too.'

J.C. looked back toward the trees. 'But I think she's gone now.'

Justine squeezed his hand. 'I guess we were too fast for her.' The absurdity of what she had just said struck her and she began to giggle, then to laugh out loud.

For a minute J.C. stared at her, then he began to laugh too. Their peals of laughter echoed high above the sullen roar of the waves, and for a few minutes the two were convulsed, laughing and hugging each other, as if they had just accomplished an unbelievable feat.

Then J.C. grew quiet. 'I have to tell you something,' he said solemnly. 'Something very bad.'

'What?'

'*She* doesn't want me. *She* wants you.'

Justine put her arms around him, resting her cheek against the top of his head. 'I think you're right, J.C.,' she said, shuddering. 'I didn't know before, but I do now.'

'I wonder why? Maybe *she* doesn't like ladies.'

'Maybe not,' Justine said, feeling a sudden and complete disconnection with reality. How unbelievable that she should be here with this child talking so calmly, so seriously about the likes and dislikes of a ghost.

They knelt together on the top of the bluff, neither speaking, somehow knowing that there was nothing more to be said.

Finally Justine got to her feet. 'And now, before we lose our nerve altogether, I think we'd better find August.'

J.C. hitched up his shorts and took her hand. He pointed. 'Let's go up there. Then we can see the whole coastline.'

They made their way a short distance along the bluff until they reached a small promontory. From there they had an unobstructed view of the shoreline in both directions. Far below, the ocean stretched grey and restless, the waves rolling in in long unbroken lines to crash on the boulders with a thunderous roar.

'Do you see anything?' Justine shouted, scanning the area.

J.C. shook his head. 'But he has to be here. This is where he was going to let the doves go.'

'What doves?'

For a minute J.C. hesitated. Then he blurted it out. 'August stole two of Marcus's doves from the aviary. To coax Strike back.'

Justine frowned. 'Your father would be mighty angry if he found out.'

J.C. nodded. 'I know. But you won't tell him, will you?'

She considered for a minute. Then she put a hand on his shoulder. 'No. I think we have enough to worry about right now, don't you?'

'We sure do. Like how do we get home?' She felt him shiver under the thin stuff of his shirt. 'I just wish we could find August.'

'Maybe he already found his falcon and went back.'

'Maybe.'

'What do you say we head for safe ground?'

J.C. didn't need any encouragement. 'But let's go a different way,' he said, and together they turned away from the sea and headed down the slope. They made a wide loop, skirting the forest, and were almost to the canefields when J.C. suddenly jerked his hand away from Justine's and darted off toward a clump of oleanders. 'Oh my gosh,' he yelled, bending over. 'Look at this!'

Strewn on the ground in every direction were the contents of August's backpack. His glove, his lures, Strike's leashes. The backpack itself was slashed to ribbons. Nearby, the cage that had once held the stolen doves lay on its side, twisted all out of shape. The door had been ripped off its hinges. The doves were gone.

J.C. felt his shock turn to panic. 'Something bad has happened to August,' he gasped. 'Something really bad.'

'Don't worry,' Justine said, forcing herself to be calm. 'We'll find him.'

Frantic, J.C. shook his head. 'We'll never find him by ourselves. We have to get Amalie and we have to get her quick.' He turned and began to run.

Justine stood still for a minute, staring down at August's backpack. She couldn't make any sense of it but she remembered Amalie's warning. *In spite of all that has happened, the worst is yet to come.*

'What next?' she whispered to herself. 'Sweet God, what next?' Then she turned and without looking back she began to run as fast as she could through the cane fields after J.C.

21

The only part of her that was visible was her face. Miraculously, it was unscarred. The rest of her was encased in a cocoon of plaster and bandages. The room was silent except for the whooshing sound of the machines that were keeping her alive. There was a crisp smell of oxygen.

Stefan and Marcus stood at the foot of the bed. Poor little Caitlin, Stefan thought. She looked so frail, so broken. He glanced at his brother and was sorry he had. Marcus's face was a death mask, his eyes polar green chips of ice.

Once outside, Stefan turned to the doctor. 'What are her chances?' he asked.

The doctor shrugged. 'We won't know for at least twenty-four hours. But at this point there is little evidence of internal bleeding and that, as you know, is good news.'

'I want her transferred,' Marcus said, his tone flat. 'I want her flown to New York.'

A polite smile creased the doctor's face. 'I would certainly advise against such a thing at this time, Mr Leyland. Her condition is very unstable. I cannot see that anything would be gained. And you might very well be putting her at risk.'

'He's right, Marcus,' Stefan said quietly.

It was as if neither of them had spoken. Marcus's face was granite. 'Caitlin is to be transferred to New York because I am leaving Barbados in three days' time. Whatever arrangements need to be made, I will make. You need only see to it that she's ready to go.' With that he turned abruptly, leaving Stefan and the doctor both stunned, staring after him.

After a long awkward moment the doctor cleared his throat. 'Does your brother realize that by insisting on this move he may be putting the patient in serious jeopardy? Does he understand the seriousness of the trauma she has suffered?'

Stefan lifted his hands in bewilderment. He couldn't imagine what was going on in Marcus's head. What did he mean, he was leaving Cristobel in three days? What was he talking about? 'I can't believe he does. I think he might be in shock himself.' He felt a sudden urgency to talk to his brother. In all the anxiety over Caitlin, he had paid little attention to Marcus or to how he was handling this latest disaster.

Stefan made a movement towards the door, then turned back, extending his hand. 'We appreciate everything you've done, Dr Joneson, and I'm sure that when my brother thinks about it, cooler heads will prevail. In any case I'll expect to hear from you as soon as you get the results of her blood tests.'

He left the hospital and hurried around to the emergency entrance where they had left the driver with instructions to wait. The area was jammed with cars, each jockeying for position, everyone honking his horn. So much for a quiet zone, Stefan thought. He made his way through the line, looking for Cristobel's driver. It didn't take long for him to realize that the car had gone. 'Thank you very much, Marcus,' he muttered under his breath. He walked two blocks and hailed a cab.

J.C. sat on the edge of his bed, waiting anxiously for Amalie to come back. She had been out looking for August for almost an hour. What could be happening? he wondered.

A small sound by the open door made him look up. One of the kitchen cats had come into his room, and although it wasn't close enough to be petted it didn't seem concerned to see him sitting there. J.C. considered that to be a major good omen. Normally the kitchen cats didn't like to be around people.

The cat sat by the door and watched him, its pale eyes unblinking, seemingly indifferent.

'Hi, kitty,' J.C. said softly. He slipped off the bed and got down on his knees. 'How come you came up here?'

At the sound of his voice, the cat moved its ears back a fraction, but it didn't seem otherwise alarmed.

J.C. inched a little closer. He had always wanted a cat. Not a half-wild thing like the ones that were kept at Cristobel to keep the rodents and lizards away, but a real pettable cat of his own. But his mother wouldn't hear of it and neither would Marcus. Maybe I could tame this one, he thought. Maybe if I give her something to eat every day she'll let me play with her and come to sleep on my bed.

The idea was intriguing. He crept closer. He was near enough now to reach out and touch her. Thus preoccupied, he never heard the door to the hall open, then close.

'You crummy little shit,' August said.

J.C. whirled around, his eyes wide with surprise and relief. 'Oh, August, what happened?' He jumped up. 'Where were you?'

August reached out and grabbed J.C. by the shirt. 'I was with Remus, you little blabbermouth. And if Amalie hadn't come along, I would have fixed that gorilla once and for all.'

J.C.'s jaw dropped open. 'But I thought . . . I thought you were in trouble. Your stuff was all wrecked. Your backpack was all cut up.'

August let his brother go with a shove, his expression one of utter contempt. 'I know that, stupid. He jumped me from behind.'

'What . . . what did he want?' J.C. stammered.

August gave a vicious kick with his foot and the cat darted out the door. 'He wanted me to tell him how Amalie uses the *gris-gris*.'

J.C.'s eyes opened even wider. 'Did you tell him?'

'Of course I didn't.' His grey eyes were narrow slits. 'But I was about to fix him good.' A faraway look came to his face, and his secret smile appeared. 'He thinks that Amalie is a *bocor*, and that when he stole Damballah he stole her power. He doesn't know how wrong he is.' His smile faded. The anger came back. 'I was going to show him how to mix a potion that would have rotted his stinking guts out. But I never got the chance because some fucking little shitass told Amalie I was missing.' He reached out to punch J.C. but J.C. dodged, fleeing to the opposite side of the room.

'How the heck was I supposed to know?' J.C. protested, ready to bolt for the door. He had never seen August so furious.

'You weren't,' Amalie said quietly, coming in from the upper gallery. She stood motionless for a minute, black eyes flashing, every muscle in her body taut. It seemed to J.C. that she was taller than ever. 'Sit!' she said to August. She pointed to a chair.

He obeyed.

'The fault is mine, not your brother's,' she said to him, her voice stern and cold. 'I expected too much of you, August. Far too much, far too soon.'

J.C. saw his brother's jaw tighten, saw the small spots of red appear high on his cheekbones. 'You don't know what's going on, Amalie. Remus thinks you are a *bocor*.'

'Let the fool think what he likes. How can it possibly concern us?'

'He wants me to teach him all I know.'

'You will teach him nothing! Do you hear?' She grew even more intense. 'I know that the fault is mine. I taught you skills before you had the maturity to know when to use them. Now, before you come to any harm, I must act. I had wanted to proceed slowly in this matter. With caution. But now I see that it is impossible.'

'I was going to kill him,' August said matter-of-factly. 'And I would have if . . .'

'Silence!' The word cracked like the lash of a whip. 'I know what you were going to do. But you succeeded only in goring the bull, making him believe that you have the knowledge he so desperately wants. That was a very foolish thing to do.'

August clenched his teeth and J.C. winced, feeling his brother's anger.

Amalie folded her arms across her chest. 'Now I must stop him before any more harm is done.

From now on, you will leave this house only when I tell you to do so.' She lowered her voice to a whisper. 'Just because you cannot see me, August, don't ever think that I am not watching.' With one last withering glance over her shoulder she left the room.

Throughout the entire discourse J.C. never saw August flinch. Not once. But by the time Amalie finished with him, his cheeks were flaming red.

After she left, neither boy spoke for several long minutes, and it was August who finally broke the silence. 'I'm hungry. Let's go get some lunch.'

J.C. was shocked to hear him sound so normal. As if nothing out of the ordinary had even happened. 'Whatever you say,' J.C. said.

He followed his brother downstairs. He was dying to find out what really had happened out there with Remus, but he didn't dare ask. If August was now in a decent mood, there was no way J.C. was going to screw it up.

Justine was in the living room waiting for Marcus and Stefan to come back from Bridgetown when she saw the two boys pass by in the hallway. She jumped to her feet and caught them just as they were about to go into the dining room. 'August,' she said, 'I'm so relieved to see you back safe and sound. What on earth happened to you this morning?'

August gave her a blank stare. 'Why? Was there a problem?' His tone was polite enough but she could sense an undercurrent of hostility. He turned to J.C. 'Did you have to tell the whole household?'

'Justine was with me when I found your stuff,' J.C.

204

said, then suddenly remembered. His face lit up. 'We were looking for you to tell you about Strike.'

August's expression changed, became slightly less hostile. 'Strike? What about her?'

'Justine saw her yesterday. Right here on the lawn.'

August looked sceptical. He turned to his stepmother. 'You saw the falcon?'

'I did. Late yesterday afternoon.'

'How do you know it was Strike?'

Justine described the bird exactly as she remembered it. 'She circled down and landed on – ' She shot a quick glance at J.C. ' – on someone's arm.'

'That's impossible,' August said. 'No one at Cristobel knows anything about falconry except me and Amalie.'

'Someone else does,' Justine said quietly.

August's eyes glazed over. He seemed to be thinking out loud. 'It wasn't Remus,' he said. 'It couldn't have been Remus. But who?'

'It was a woman,' Justine said. 'A woman in a long white dress.'

A look of suspicion came into his eyes. 'Have you told my father?'

'No.'

'Are you going to?'

'I can't think of a reason to. Can you?'

August stood considering for a minute, then turned and headed back across the hallway toward the stairs.

'Where are you going?' J.C. yelled.

'To get my other glove and tackle. And then I'm going to find Strike before Marcus does.'

'But . . . but what about Amalie?'

Slowly August turned. 'I suppose as usual you're going to tell her.' For a minute he stood motionless, looking pensive, then he walked back to where Justine

205

and J.C. stood, the two small red spots on his cheeks the only sign that he had ever been angry. He smiled. 'I'm sorry, Justine. I guess I lost my temper.' Then he went into the dining room without so much as a glance at his brother.

22

Stefan sat in silence as his cab moved up through the rainforest, heading toward Cristobel. He couldn't believe he had been so stupid last night. Why in hell had he thought that the woman in white was out there somewhere, when in fact it had been Caitlin? Unless, he thought grimly, the woman had really been following him and he just hadn't seen her.

The cab stopped at the top of the hill and he got out. It had started to rain again but the trees gave him shelter until he was almost to the edge of the lawn. He wondered if Marcus had come back yet. As far as he was concerned, right now an awful lot hinged on his brother and what was going on in his head. 'I am leaving Barbados in three days' time,' Marcus had said. But what the hell was he talking about? What kind of plans had he made that no one else knew about? And in the last analysis, what does he expect from me? Stefan wondered.

And to add insult to injury, Marcus had left the hospital without so much as a backward glance in Stefan's direction. It was as if he had ceased to exist.

Stefan ran the last hundred yards to the house. Once on the veranda he stopped to catch his breath and shake the water off his windbreaker. The front of the house was quiet, but it was an eerie quiet, as if the entire household had already packed up and gone away. He felt an uneasy prickle at the back of his neck at the thought of being left all alone at Cristobel. 'You're beginning to get on my nerves, Leyland,' he muttered to himself. 'Try to behave like an adult, will you?'

The front door was closed, the first time he had ever seen it so. He opened it slowly, cautiously, and stepped into the entrance hall. Normally the breeze blew through the house from front to back, keeping the air inside fresh and cool, but today it was damp and musty smelling. In spite of his resolve, there was something about the house that gave him the creeps, and when Justine came up behind and tapped him lightly on the shoulder, he couldn't help it. He yelped.

'I'm sorry,' she said, jerking her hand back. 'I didn't mean to startle you. But I'm so glad you're back. I have to talk to you.' She took his arm and led him into the living room.

'Where's Marcus?' he asked.

'He's in his studio.' She frowned. 'That's one of the reasons I need to talk.' She sat down on the edge of a chair and stuck her hands between her knees. 'My fingers are frozen. Have been all day.' She smiled a weak smile. 'How's Caitlin?'

'Holding her own.'

'Did she . . . did she tell you anything about what happened last night?'

'No. She's still in a coma. We won't know much for another twenty-four hours.' He sat down across from her. 'Didn't Marcus tell you anything about her condition?'

She shook her head. 'He barely spoke two words to me. He just told me he didn't want to discuss it, then disappeared before I had a chance to say another word.' She shivered, 'I have never seen him so withdrawn, Stefan. So unapproachable. I don't know what he's thinking any more and it scares me.' She threw up her hands. 'But then, what doesn't these days? Anyway, I wish you would talk to him, find out what he's thinking about, what he's planning to do, if anything.'

He nodded. 'I can try. Not that there's any guarantee. Marcus has never considered me a confidant. But I agree that he's behaving oddly even for Marcus. The sooner I talk to him the better I'll feel.' He started to get up but she motioned him back.

'That's not all,' she said, looking down at her hands. 'I . . . I saw the woman again.'

Stefan leaned forward. 'When?'

'Last night. Just before dinner.'

He was astonished at her composure. 'Why didn't you tell me?'

'I couldn't. There just wasn't a good time. But I think you'd have been proud of me. I didn't freak out.' She made a face. 'At least not then, I didn't.' Then she told him about the whispered warnings that both she and J.C. had heard. How they had spent most of the night huddled together, waiting. And finally she told him about being chased through the rainforest.

Stefan listened to it all in silence. He didn't dare tell her what he had imagined last night before Caitlin went off the cliff. Maybe he should have had his own blood tested. 'You seem very calm,' he said finally.

'I know. I keep wondering when the breakdown comes. When the horror becomes too much for even a crazy lady.'

'You're not crazy. I've told you before, there is only

one answer to all of this.' He took her hands. She was right. They were frigid. Her face was pale and drawn and in her eyes he could see a plea for help. A lump came into his throat. *Please God, let me save her. Don't let me screw this up.* 'There is only one answer,' he repeated. 'And as soon as I get that call . . .' He stopped mid-sentence and pulled her to her feet. 'Come with me. I'm going to phone VonVost right now. Maybe we'll be lucky. Maybe he already has the results.'

They crossed the hallway, heading towards the phone in the library when the sound of voices inside the room stopped them. The door was ajar and Stefan could see Marcus standing by the window. The only other person in the room was Amalie.

'I have watched disaster come to Cristobel,' she was saying, and there was something so ominous in her tone that Stefan held up his hand to keep Justine from going in. 'When you divorced my Caroline, I kept my own counsel. And when you brought another woman to live here in her stead, still I kept silent, waiting for things to be made right. Now I will wait no longer.'

Marcus's tone was equally chilling. 'I have little time for theatrics, Amalie. Say what you have to say. Then leave.'

Stefan turned away. The last thing he had the stomach for right now was an argument between Amalie and Marcus. 'Is there another phone down here?' he asked Justine.

She nodded. 'In the breakfast room.'

'Amalie didn't sound very happy,' he said, taking her arm.

'I think I know why.' Justine told him about her

210

strange encounter with Amalie this morning. 'You know how bloodless she seems, but when I told her that Marcus was trying to sell Cristobel, I could tell she was shocked.'

They walked across the rear courtyard and into the breakfast room. 'This place is creepy enough without adding to it by talking about Amalie,' Stefan said. 'Right now let's put in our call and see what Dr VonVost has to say.'

J.C. and August stood on the veranda just outside the library, listening. When J.C. first heard their voices he wanted to leave. He knew how Amalie felt about eavesdroppers, but August refused to budge.

'She's going to tell him about me,' August whispered, and the two angry red spots appeared again on his cheekbones. 'You can drag your ass out of here if you want to, but I'm staying.'

J.C. turned to go but Amalie's next words brought him up short. 'I understand you want to sell Cristobel, and I want to know how you think you can.' The boy threw a startled look at August but his brother was staring down at his feet, his hands clenched into tight fists.

'I don't see that it's any of your concern,' Marcus answered.

'Not my concern?' Her voice was so low that J.C. had to strain to hear. 'You foolish, foolish man. Surely you know that Cristobel is my *only* concern. Cristobel and those who belong here. It was the order of the court that you were not to consider selling until the boys reached maturity. So how do you imagine you can do it?'

J.C. didn't dare look, but he heard the clinking of ice cubes in a glass. 'It's none of your business,' Marcus said quietly.

'It *is* my business. You, of all people, should know that I will never allow it to happen.'

'You never cease to amaze me, Amalie. Not only are you the most arrogant woman I have ever had the misfortune to know but you are also the most unrealistic. You refuse to accept the facts. Your precious Caroline has deserted the ship, leaving me to deal with her sons and with Cristobel, and there's nothing you can do about it. I have finally decided what must be done. And it will be done, regardless of how you feel about it.' There was a pause, then he continued. 'Whatever happens, there will no longer be a position for you in the Leyland household.'

J.C. couldn't stop himself. He gasped out loud. Amalie not a part of their lives? Impossible. He could sooner imagine himself without his right arm. Beside him, he felt August tense up, and he knew that his brother was thinking the same thing.

Inside the library there was a long silence and finally Amalie spoke. She sounded tired. 'I have waited too long for things to be made right. My patience is at an end. Now you have been warned. I will not rest until Cristobel is safe.'

Marcus laughed, a harsh unpleasant bark. 'What do you plan to do? Conjure up some kind of spell? Summon up your spirits? Have them drag Caroline back kicking and screaming from wherever she is? You are a hoax, Amalie. I always gave you the benefit of the doubt – a credit, I must admit, to your ability to create an illusion of power – but now I realize that you are nothing but a charlatan. You haven't even been able to control Remus Hastings. How, may I ask, do you expect to control me?'

J.C. shuddered, waiting for the explosion, but when Amalie spoke, her voice was calm, silky smooth. 'I see that you find this amusing, Monsieur Leyland. I, on the other hand, do not. I am afraid your ignorance will prove to be your undoing.'

J.C. held his breath, waiting for his father's response but it never came. The next thing they heard was the opening and closing of the door.

All the circuits were busy. It would be a few minutes, the operator said.

Stefan and Justine sat in the breakfast room and waited, but Justine couldn't sit still. Her stomach was churning, her palms wet and sticky. With a trembling hand she poured herself a cup of coffee from the urn on the sideboard, took a sip, then pushed it away. She could feel Stefan's eyes watching her, full of concern for her, confident that this would soon be over. But this time his confidence wasn't contagious. Now, waiting for this phone call, she was suddenly filled with an awful certainty that he was wrong. That there had been no poisoning. That there were only two possible explanations for what was happening to her here at Cristobel. One was insanity.

The other terrified her even more.

'What is it?' Stefan asked, touching her hand.

'I'm afraid.'

'I know. And I don't blame you. But I also know what VonVost is going to tell me. So I'm going to say it again.'

She listened intently, wanting him to repeat it endlessly, even if it didn't begin to dispel her paralyzing doubt.

'The woman in white is real, but you and J.C. have been systematically poisoned and it has altered your perception of her.' He squeezed her hand. 'You are not insane.'

A look passed between them then that made her feel almost safe. After all, she thought, what could possibly harm her if he were here beside her?

You know what, her voice said. *This is something that nobody can protect you from.* She covered her face with her hands.

At that moment the phone rang.

Stefan dropped the phone back into the cradle and sat perfectly still, VonVost's words ringing in his ears. A dark slippery chill of fear slid up his spine. 'We've done every test we can think of, Dr Leyland,' VonVost had said. 'We found no trace of any kind of toxic substance. None whatsoever.'

23

'What are you going to do to Remus?'

'I'm going to fix him good. And then Strike and I are leaving and we're never coming back.'

J.C. felt sick. He knew August wasn't bluffing. 'But where will you go?'

'None of your business,' August said, jamming his clothes into a duffel bag.

J.C. didn't know what to say. His stomach was in knots. There was no doubt in his mind that August meant every word. He was going to do something bad to Remus and then he was going to leave Cristobel forever.

'But what will I tell Amalie when she finds out you've gone?'

August shrugged. 'Tell her whatever you want. I don't care.' He picked up a shirt with their school insignia on the pocket, considered it for a minute, then tossed it on the floor.

J.C. shot an anxious look toward the window. 'What if you can't find Strike? It's still raining so maybe she won't come out from wherever she's hiding.'

'She'll come. If she's anywhere around here, she'll come.'

'Well, what if you can't find Remus?'

August's answer was chilling in its certainty. 'I

won't have to find him. He'll find me.'

J.C. shivered. He couldn't imagine going off alone. Not even for a minute, never mind forever. 'Aren't you scared to leave?'

'Why should I be? What is there to be afraid of? Certainly not that chickenshit Remus.'

'What about Amalie? Aren't you afraid of her?

'I might be if I thought she'd catch me. But I'll be long gone before she even knows.'

J.C. looked down at his feet. 'Aren't you going to miss her?'

August shot a scornful look at his brother. 'Don't you ever listen to anything? Didn't you hear what Marcus said? Amalie isn't going to live with us any more, so what's the difference?' He opened the bottom drawer of his chest, took out a few things, leaving most behind.

Thinking about losing Amalie brought J.C. to the brink of despair but he pushed the tears back. He was never going to let August see him cry again. He stiffened his lip. 'If you leave, that means you don't believe in Amalie's power anymore. You don't think the *loa* will bring Mother back.'

'If she comes back, maybe I will too. But I wouldn't count on it if I were you.' August pointed to the clothes still in the drawer. 'You can have what's left, but then you're such a skinny runt, you'll probably never fit into anything.'

J.C. felt a flash of anger. 'I will too. Someday I'll be a lot bigger than you.'

August rolled his eyes upward. 'Oh yeah. Sure you will. And someday I'm going to be the Pope.'

For a few minutes neither boy spoke. Finally J.C. said, 'After you leave, how will you find enough to eat?'

216

'I have some stuff.' August pointed to the duffel bag. 'And when that's gone, I'll buy more. I've got plenty of money.'

J.C. chuckled. 'You do not. You only have sixteen dollars.'

'That's what you think.'

'Well, how much then?'

August looked smug. 'None of your business. But I'll tell you one thing. Marcus is very careless with his cash.'

J.C. couldn't believe his ears. 'You stole? You stole money from Marcus?'

August grinned. 'Let's just say I borrowed it. Against my inheritance. That is if there's anything left when Mother dies. But the way she spends money, I'm not holding my breath.' He zipped up his bag, then went to the closet, reached up and took down his treasure box, the round tin with the Christmas scene on the lid. He opened it and sorted through the contents, taking out the five silver dollars that their grandmother had given him before J.C. was even born, and the gold watch with the long chain. Then he put the box back in its place on the closet shelf. 'Even though I'll have gone,' he said, glaring at J.C., his grey eyes flashing, 'don't think that my box is yours. You keep out.'

'I don't want your old junk,' J.C. said.

August shrugged. 'Whatever. Anyway, I need your backpack.'

'What for?'

'Mine's gone, stupid. I don't have room for Strike's lures and tackle in there.' He pointed to his duffel bag.

Reluctantly J.C. slid off the bed and headed for the

217

door. 'You better not wreck it like you did yours,' he said, then stopped. 'Hey, wait a minute. If you're going away for good, how will I get it back?'

'You won't. But don't worry. You can ask Marcus to buy you a new one.'

For some reason that answer made J.C. feel even worse. 'I don't want a new one. I want my old one.'

August looked exasperated. 'Oh, for Christ's sake, I'll mail it to you when I get where I'm going.'

'Where's that?'

'I already told you. None of your business.' He sat down on the edge of the bed and began to lace up his shoes. 'Hurry up and get it. I want to be out of here before Amalie finishes her afternoon meditation and comes looking for us.'

J.C. walked slowly down the hallway to his own room, hoping against hope that something would occur to him that would keep August from doing this unbelievable thing. He considered telling Amalie, but discarded the thought almost as soon as it occurred to him. Amalie always spent the late afternoon behind closed doors. It was an ironclad rule that during her meditation she was never to be disturbed. So if she went to August's room now, he would know right away that J.C. had squealed. 'Then instead of kicking the shit out of Remus,' J.C. muttered under his breath, 'August'll do it to me.'

He took a few more steps, then stopped. I know what I should do, he said to himself. I should tell Justine. Maybe she can think of some way to stop August without getting me into trouble. He sprinted down the hall to her bedroom, but she wasn't there. He went into her studio but it was empty. And then he heard the clock strike four and he knew he had no more time to look. If he didn't come right back, August would surely suspect something. Frantic, he ran to his own room, grabbed his backpack off the hook in the closet, and streaked down the hall.

Outside August's room he stopped just for a second to catch his breath, then he threw the door open.

The room was deserted.

August was gone.

Justine looked down at the long angry scratch on the back of her hand and wondered how it got there. How odd that something like that could happen without a person even knowing. It must have hurt at the time and yet she had no recollection.

'Are you okay?' Stefan asked.

She nodded.

He stood up and began to pace, thinking out loud. 'What he said is impossible. There has to be some mistake.'

'There's no mistake,' she said quietly. Why do I feel so calm, she wondered. Why am I not screaming?

Because you've known all along, the voice said.

Known what?

That there was no poison. That J.C. was right. That the woman in white is dead.

Something like a small electric shock ran through her. 'Do you believe in ghosts?' she asked suddenly.

He stopped his pacing and sat down next to her. He didn't have to ask why she wanted to know. 'Do you?'

'I didn't. But I do now.' She looked at him hard, tears stinging her eyes. 'And I know something else. The fear I lived with when I thought I might be insane is nothing compared to what I'm feeling right now.'

Her lip quivered. 'So now, Dr Leyland, tell me again that you don't think I'm crazy.'

Stefan didn't answer right away. He was still numb. Finally he spoke, 'Do you want to know what I think?'

'You know I do.'

'I think you should leave Cristobel. Right now. Marcus or no Marcus. Sale or no sale.' Once it was said, he felt a tremendous sense of relief, as if somehow by accident he had stumbled on the only solution. Forget about hallucinogens. Forget about rational answers. Think about only one thing. Escape. There was no more time to lose.

He put one finger under her chin. 'Go tell him you want to leave. Right now. On the next plane. Tell you'll wait for him in New York or wherever.' A thrill of fear touched him. 'I don't know what's going on here, Justine. I really don't. But it doesn't matter, because ghost or no ghost, understanding or no understanding, I think you should get the hell out.'

A tremor went through her body, an odd mixture of gratitude and blind terror. Gratitude because Stefan didn't think she was being a fool. But he was afraid for her, and that terrified her. She was filled with a sudden hopelessness. That no matter what, it was too late to be saved.

'Justine?' he said softly, understanding as he always did when she needed help. 'Let's go find Marcus. Let's put an end to this nightmare.'

She sat for a minute, her heart beating wildly in her chest. Slowly she shook her head. 'I know you're right but it's impossible,' she said. 'Marcus and I have no money. I don't even have enough to get to Saint Vincent, never mind New York.'

'Now you *are* being stupid. I'll buy your ticket. You

220

can pay me back whenever you can. And you can stay in my apartment until you get settled.'

Tears of gratitude filled her eyes. She felt a tremendous urge to throw her arms around him and kiss him, because somehow she knew that this was her very last chance. 'You have yourself a deal,' she said simply.

They went to the library where they had last seen Marcus, but the room was empty. 'Where the hell has he gone now?' Stefan muttered.

'He's probably back in his studio.'

They headed for the stairs and were almost to the top when they heard the phone ring. Such a normal, harmless sound and yet it made her want to scream. Get a grip on yourself, Justine, she thought, clenching her teeth. Get a grip.

One of the servants appeared at the foot of the staircase. 'Dr Leyland, the call is for you.'

Justine and Stefan exchanged startled glances. 'Who do you suppose it is?' she asked.

'I don't know. Maybe it's about Caitlin. In any case, while I'm gone you see if you can find Marcus.'

The connection was a clear one. VonVost sounded as if he were in the next room. Even so, Stefan had to ask him to repeat himself twice.

'When we talked earlier,' the doctor said, 'I forgot to tell you about what we found on the handkerchief you sent up. A strange combination, I must say. We found traces of rum mixed with traces of decomposing human tissue.'

What the hell? Stefan thought. *What the sweet hell? How am I supposed to make any bloody sense out of any of this at all?*

24

J.C. never took his eyes off the clock. It was twenty-seven minutes after four. He was going to wait three more minutes and then, closed door or no closed door, he was going to get Amalie. Ever since he had found August's room empty – exactly twenty-seven minutes ago – he had wrestled with indecision. What should he do? If he told Amalie too quickly, August would know he had blabbed. But if he gave him too big a headstart, Amalie might never find him. A dozen times he headed for the door, then stopped, afraid that he might be getting himself into worse trouble than he was already in.

That was how his thinking had gone, back and forth, tell, don't tell, until finally he made his decision. 'At four-thirty sharp, I'm going to get Amalie!' he yelled out loud. 'And if August beats me up, too bad.'

Once the decision was made he felt much better, and when he heard the single chime of the clock signaling the half hour, he didn't waste a minute. He tore down the back stairs, across the courtyard, and through the arch that led to Amalie's room, all the while something inside him telling him he shouldn't have waited. That he should have told Amalie right away.

He slid to a halt in front of her door. It was still closed

tight. He inhaled, raised his hand and knocked. It was a light, timid knock, but to J.C. it echoed like a clap of thunder down the long, deserted gallery.

There was no answer.

He swallowed hard, straightened his shoulders, then knocked again, this time more forcefully.

Slowly the door opened. Amalie stood there, a towering giantess, arms folded across her chest, black eyes piercing his defences. Behind her, he could see the flickering reflections of scores of lighted candles.

'A – Amalie, I know we're never supposed to bother you when – when your door is closed.' In the face of her displeasure his courage faded fast. He rubbed his eyes hard with his fists. 'But I had to tell you. It's about August,' he said, choking back the tears. 'He's gone.'

Her expression changed instantly, became sharp, intent on what he was saying. 'What are you talking about, Jean-Claude? Gone where?'

The words tumbled out. 'He's gone to find Strike and then he's going to fix Remus good and then he's going away and he's never coming back.'

Amalie stepped into the hallway and closed the door behind her. Her voice was low, steady. 'When did this happen?'

'He's been gone exactly thirty minutes. That's how long I waited, but even so, I know he's going to kill me when he finds out I told.'

She bent over and put a firm hand on his shoulder. 'You have nothing to fear from your brother, *mon petit*. Nothing. You did the right thing. Now listen to what I tell you. Go back to your room and wait there until I come.' She drew herself up to her full height. 'You go now. I won't be long.'

She waited until he was almost to the end of the gallery. Then she turned and, moving swiftly, she left the house.

As was the custom at Cristobel, once the sun had set all the candles in the entrance hall were lit, casting an eerie, flickering glow on the white ceilings and walls. If I owned this place, Stefan thought, shivering, the first thing I'd get rid of would be the goddamned candles.

He went into the living room to find Marcus already there. He couldn't keep the irritation out of his voice. 'Where the hell have you been? Justine and I have spent the past hour trying to track you down.'

Marcus studiously inspected one fingernail. 'I don't remember appointing you guardian over my comings and goings. But if you must know, I had things to attend to.' He crossed the room. 'Can I fix you a drink? You sound as if you need one.'

'I do.' Stefan eased himself into a chair, suddenly realizing that every bone in his body ached. He needed a good night's sleep as well, but there was little chance of that until he got a few things straightened out. He was less than eager to tell Marcus about the negative blood test results. He knew what his brother's reaction was going to be. He could already see the sardonic curl of Marcus's lip, hear the derision in his voice. Oh well, Stefan thought, Marcus has always considered me something of a jackass, so this will come as no great surprise.

He leaned back in his chair and took a deep breath. He had to admit that thus far he hadn't been able to do much to help Justine. If anything, he had followed her into a quagmire of uncertainty. Without question he had missed wide of the mark when it came to the blood tests. Maybe Marcus is right, he thought wryly. Maybe I am a jackass.

But then in his own defence, the test results hadn't all been normal. He remembered the last of what VonVost had told him: We found traces of rum mixed with traces of decomposing human tissue. But what the hell did it mean? Stefan hadn't told Justine about it yet and he wasn't sure if he should. It might trigger something in her memory. On the other hand it might scare her even more. Until he made up his mind he decided not to mention it to Marcus. 'Will Justine be joining us?' he asked.

'She should be down shortly.' Marcus dropped two cubes into a glass, poured a double measure of vodka, and handed it to Stefan.

'Has she talked to you yet?'

'What about?'

'I'd rather she told you herself.' He took a sip. It burned all the way down. 'In the meantime, there are a few other things that need to be discussed.'

Marcus made himself a drink. 'Well?'

'At the hospital you said you were leaving Barbados in three days.'

'That's right.'

'What did you mean?'

The tone was arrogant. 'I meant exactly what I said.'

'You're leaving the island?'

'I am.'

'And what about Justine?'

Marcus didn't answer at once. With a slow deliberate motion he walked around the end of the sofa and sat down. How very much like a cat he is, Stefan thought, watching. How very cool and unemotional. 'What about her?' Marcus asked.

Stefan cleared his throat. 'Is she leaving with you?'

Marcus raised an amused eyebrow. 'Of course she is. But how typical of you to have to ask.'

Stefan felt a stab of anger. They were leaving Cristobel, so all Justine's agonizing had been for nothing. 'Just when did you plan to tell her about it?'

'Tell her what?' Justine said, coming into the room. She looked drawn, with deep circles under her eyes, but she still moved with that exquisite fluid grace that Stefan found so incredible.

He and Marcus both stood up.

She stopped, seeming confused, as if for a moment she weren't certain what to do. Then she crossed the room and stood beside her husband. 'We have to talk.' There was an edge to her voice.

'I'm sure we do, my darling.' Unlike hers, his tone was adoring. He bent and kissed the top of her head. 'But first let me pour you a glass of wine.'

She was clearly taken aback by the sudden change in his attitude. She turned to Stefan, a bewildered expression on her face and he knew what she was thinking. Marcus seemed more at ease tonight, more like his old self than he had in days. He sounded almost happy. Stefan couldn't imagine what had happened to alter his brother's mood so dramatically.

Marcus handed Justine a drink, then raised his own. 'May I propose a toast?'

Stefan and Justine exchanged glances, then lifted their glasses.

'To a new beginning,' Marcus said. 'And a farewell

to Cristobel.' He held his glass still for a minute, then put it to his lips and drank.

Justine froze, her arm suspended in place. 'Marcus,' she breathed, 'what are you talking about?'

'We are leaving Cristobel,' he said, obviously taking great pleasure in her astonishment.

'When?'

'On Friday.'

'*This* Friday?'

He nodded. 'I've made all the arrangements. We leave on the four o'clock plane for New York.'

'But how – ' she stammered, looking from Marcus to Stefan.

'Did you know?

He shook his head.

She turned back to her husband. 'But where will we stay? How will we afford it?' Her face was suddenly flushed with colour, her eyes sparkled. 'Don't answer. I don't care how you managed. The important thing is that you did it. We're leaving this wretched place and that's all I care about.' She reached over and grabbed Stefan by the hand. 'Isn't it wonderful? It's as if he read my mind.'

Marcus's eyes grew cold. 'Is there something going on here that I don't know about?'

Justine smiled. 'Nothing that matters now. Stefan and I had decided this afternoon that the very best thing for me would be to leave Cristobel. But I wasn't sure how to tell you that I couldn't stay here any longer. But now you've taken care of everything just like Caitlin said you would.' She set her drink down on the end table. She grew solemn. 'You've saved my life, Marcus. I don't imagine you'll ever fully understand, but it's true all the same.'

Stefan couldn't bear watching them. He stared down into his glass, swirling the ice around with a nervous motion. Why was he feeling so depressed? After all, wasn't this the best thing that could have happened? For all of them to leave Cristobel before any more tragedy struck? Of course it was. He didn't know how Marcus had found a way to cut free from the place, but he had. And as a result Justine was getting out. So why this feeling of loss? Why wasn't he feeling a great sense of relief? He should be, but he wasn't. And with deepening concern he realized why. It had nothing to do with Marcus. It had to do with Justine and how he had come to feel about her.

'What about the boys?' Justine was saying. 'Have you told them? J.C. will be so excited.'

'The boys will be staying here at Cristobel with Amalie for a time. They'll join us later.'

Stefan saw the colour drain from her face, surmised she was wondering how J.C. would deal with his fears alone. He couldn't help but wonder himself.

'Can't they go with us?' she asked.

'No. They can't.' His tone ruled out any further discussion.

The sparkle went out of her eyes.

'Where will you be staying?' Stefan asked, trying to lighten the mood. 'You're more than welcome to stay with me until you get settled.'

Marcus didn't even acknowledge the offer. He crossed to the sideboard and made himself a fresh drink.

There was a moment of awkward silence. Finally Justine said, 'Have you heard anything about Caitlin?'

'I spoke to her doctor this afternoon.' Marcus's

voice was brittle now. 'Although, to tell the truth, witch doctor might be a more appropriate title.'

How typical of Marcus, Stefan thought, and he felt the old hostility towards his brother stirring. He struggled to repress it. 'Has there been any change in her condition?' he asked.

'She's stabilized. That's all the fool could tell me.'

'He's not a fool, Marcus,' Stefan said.

'I didn't ask your opinion. In any case it won't be long before Caitlin is back in civilization. In order to provide her with the best care available, I've liquidated whatever securities I had. And I received a modest advance from Jack Thomas which should be enough for us to live on until . . .' He paused and his expression changed, became thoughtful, pensive. 'Ah well,' he mused. 'Who knows what may happen? In any case I've made all the arrangements for Caitlin. In three days' time she'll be in a good hospital with a competent staff where they know what they're doing.'

Stefan shut his mouth. If he was going to get into a brawl with Marcus, he wanted to be sure he knew why. He wanted to make sure it had nothing to do with how he felt about Justine.

'By the way, Stefan,' Marcus said coolly, 'just so you give yourself plenty of time to prepare, your flight leaves tomorrow morning for St Croix. Connecting to New York.'

Justine's hand jerked, knocking her drink to the floor. 'You mean . . . you mean Stefan isn't going with us?'

Something dark moved across the planes of Marcus's face. 'I hardly think, my dear, that at our age we require a chaperone.'

'I just thought . . .' Justine flushed, then threw her

hands up, wondering how she could possibly explain, wondering if she even knew herself. 'It's just . . . it's just that I've come to depend on Stefan.'

'I'm sure we can find you another therapist.' Marcus smiled, but Stefan saw beyond the smile and suddenly out of nowhere a single shocking thought came into his mind. *My God, this man is dangerous.*

At that moment a servant appeared in the doorway to announce that dinner was served, and Stefan heard Justine sigh. 'I wonder if the day will ever come when I'll feel like enjoying a meal,' she said.

For as long as he lived, Stefan would never forget the next sequence of events. They were inscribed in his memory as sharply as if they had been carved there with a knife.

Justine was several steps in front of him, Marcus by her side, holding her arm. Stefan was deliberately lagging behind, his stomach in knots.

They were almost to the arch that led into the dining room when Justine suddenly stopped. She turned back and stared at Stefan with an expression of absolute horror on her face. Her hand flew out and grabbed his, holding it tight. 'Something terrible has happened,' she whispered. 'Something – something ungodly.'

At the same time, the front doors swung open, and the wind came whistling through. All the candles flared up for an instant, then guttered out, leaving the hallway in semi-darkness.

The three turned and stared.

Amalie stood in the open doorway. In her arms she held the limp body of a twelve-year-old boy, but she

carried him as effortlessly, as lovingly as if he were an
infant. It was August. His shirt was blood-soaked, his
head tipped back at such a grotesque angle that it was
impossible not to see the mortal gaping gash across
his throat.

25

There were no sounds of sirens. No ambulance. There was no need. They covered up the mutilated body and took it away quickly, shaking their heads that something so hideous could have happened on their island.

Justine stood in the shadow of the stairs and listened, her eyes dry, aching. Inside the library Marcus was giving the police a description of Remus Hastings, describing the attack on the birds, the threats made against his sons. She heard the low murmur of other voices responding, asking more questions, but it meant nothing to her. Only one phrase kept going round and round in her head. *Get out, Justine. While you still can, get out.*

Dimly she became aware that Stefan had come from somewhere to stand beside her. 'Do you suppose anyone has told J.C.?' he asked quietly.

The question jolted her out of her stupor. 'Oh damn,' she said. 'Is there no end to this nightmare?' She looked up at Stefan. 'Do you think I should look for him? To see if he's all right?'

'Please do. You have a better rapport with him than anyone except Amalie.' He stood and watched until she had disappeared up the stairs.

'Stefan,' Marcus said, appearing in the library door.

His voice was cool, businesslike. 'Will you step in here for a minute? These gentlemen would like to ask you a few questions, and since I told them you'd be leaving Barbados tomorrow, they'd like to speak with you now.'

Stefan walked across the hall and into the library. Besides Marcus there were three other men in the room. 'Ask away, gentlemen,' Stefan said, 'though I can't imagine I have anything to add that you haven't already heard.' He paused. 'I'm sure you've talked to Amalie.'

There was a brief shuffling of feet and then one man who Stefan assumed was the Chief Inspector said, 'We haven't seen Amalie yet. But she isn't leaving the island, Dr Leyland. You, it seems, are.'

Stefan shook his head. 'I was. But not now.'

'There is no reason for you to change your plans,' Marcus quickly interrupted. 'There is nothing you can do here. We have suffered a tragic loss. We need our privacy.'

Stefan couldn't hide his surprise. He turned to stare at his brother. 'I thought you might want me to stay.'

Marcus didn't reply. His frigid glance moved past Stefan to the Inspector. 'What is it you'd like to know? Dr Leyland hasn't much time.'

The Inspector cleared his throat. 'Early this morning a certain young woman fell off a cliff not far from here. I understand you were the only witness.'

'As far as I know, yes.'

'Do you think there could be any connection between what happened to her and this unfortunate incident?'

'No.' That was one thing he was sure of. August's killing was the work of a fiend but clearly a human

233

one. Stefan still had no idea who or what had driven Caitlin to plunge into the sea, but he had no intention of mentioning the woman in white. It was too bizarre. 'I saw Caitlin fall,' he said. 'There was no one else in sight.'

'Except you.'

'That's right.'

'I'm sure when the lady regains consciousness she will confirm that.'

'I'm sure.' Stefan paused. 'But if it would make you more comfortable, it's not critical that I leave tomorrow.'

'As I said before, gentlemen,' Marcus said quietly, 'Dr Leyland is leaving on the morning flight to New York.'

There was another shuffling of feet. 'I don't think it will be necessary for you to change your plans, Dr Leyland,' the Inspector said quickly. He asked a few questions about Remus Hastings, none of which Stefan could answer. 'I really know nothing about the boy,' Stefan said. 'Except what's been told to me.'

The Inspector turned to Marcus. 'If I may I'd like to talk to your younger son.'

'I'm afraid that will have to wait until tomorrow,' Marcus said. 'Jean-Claude needs a little time to absorb what has happened. August was his only brother.' He sounded irritated. 'Frankly I think justice would be better served if you were to look for Remus Hastings.'

'We are already doing that, Mr Leyland,' the Inspector said quietly. 'Barbados is not a large island. The boy cannot hide for long.'

'He can hide for as long as he chooses to do so.' Amalie stepped into the room. Her voice sounded whispery, like the rustle of dry leaves.

234

Stefan couldn't help but stare. In the dim light Amalie's skin looked almost grey, her eyes sunken deep beneath hooded lids. And yet somehow in her grief she seemed more formidable than ever.

Two of the policemen shrank back a little, clearly intimidated, but the Inspector stepped forward. 'I'm pleased to see you again, Amalie. I'm just sorry that it has to be under such trying circumstances.' There was a certain measure of respect in his tone. 'I have some questions.'

'I was sure you would.'

'You found the boy?'

She nodded.

'Did you see anyone?'

'No. Only the child. Only August.' The last two words were almost inaudible.

'We understand from Mr Leyland that you have been having problems with the Hastings boy.'

'Nothing I could not deal with.'

'Is *this* how you deal, Amalie?' Marcus interrupted again, and there was such venom in his tone that Stefan winced. 'Is this how you protected my children? My son, whom you claimed to love?'

Stefan searched her face for some sign of a reaction but she remained expressionless. Only the faintest tightening of the muscle along her jaw showed that she had even heard. She addressed her next remark to the Inspector. 'I made a serious misjudgment, Monsieur. One for which I will pay dearly for the rest of my life.' She turned and impaled Marcus with a piercing glance. 'But now at least August's mother will come home.'

Something dark passed across Marcus's face but he said nothing.

The Inspector cleared his throat. 'Do either of you have any idea how we might contact Mrs Leyland?'

'The *ex* Mrs Leyland,' Marcus said. 'The last time we heard from her she was somewhere in Asia.'

'We will do our best to locate her.' The Inspector narrowed his eyes and looked back at Amalie. 'And Remus Hastings? Do you have any idea where he might be?'

'No. I do not.' She spoke clearly, without hesitation, but Stefan wondered if she was telling the truth. Justine's words echoed in his mind. *Nothing happens at Cristobel that Amalie doesn't know about.* If Amalie really didn't know where Remus was hiding, he bet it wouldn't be long before she found out. Remus Hastings had committed an appallingly vicious act, but Stefan couldn't help but hope that the police found him before Amalie did.

'If you will come outside,' the Inspector said, 'I would like you to show me exactly where you found the boy.'

'As you wish.' Like an empress leaving her court, Amalie followed the Inspector to the door.

Stefan watched her go and suddenly he felt a great rush of sympathy for her, somehow certain that besides J.C., the only other person truly devastated by August's death was Amalie.

August, oh shit, August. How could this have happened? Why didn't you listen to Amalie? But why, oh why, he asked himself, hadn't he told Amalie right away that August was gone? Maybe she would have found him in time, kept Remus from hurting him. With broken sobs he had poured out all his feelings of desolation and guilt to Amalie and she had tried to comfort him. But it was hard for her to help, J.C. knew, because Amalie was struggling with her own grief. Her own guilt. 'It was not your fault, Jean-Claude,' she had said. 'If there is any blame to be laid it is on my head. Besides, now is not the time for you to be weak. Now is the time for strength. Your mother will be home soon and when she comes she must find a tall brave son waiting for her. Not a snivelling infant.'

She had left him then, ordering him to stay in his room until she came for him. She said she had to speak to the police, but J.C. was sure that as soon as they were gone, she was going to search for Remus.

His stomach ached, his throat burned, his eyes were sore from crying. He sat up, blew his nose, then swung his legs over the edge of the bed. What will become of me now? he wondered. Who will be my friend? True, August had never been very nice to me, but he had always been there. Now I'm all by myself. August really wasn't ever coming back.

J.C. felt doomed.

All at once he heard a sound and instantly his sadness changed to fear. He jerked his head to one side, listening. Was someone coming? Was someone sneaking along the gallery? Could it be Remus coming to get him? To finish the job? Get rid of the other white maggot? Or was it someone else? He felt his pulse quicken. Ever since Amalie had told him about August he had forgotten all about *her*. Now with a jolt he remembered. And the thought of *her* made Remus Hastings seem like nothing. After all, at least Remus was a human.

His heart in his mouth, he leaned back against the headboard and listened. How quiet it seemed. Even the night birds were still. And then he heard a faint knock on the door. He caught his breath and held it.

The knock came again. And a soft, recognizable voice called, 'J.C.?'

He exhaled and jumped off the bed. He opened the door and threw his arms around Justine, all his heartbreak and bewilderment and fear coming out in long gulping sobs.

'It's all right to cry,' she said. She came into the room and knelt on the floor and held him tight, soothing him, comforting. 'I know it's awful, J.C. I know. I know.'

He cried for a very long time. He just couldn't seem to stop, but Justine never pushed him away, never told him to be brave, never told him to hush. She just kept rocking him and rubbing his back with a gentle, comforting touch.

When he finally felt able, he straightened up and wiped his eyes on his shirt-tail. 'What's – what's going to become of me?' he asked. 'August is dead. My mother is gone. Now I don't have any family at all.'

'Of course you do,' Justine said. 'You still have your father. And you have me. Besides, as soon as your mother hears what happened, she'll come home.'

He shook his head. 'There isn't going to be any home to come back to. I heard my father say he wants to sell Cristobel.' He blinked hard, squeezing back the tears.

'Your father can't sell Cristobel, J.C. Not for a long time,' she said softly. 'There'll always be a home here for you. And with us. Wherever we go.'

Something tight inside his throat eased a little but he still felt a terrible cloud of doom hanging over his head. August was dead. And even if his father didn't sell Cristobel, soon Amalie would no longer be part of his life.

A tremor went through his body, and Justine, seeing it, pulled him close again. 'It's going to be all right, J.C.,' she said firmly. 'You don't have to go anywhere if you don't want to. I promise. Your mother is going to come home, I'm sure. And then you won't have to leave Cristobel. Or Amalie. Ever.' Even as she said it she wondered what in the world she was talking about.

And then another thought came into her mind. What if *Caroline* does come back? What will happen to Marcus? What will happen to me?

26

The air was thick with moisture and the rustling sounds of small nocturnal creatures. The candle on the table beside him burned without flickering; mute testimony to the stillness of the night.

Stefan sat on the veranda alone. After the Inspector and his men had left, Stefan had tried to talk to Marcus. He wanted to tell him about the blood tests, to talk about this woman in white, and most of all, to tell his brother that he wanted to stay until Justine was safely away from Cristobel. But Marcus was in no mood to discuss anything. With a wave of his hand he put Stefan off, then vanished into his own inner sanctum without another word. Apparently as far as Marcus was concerned there was nothing left to be said.

Stefan heard the clock strike eleven and he wondered if Justine had gone to bed. He really wanted to talk to her, see if she was all right, see if she had seen J.C.

A maid stepped out onto the veranda and offered him something to eat but he wasn't hungry. He thought about going to look for Justine, then decided against it. Marcus had made it crystal clear that he was no longer welcome at Cristobel. He had no choice but to disengage himself.

A cooling breeze stirred along the edge of the lawn

and wafted across the terrace. It touched the candle and the flame flared up, then died back down, leaving the place bathed once more in dim, eerie light, and all at once Stefan was filled with the old familiar sense of foreboding. As if something ghastly were still waiting to happen. 'As of tomorrow it'll be of no consequence to you,' he said out loud. 'As of tomorrow you'll be back in New York, and all this will be but a strange memory.'

'So you're still planning to leave?' Justine had come up behind him. She sat down on the edge of the chair. 'I know it's cowardly of me but I had hoped you'd stay.'

'It doesn't seem as though I have much choice. Marcus has made it clear that he no longer requires my services or desires my presence.'

She put her hands to her head in a gesture of desperation.

'He no longer requires? What about me? What about what I require?'

He couldn't look at her. He didn't want her to see how he felt. 'You'll be just fine,' he said, keeping his tone light. 'You'll be leaving Cristobel yourself in a few days.'

Justine closed her eyes. 'Why doesn't that make me feel comforted?'

'It should. Have you forgotten what the real world is like? How normal it is?'

She tried to smile but it was a sickly attempt. 'Normal? What the hell is that?'

He had to laugh. 'Thanks to Cristobel I'm not sure myself. But once we're away from here, I think we'll remember what it's like.'

She was sombre. 'If I live long enough, maybe so.'

He felt a sudden urge to be with her somewhere, *anywhere*, just so long as it wasn't here at Cristobel. To see what she would look like without the hunted expression in her eyes. Without the fear. 'Will you come to see me in New York?'

She reached out and grabbed his hand. 'Of course I will.' For a moment she held on tight, then seemed to realize what she was doing and with a look of embarrassment she let go. She wrapped her arms around herself and shivered. 'I'm cold. I think I'd better go inside. See how J.C. is doing.'

'Where is he?'

'In my room.'

'Were you able to talk to him earlier?'

She nodded.

'How did he seem?'

'Sad. Frightened. Lost. A lot like me, I guess. I told him he could sleep in my room tonight. I settled him down on the sofa and he went right to sleep. Marcus would be furious if he knew, I'm sure. But I don't care anymore. My husband seems to have lost his sense of compassion in all of this. That is if he ever had any.' She looked at Stefan. 'You know, it's strange how little we really know about people. Even the ones we think we love.'

'Marcus was never famous for his compassion,' he said quietly.

She looked wistful. 'I didn't know that. Stupid me.' She shrugged. 'Anyway, I hope J.C. gets through the night without waking. I can tell you right now, I'll be of little use to him if he has a nightmare. Lately I don't seem to be able to tell where the nightmare ends and the real world begins.' She stood up and took a few steps toward the door, then stopped. She didn't turn.

'If I asked you to stay – no, if I begged you – would you do it?'

'Yes.'

She expelled all her breath. 'Well, I'm not going to ask. I can't. I just wanted to know.' Then she moved away. And in the next moment she was gone.

When Justine tiptoed in, J.C. was crying in his sleep, making soft whimpering sounds like a baby animal. Her first instinct was to wake him but she decided against it. Whatever his pain, at least he wasn't aware of it. And hopefully, if he slept until morning he wouldn't remember dreaming at all.

She undressed in the bathroom, making as little noise as she could. Then, as had become her habit, she left the light on and slipped into bed. The clock on the nightstand read eleven-thirty.

She lay on her back and looked up at the fan turning soundlessly above. Her eyes burned from exhaustion but she couldn't close them. The fear was still inside her. It lay like a small malignant lump, too small to be felt by touch, but there all the same, pulsing with a life of its own, a life over which she had no control. She lay still, hoping that at least for tonight it would stay small, stay where it was, quietly pulsing there under her heart. If she didn't allow herself to think about what had happened to August or Caitlin, maybe it wouldn't grow. She wouldn't allow herself to think about Stefan leaving either. *God, how could she bear him leaving?*

She rolled over on her side. She would put everything out of her mind, especially thoughts of *her* – the woman in white. Whoever or whatever she was.

Under her heart she felt the lump stir, begin to

243

thicken. *Think of something else. Anything. Quickly. A B C D E F G. Red, orange, yellow, green, blue, purple, brown, black. Thirty days hath September. I have a little shadow* . . . *Sleep, Justine,* she pleaded. *Please. Please.*

And then somehow, miraculously, she did.

She dreamed. There were gardenias in her hair and she danced along a gently curving path lined with summer flowers of every description. The whole world was tinted with colour: pink and rose and apricot.

She passed through a garden with a singing fountain and she stopped to wet her fingers. She had no memory of fear. Only a deep sense of anticipation.

'Come along, Justine,' a gentle voice called. 'It's time.' A rustling current of air fluttered around her, lifting her up, encouraging her to move on. Her long, ruffled skirt whispered along the stones. She felt weightless, as if she had no substance, and she heard herself laugh. 'You're weightless because you're dreaming, silly,' she said, and she wished she would never wake up.

'Come along,' the voice called again.

She tipped her head to one side, listening. There was something vaguely familiar about the voice. And something disturbing. And suddenly she was filled with uncertainty. She squinted, trying to see, but the path ahead was clouded in pale green mist.

'Justine!' A new voice. This one was high-pitched, filled with anxiety, but it was far away.

Her uncertainty vanished. She knew now that she had to hurry, to run, to disappear into the dreamy mist before whoever it was could catch her and ruin everything.

'Justine!' This time the voice was almost on top of her. And all at once she felt a sharp stab of pain. Incredulous, she opened her eyes and stared down at her hand. On the fleshy part of her palm just below the thumb was a perfect crescent-shaped bite. Reddish-purple toothmarks that were slowly filling with blood.

'I'm sorry, Justine!' J.C.'s voice was a strangled cry. 'But you were walking in your sleep and you wouldn't wake up and I couldn't think of anything else to do!'

Instantly she was wide awake and her terror was infinite. She looked around. It was the dead of night. She was standing in the middle of a tangle of vegetation in her bare feet and she could hear the roar of the ocean not fifty yards away.

'We have to get away from here!' J.C. cried, pulling frantically at her sleeve. 'Don't you know? *She's* here! *She* wants you!'

Justine stared down at the boy and saw her own horror reflected in his eyes.

In the next instant they were running, stumbling over roots and stumps, fleeing for their lives. Justine had no idea where they were or where they were going. She had stopped thinking, conscious only of the boy just ahead, and whatever it was that was coming behind.

'Don't look back!' J.C. screamed.

Buffeted by waves of terror, she crashed through the underbrush, her arms stretched out to keep the sharp branches from ripping her face. She was only dimly conscious of sudden pain across her forehead, of something dripping.

Once, J.C. fell and she had just enough instinct left to lift him to his feet, drag him along. Behind

245

them she could hear the echo of cruel laughter, a sound that seemed far, far away, and yet at the same time, horrifyingly near. And then her worst nightmare became reality. *She felt something touch the back of her neck.* Something paralysingly cold, sickeningly wet. I'm caught! she thought wildly. Oh my God, she's caught me!

She heard herself scream.

In the same instant they broke into the open. Through the tears and blood and mist she could see the lights of Cristobel. She and J.C. staggered across the lawn, holding each other up, sucking in great gulps of air.

'We – we did it – we – we escaped,' J.C. gasped, collapsing on the veranda.

Justine sank down beside him. 'We escaped,' she whispered. But she knew better. They hadn't escaped at all. They only *thought* they had. She was suddenly filled with a horrible suspicion that this was all some kind of monstrous game. That when *she* grew tired of the game, there would be nowhere for Justine to run. Nowhere at all.

27

Stefan woke up to find J.C. standing at the head of his bed. 'You've got to come right away, Uncle Stefan,' he panted. 'Justine is hurt, and I can't find Amalie anywhere.'

Stefan jumped out of bed and pulled on a pair of slacks. 'What happened? Where is she?' He grabbed a shirt from the back of the chair as he went by.

'She's got a lot of scratches.' J.C. led the way down the long dark corridor and down the back stairway. 'She's in the kitchen.'

When he saw Justine, he was stunned. Her night-dress was stained with blood, and now, looking at both of them in the light, he wasn't sure how much was hers and how much was J.C.'s. Wherever there was exposed skin, the two were covered with cuts and scratches. 'Holy hell,' he breathed. 'What happened?'

He took a roll of paper towels from the counter and began to clean off the blood. He could see now that most of their injuries were superficial except for one deep gash on Justine's forehead.

They both began to talk at once, then Justine stopped. 'You tell him, J.C.,' she said. 'I don't think I can.' Her tone was almost robotic.

'I woke up and I saw Justine going out onto the veranda.' His words tumbled over each other. 'I tried to call her back but she didn't pay any attention so I went after her. She walked out across the lawn to the edge of the trees. She didn't use the path. She just went right through the underbrush. Through the bougainvillea thorns and everything. And then she started to run real fast.' He looked over at Justine. 'You're a very fast runner.'

'I know,' she said, taking the cold compress from Stefan, pressing it against the gash on her forehead. 'So are you.' A private look passed between them.

J.C. nodded, then turned back to Stefan. 'I finally caught up with her. She was almost to the ocean and I knew she was in terrible trouble.' He lowered his voice. 'Because I knew *she* was there. But Justine wouldn't wake up.' He stared down at his bare feet. 'So I bit her,' he mumbled.

'You what?'

Justine held up her hand so Stefan could see the livid purple toothmarks on her palm.

Stefan gave a low whistle. 'Now *that's* ugly. We'd better put something on it,' he said.

'I'm sorry, Justine,' J.C. whispered. 'But I didn't know what else to do.'

She reached out and touched him gently on the arm. 'You did the right thing, J.C. We both know what would've happened if you hadn't. So anytime you need to bite me to save my life, go right ahead.' The quick look passed between them again, and J.C. managed a half-hearted smile.

Stefan cleared his throat. 'Would someone like to tell me what this is all about? If either of you knows, that is.'

J.C. looked nervous.

'I heard the woman again,' Justine said and there

was something in her voice that went beyond fear. She seemed resigned. 'I went where she told me to go. Because just like the first time, I had no choice. And if it hadn't been for J.C., I would have jumped off the cliff.'

Stefan sat down hard and looked from the boy to Justine and back. He couldn't believe it. Here they were, back to square one, except that now he had no possible explanation. What he had counted on didn't exist. There were no toxins involved. He could feel a monster headache beginning to pound at his temples. All logic, all ability to make sense of this was lost. There was no such thing as going from A to B to C. He looked from one to the other. This must be some kind of group hysteria, he thought wildly. Some kind of weird psychic phenomenon. He felt a sharp cramp of fear. *Or is it something else? Something I can't begin to imagine?*

'The woman is dead,' Justine said flatly. 'J.C. knows it and I know it and I'll bet that Caitlin knows it too.' She bit her lip hard. 'And I'll tell you something else. I don't think in my whole life I've ever been so terrified as I am right now.'

J.C. inched closer to her. 'You don't sound scared,' he said.

'I know. You don't either. But we are, aren't we?'

He nodded. 'We sure are.'

'That settles it,' Stefan said.

'Settles what?'

'I'm not leaving Cristobel until you are both safe on an airplane out of here. Not that I seem to be able to do anything about what's happening. But at least I can be here.' He snorted. 'Big deal, right?'

What little colour J.C. had in his face drained away.

'I . . . I don't want either of you to leave,' he stammered, tears stinging his eyes. 'Because I can't go away right now. I'm scared to stay here, but I can't leave Amalie. And if my mother comes home I have to be here waiting. Amalie said so.'

'Amalie doesn't know about the woman in white,' Stefan said quietly. *Or does she?* 'In any case you can leave with Justine, and when your mother comes home, you can fly right back.'

'Your uncle is right, J.C.,' Justine said. 'You can't stay here without us. I'm going to talk to Marcus.'

Stefan got up. 'I'd better get some ointment for that hand,' he said to Justine. 'You guys wait here. I'll be right back.' As he passed behind them, he gave Justine a reassuring pat on the shoulder. And then he saw it. On the back of her nightdress just below the neckline was a large splotch. Not reddish-purple like the bloodstains. This one was rust-coloured. 'What's this?' he said, touching it with his fingers. It was still wet.

Justine turned and in the next instant memory flooded back, stunning her. She covered her face with her hands. 'My God,' she choked, almost gagging. 'Jesus God, how could I have forgotten? *She touched me!*'

J.C.'s expression changed to one of sheer horror. '*She* touched you?'

Something went *click* in Stefan's brain. 'Rum,' he said almost to himself. 'I'll lay odds that it's rum.' He didn't mention the part about the decomposing human tissue.

It was early morning. Stefan was alone in the breakfast room when Marcus came in. 'Glad to see you're up and about,' Marcus said, sitting down. 'The driver will be here at eight-thirty sharp.'

Stefan didn't look up. 'I don't think I should leave Cristobel,' he said, pouring himself a cup of coffee. 'And when you hear what happened last night, I'm sure you'll agree with me.' Then he told his brother about Justine and J.C. and their midnight flight from the spectral woman who had been terrorizing them.

Marcus listened without comment until Stefan had finished. Then he said, 'I thought you told me that this was all going to be resolved once you got the results from the blood tests.'

'The results were negative.'

Marcus's face took on a distant, dispassionate look, as if for a moment he had forgotten who Stefan was. 'In any case it doesn't matter any more. Once we leave Cristobel, Justine will forget any of it ever happened. I see no reason for you to remain here. None whatsoever.' He glanced at his watch. 'Are you packed? It's nearly eight.'

'I'd like to stay, Marcus. Just until you and Justine and J.C. are ready to go. Whatever the cause, they suffered a real trauma last night. I think they need all the support they can get. Whoever this woman in white is, she is causing terror out of all proportion.'

Something flickered behind Marcus's eyes then, something so cold and uncompromising that Stefan was caught off guard. 'We are leaving Cristobel. This woman in white is no longer of any importance at all.' He spoke in a monotone, each word receiving the same degree of inflection. 'And now I would suggest you get your things. As you know, it takes almost ten minutes to walk down to the road. I don't want the driver to be kept waiting.'

Stefan opened his mouth, then closed it. He knew there was no point in saying anything further. Clearly Marcus wanted him gone. This morning. To the point where he had made the most inconvenient travel arrangements; Stefan was going to have to fly to St Croix, then to San Juan, and finally to New York. It made no sense, considering the fact that most of the afternoon flights went direct to Kennedy.

Stefan felt an overwhelming urge to tell Marcus to go to hell. He'd taken enough garbage from him to last a lifetime. He set his cup down in the saucer and looked across the table to find Marcus regarding him with an expression that shocked Stefan into silence. The mask of indifference had vanished. In its place was a look of pure contempt.

'Before you leave I need to ask you a question.' Marcus's tone was scathing. 'How long, dear brother? How long have you been in love with my wife? And how long did you think you could play me for a fool?'

Hearing Marcus say it out loud left Stefan speechless. He was guilty as charged and he suddenly realized that he did not have a single moral ground left to question his brother's right to send him away. 'I'll get my gear,' he said, getting up from the table. At the door he turned. 'Best of luck, Marcus. I mean that. If you ever need anything, please call.'

There was no reply.

Stefan took the stairs two at a time. He had only a few minutes left and he couldn't leave without saying goodbye to Justine. No matter what, he had to do that.

He was almost to her room when the door opened and she came out. She held one finger up to her lips. 'Sshhh,' she whispered. 'J.C. has finally fallen asleep.'

Stefan could hear the weariness in her voice. 'I don't suppose you slept much either,' he said.

'Not a wink.' She made a face. 'Would you believe me if I said I was afraid to? Tonight I think I might tie myself to the bed.'

'How's the forehead? Maybe I should take a quick look before I leave.'

She went white. 'Before you leave? But I thought . . .' She looked down.

In spite of his heartache he kept his tone level. 'I have to leave. Marcus insists. Anyway, there's enough trouble here at Cristobel without me making things worse. You and Marcus and J.C. will be out of harm's way in just two more days. And then, I promise, everything will be A-okay. You wait and see.' He tipped her chin up with one finger. 'If you and J.C. stick together like glue, no one will hurt you. Not even the woman in white.' He was surprised at how casually he had mentioned it. As if there were nothing out of the ordinary about it at all. 'Anyway,' he added, 'just keep telling yourself, it's only two more days.'

Her breath came out in a low moan. She put her hand on his arm to steady herself. He could feel it trembling. He took it and held it for a moment, then he let go. 'I have to hurry,' he said. 'Marcus will have my head if I keep his driver waiting.'

He turned quickly and left her standing there. He didn't look back.

There was no one around to bid him farewell. He stood for a minute on the edge of the veranda, then picked up his duffel bag and headed out across the lawn the way he had come that first day. Only four days had passed but it seemed like an eternity. He didn't look back so he didn't see a pale, shivering Justine watching from the upper gallery. If he had, he might not have left.

He walked quickly, eager now to be gone, eager to put Cristobel behind him. He should never have allowed himself to become involved in any way except as a physician.

By the time he reached the road he had convinced himself that he was doing the best, the *only* thing he could do and still maintain some sense of self-respect.

The driver was waiting.

Stefan stopped at the edge of the road and turned for one last glance back. His breath caught in his throat. Incredibly, where he had just walked, the thick lush vegetation seemed to be closing in, obliterating the path, forming an impenetrable barrier. As if to keep whoever was in, in. And whoever was out, out.

Impossible, he said to himself. What the hell are you imagining? And yet, even as he denied what he was seeing, through the twisted underbrush he could *feel* someone watching.

'Who's there?' he yelled. 'Who are you?'

But all he heard in response was the sound of the wind.

The driver opened the door and got out of the car. He stood looking at Stefan with nervous concern. 'You okay, Dr Leyland? We best hurry if you gonna make that flight.' He took Stefan's duffel bag and threw it into the back seat.

For one insane moment Stefan thought about going

back, but a last shred of reason stopped him. If he was to regain his balance he had to get away from Cristobel. Get control of himself. He couldn't save Justine if he couldn't save himself. He needed distance. Then maybe he could make some sense of it all. Then maybe he could help.

He got into the car and leaned back against the seat, taking deep breaths of air, still shaken, trying desperately to recover his balance. The driver pulled away. But not in time to keep Stefan from hearing what he thought was the distant echo of high mocking laughter.

28

J.C. wondered what it would be like to be dead. Like
August. He wondered if August was in Hell. He hoped
not. There was a book in his father's library, filled with
horrible pictures of what Hell was supposed to be
like. J.C. and August had spent many a long summer afternoon pouring over the illustrations, trying
to decide which circle of Hell they thought was the
worst. August could never make up his mind, but
J.C. never had any doubt. The worst was the seventh
circle because that's where you ended up in the river
of blood. J.C. hoped that before August died he had
had time enough to say his prayers.

He walked across the veranda and sat down on the
edge of the step. A small grey lizard scurried along
the sand beneath the hibiscus hedge, then stopped.
Its throat pulsed orange.

J.C. watched.

The lizard moved a fraction of an inch, then froze.

J.C. could see a blue-winged wasp a few feet away,
burrowing into the sand. She had no awareness of
the lizard. She whirred her wings, intent on finding
a cool spot.

The lizard watched, motionless.

Normally J.C. would have stayed where he was until
the scene was played out. But not this morning. This

morning he felt a tremendous rush of sympathy for the wasp. He stood up and kicked a cloud of sand in the lizard's direction.

It slithered off into the shrubbery.

J.C. sat back down, feeling very tired. He wished he had had a chance to talk to August before he died, in that last second before Remus killed him. To see if he was scared. But then maybe his brother hadn't had a chance to be scared. Maybe Remus had jumped him from behind.

J.C. shot a nervous glance over his shoulder. Behind him, the veranda was deserted.

He turned his attention to one of the scratches on his leg. It made a long curving line along his calf muscle, and during the night it had turned an angry red. He flicked a scab of dried blood off one edge. It stung and he blew on it to ease the pain.

Beyond the terrace the sun had just cleared the tops of the trees, and the air turned sultry, steaming hot. He scanned the horizon, wondering where Amalie was. First thing this morning he had gone in search of her, but her door was still closed tight. He hadn't bothered to knock. Not because he was afraid to. Instinctively he had known that she wasn't there. And that knowledge had started the creepy tingling in his spine, because in the early morning Amalie was *always* there. He couldn't remember a day when she hadn't been.

She'll be back any minute now, he told himself. And I'll tell her all about what happened last night. And then she'll tell me what I should do. He had lost all faith in himself and in Justine. They both needed help. Powerful magic help. The kind only Amalie had. Now all he had to do was convince her that he wasn't imagining.

257

Squinting, he watched for her to come. I'll count to fifty, he thought. One, two, three . . .

A small flock of chattering sugar birds landed in the banyan tree on the edge of the lawn, distracting him for a minute. Then he went back to his counting.

He was almost to one hundred when suddenly he saw it. A winged shadow moving fast across the dark grass. He looked up. High above, riding a spiral of air, the huge falcon circled.

'Strike!' J.C. jumped to his feet. 'Holy shit, it's Strike!' His first instinct was to run and find August, to tell him the good news. But then he remembered. August was dead.

He stopped short, his breath coming out in a long groan. His arms fell limp to his sides and he stood watching the falcon, a single tear sliding down his cheek. 'Oh Strike,' he said, 'You shouldn't have come back. Who's going to take care of you now?'

At the same moment far across the lawn there was a flicker of movement that might have gone unnoticed had it not been for the bird. Circling down, Strike had settled to earth beside the giant banyan tree, and as J.C. watched, his eye caught an almost imperceptible stirring just beyond, in the thick cover of vegetation.

It's Amalie, he thought, breathing a huge sigh of relief. He took a few quick steps forward, then pulled up short, suddenly unsure. What if – ? What if it wasn't Amalie at all? 'Amalie?' He hunched up his shoulders and stared without blinking. And suddenly he heard a warning voice in the back of his head. *Don't look! Whatever you do, don't look!* He tried to put his hands over his eyes but his arms stayed stiff at his side. Powerless to turn away, he began to make a whimpering sound low in his throat.

In the next instant the woman in white appeared. Still half-hidden in grey-green shadow, she held out her arm, beckoning.

Horror-stricken, his eyes starting from their sockets, J.C. stared. Was it possible? Was *she* motioning for him to come? And then through a haze of terror he saw Strike spread her wings and in one fluid motion she took flight to settle on the outstretched arm.

The world swam in front of J.C. and his legs gave way. He collapsed in a heap, finally managing to bring his hands up to cover his eyes with small groping fingers. 'Go away,' he sobbed. 'Go away. Go away.'

And dimly, through the sound of his own pathetic gasps, he heard laughter. Cruel, malevolent, and somehow, terrifyingly familiar.

From the upper gallery Justine watched until Stefan had disappeared from sight. She felt stunned. She felt abandoned. She felt doomed. She had put all of her hope in Stefan. He was her one link to the outside world, the world beyond madness, beyond Cristobel. And more than that, he had been her friend. She was filled with a terrible sense of loss. If only . . .

Stop it, she said to herself. He's gone and there's nothing you can do to change it. She shook her head, trying to clear her mind. Two more days. She didn't even know what that meant anymore. Measures of time had ceased to have any relevance. Two more days. Two more weeks. Two more years. What difference, when each second that passed seemed like an eternity. An eternity spent waiting for something else unthinkable to happen.

What next? she wondered. What happens now? She

put her hand to her face and it came away wet. She had been crying like a baby without even knowing.

She walked down the gallery and stopped at the corner of the house. The sun had come burning up over the tops of the trees and she realized suddenly that it was a scorching hot day. The grass actually shimmered in the heat. She stepped back under the shaded overhang of the roof. Not that it mattered what the weather was like. Hot or cold, she didn't want to be outside.

Two more days, she said to herself, her arms hugging her shoulders as she took a deep breath. 'And now,' she muttered, 'if you can keep your wits about you for more than thirty seconds, you'd better find Marcus and have him see to getting a ticket to New York for J.C.' She gave a last nervous glance out across the lawn.

Your time is almost up, Justine.

The words came into her head so clearly that for a moment she thought she had spoken them herself.

Your time is almost up.

Again. Unmistakable. Malicious.

Justine knew whose words they were, and she was stricken with the kind of giddy weakness that only sheer terror can create. She looked out across the gardens. The woman in white was nowhere to be seen. But something else was. A small shuddering heap on the grass. It was J.C.

As she flew down the stairs and raced across the lawn she thought only one thing. Get J.C. inside. Maybe inside they would be safe. She tried to lift him but he was a dead weight, so she held him under the arms and half carried, half dragged the boy across the terrace and into the conservatory.

She sank down in a wicker chair beside the door and held him, rocking back and forth, crooning the same words over and over. 'It's all right, J.C. You're safe. It's all right. You're safe.'

J.C. didn't pull away, nor did he respond. He just lay against her, his head lolled to one side, his eyes half-open, unfocused, blank.

Oh God, Stefan, please come back, she prayed, holding J.C. tight. Please. I don't know what to do. I don't know what to do.

The car made its way past a line of taxicabs and pulled up in front of the BWIA terminal. 'Here we are, Dr Leyland,' the driver said. 'You best hurry.'

Stefan nodded and got out.

Almost before he could close the door, the driver pulled away, easing his way back into traffic.

Stefan waited until the car was out of sight. Then, slinging his duffel bag over his shoulder, he crossed the road and hailed a cab.

29

You cannot sit here any longer, she told herself. You have to get help. She put her hand on one side of his face and gently moved his head away from the curve of her shoulder.

She felt him stir. 'J.C.,' she said softly. 'Wake up. Come on, sweetheart, please. You're safe now.' What a simple word, safe. And how distant, how far out of her reach.

He lifted his head and looked at her, bewildered. Then bewilderment changed to terror and he buried his face against her shoulder, his thin body racked with sobs. Words tumbled out of his mouth in an incomprehensible babble.

'Easy, J.C.,' she said. 'It's all right. You're safe.' She marvelled at how calm she sounded. Her own sobs were lurking just below the surface. She bit down hard on her lip. She knew that if she lost control, she would never get it back. She would cry, then she would scream. And screaming, she would scream and scream forever. Long after they came and took her away she would still be screaming.

She held him for a long time, not speaking, and finally J.C.'s tremors began to subside. At last he raised his eyes and looked at her. 'We're in terrible trouble.' His voice was quavering but now at least the words were intelligible.

'I know,' she said. 'Do you want to tell me what happened out there?' She looked over the top of his head, wondering what she would do when she heard the answer.

J.C. was silent for a minute, then he answered in a ragged voice. 'I ... I saw *her*.' He shook his head back and forth, back and forth, as if he still couldn't believe it.

Justine made herself breathe normally. *Your time is almost up, Justine.* 'Where?' she managed.

'On the edge of the wood. I thought she was motioning for me to come. But she wasn't. She was calling Strike. I tried not to look.' His hands came together convulsively. 'I tried to cover my eyes but I couldn't.' The last was a frightened wail.

Justine pulled him close again, wondering what she could possibly say that would give him comfort. But her own mind was so filled with dread that she couldn't speak. All she could do was pat him on the back.

'You know what else?' he said, not looking up.

She waited.

His voice was low, shaky. 'I think ... I think *she's* someone I know.'

Someone I know. Her mind raced, trying to grasp what he had just said, to make some sense of it, to find some spark of sanity in the words. *Someone I know.*

The sudden sound of footsteps on the marble floor behind them brought her spinning around, almost knocking J.C. off her lap.

He slid off by himself and stood up, wobbly, still holding onto her hand.

'There you are,' Marcus said briskly. 'I've been looking everywhere for you.'

Justine felt an unexpected rush of anger. It wasn't fair. Here they were, she and J.C., on the sheer edge of hysteria. And now Marcus appears, clearly unconcerned, untouched by any of it. 'We've been right here,' she snapped.

He ignored the sharpness. In fact it didn't seem as if he had even heard her. Clearly his mind was on something else. 'There's been a change in plan,' he said. Then he turned to the boy. 'You are excused. You may go to your room until I send for you.'

J.C. shot a frightened look at Justine.

'I'd like him to stay with me, Marcus,' she said, making a tremendous effort to keep her voice level. 'We both have had a terribly trying morning.'

There was no spark of interest. 'Indeed? Well, you can tell me all about it later. Right now I'd like you to go upstairs and pack. We're leaving Cristobel today. At four-fifteen this afternoon to be exact.'

She felt the colour rush to her face. She was caught up in a maelstrom of emotion: disbelief, hope, and an overwhelming feeling of relief. 'Are you serious?' she breathed.

'I am.'

She jumped to her feet. 'Oh, Marcus, thank you. Thank you.' She pulled J.C. close and hugged him. 'Did you hear? Did you? We're leaving! We're leaving today!' In her rush of joy she barely heard her husband's next words.

'I'm sure Jean-Claude will miss you,' he said.

She turned, frowning. What was Marcus saying? Then she remembered. Marcus wasn't yet aware that she intended to bring J.C. with them to New York. Still flushed with excitement, her frown changed to a smile. 'How stupid I am. In all the turmoil I haven't had a chance to tell you. J.C. is going with us. He needs a ticket but I know you can arrange it.'

Marcus's expression didn't change. His eyes were like glass. 'Jean-Claude is to stay here at Cristobel with Amalie.'

Justine shook her head. 'That's impossible, Marcus,' she said firmly. 'J.C. cannot stay here without us. He has been through a terrifying experience. To abandon him now would be unthinkable. His brother has just been murdered and . . .'

'This is Jean-Claude's home,' Marcus interrupted. 'He does not wish to leave it.'

Justine turned to J.C., feeling a stab of panic at the thought of leaving him behind. 'Tell him, J.C. Tell him you want to go with us.'

J.C.'s face was pale and pinched. Miserable, he looked from Justine to Marcus, then down at his feet.

'You see, Justine?' Marcus said quietly. 'The boy wants to stay here at Cristobel. I'm sure he appreciates your concern, but it's unnecessary. Isn't that right, Jean-Claude?'

Still staring down at his feet, J.C. managed an almost imperceptible nod.

'Very well. Now you may be excused.'

Without looking at either Justine or his father, J.C. turned and fled the room.

Justine was furious. 'How can you be so unfeeling? Don't you see that the last thing your son needs now is to be left here alone?'

'What my son needs,' Marcus replied, his voice barely controlled, 'is for me to determine. I'm sure you would never think of interfering where he is concerned.'

She was shocked into silence by what she heard

in his tone. Anger. And something more. Something threatening.

He glanced at his watch. 'Now I have some last minute things to take care of in my workroom. And you, my darling, had better hurry and get our things packed.' He leaned over to kiss her but she pulled away.

Whatever warmth there had been in his eyes vanished. He stood looking at her as if she had struck him, and she felt a terrible thud in the pit of her stomach. 'I don't know who you are any more,' she whispered numbly. 'I really don't.'

He stared for a moment, then smiled as if she had just said the most absurd thing. He reached out to touch her arm, then slowly he dropped his hand to his side. 'You'd better pack,' he said coldly. 'That is, if you don't want to spend another night at Cristobel.'

With that, he left her.

The farther away he got from the airport, the more convinced Stefan was that he had done the right thing in not leaving the island. He hadn't been away from the madness of Cristobel for more than a few minutes when his mind had begun to clear. He didn't know who the woman was or why she had been there, but he had no doubt that as he was leaving she had been watching. And he knew without question that she was a threat to Justine and to J.C. So what was he going to do about it? For one thing he wasn't going to run. He wasn't going to follow Marcus's orders. He wasn't going to abandon Justine and J.C. just because he had made a mistake and had fallen in love with her. There was something happening at Cristobel that

266

made everything else seem irrelevant. Until everyone was safely away, he wasn't going to abandon them.

By the time they had reached the airport he had made some decisions. He wasn't going to go to St Croix or anywhere else for that matter. Just because Marcus didn't want him at Cristobel didn't mean he had to leave Barbados. He'd find a hotel and call Justine, tell her where he was. And if she needed him, he'd go back. No matter what.

But first he decided to go to the hospital to see how Caitlin was doing. See if she was conscious. And if she was, he thought grimly, maybe she would be able to tell him who or what had driven her off the cliff.

He got out of the cab and paid the driver. He walked across the street and stood for a minute staring up at the second-storey windows. Then he went inside to look for Caitlin's doctor.

30

It seemed to J.C. that there was nothing left in the world that didn't terrify him. His throat tight with fear, he sat cross-legged on his bed and began to count on his fingers. First, there was Remus Hastings. Second, there was Cane Cave. Third, snakes. Fourth, his father. Fifth, August being dead. Sixth, Amalie. He shivered. Where *was* Amalie, anyway? Seventh, there was Justine going away. And finally the most frightening thing of all. *Her.* He let out a long shuddering breath. At least he hadn't seen her face, thank God. If he had he knew he would be dead right now just like August.

And then something struck him, something peculiar. If he hadn't seen her face, how could he think he knew her? And furthermore, J.C. knew that *she* was dead, and he didn't know any dead people. Except August.

You were imagining, he said to himself. You don't know who *she* is. August was right. You are a dumb shit. You are a cry-baby shivering miserable puking dumb shit. But admitting it didn't make him feel any less terrified.

He threw a nervous glance over his shoulder, then inched his way up the bed to sit with his back wedged against the headboard. It wasn't very comfortable but at least this way no one could sneak up on him from behind.

He sat without moving, listening to his heart beat, listening to his stomach growling. It was almost past lunchtime. Why hadn't Amalie come to get him? Surely she was back by now. Unless . . .

Unless Remus Hastings had done something horrible to her.

That's ridiculous, he said to himself. Amalie is too powerful. But then he remembered that Remus had the Lord Damballah, and he slid from hope to despair. He shuddered again, picturing the snake god's head with its hideous open jaws. He threw his hands over his eyes and sat stiff as a board, suddenly afraid to move another inch. They're going to find you here a hundred years from now, he whispered to himself. Right here on this bed. With all the skin rotted off your bones. Justine and Marcus are going to leave, and Amalie is never coming back, and no one will even know you're here. No one but *her*.

He spread his fingers and sneaked a fearful look toward the door that opened onto the outer gallery.

Nothing there.

He listened, his skin crawling. Had he heard something? The sound of something creeping along in the shadows just beyond his door?

At that moment a gust of wind blew into the room. The door moved.

J.C.'s breath caught in his throat and he clasped his hands together and stared. Had it been the wind? Or had something else touched the door?

'Jean-Claude.'

J.C. let out a high-pitched shriek and whirled around, his eyes wide with fear.

His father stood beside the bed.

J.C. felt his cheeks burn with embarrassment. 'I'm – I'm sorry,' he stammered. 'I thought – ' He looked down at his hands.

His father's voice was dry, emotionless. 'I've come to take you to Bathsheba,' he said. 'Amalie is there waiting for you.'

Relief flooded over J.C. and he jumped off the bed. 'So *that's* where she is,' he said. 'With Lebon. I should've guessed.'

Marcus nodded. 'The car is waiting. Come along.'

J.C. followed his father into the hall. 'Can I say goodbye to Justine?'

'There isn't time. Amalie is waiting.' His tone left no room for objection.

As J.C. hurried out the front door, he threw one quick glance back over his shoulder, hoping to see Justine so he could at least wave goodbye, but behind him the hallway was deserted. As if no one lived there anymore.

'Goodbye, Justine,' he whispered.

His father closed the door quietly behind them.

Anger smothered her fear. She threw their clothes helter-skelter into suitcases without any consciousness of what she was doing. All she knew was that her husband was an unfeeling bastard. A monster. How could he possibly consider leaving his son behind in this hellish place?

Don't think you're such a saint, said a voice in the back of her head. You could refuse to go.

Something inside twisted into a hard knot. She stopped what she was doing and sat down on the edge of the bed. It was true. If she was so concerned about J.C., she could simply refuse to go. She could tell Marcus that unless the boy went with them, she would not leave.

Not leave Cristobel?

She heard a rasping sound and realized that it was her own breath. Not leave Cristobel? Was she heroic enough – or fool enough – not to leave, given the chance?

If you stay with J.C., you'll both die together.

'Oh, my God,' she whispered, clasping her hands together in supplication, 'what am I to do? What am I to do?'

You handled it badly with Marcus, she told herself. You never should have become angry. Never should have told him what to do. Now you have only one hope. You have to find Marcus and talk to him. Don't demand. Beg. Beg him to take the boy. He'll do it for you if you beg. You know he will. He loves you. He has never refused you anything. Just don't order him.

She gathered herself together. All she had to do was make him see how critical this was to her. A threat to her very life.

Your time is almost up, Justine.

She left her room and started down the hall. Marcus had said he was going to his workroom and she headed there, vaguely conscious of a peculiar stillness in the house. A feeling of emptiness.

At the foot of the stairs she stopped. The front doors were closed. There was no air blowing through. She walked across the hallway, her sandals making their sharp tapping sounds on the marble floor. But she didn't care. At least it was a sound in an otherwise silent world.

271

Like the rest of the rooms, the kitchen was deserted. She glanced at her watch. It was almost twelve-thirty and yet there was no sign of the luncheon staff.

Now she felt truly unnerved. She walked quickly across the rear courtyard.

Marcus's workroom was empty.

You're alone in this house. She felt the last remnants of control slipping away. Find J.C., she thought wildly. At least you know that he's still here. Breathless, she ran up the back stairs and down the corridor to his room. His door was ajar.

She pushed it open. 'J.C.?' she called.

No one answered.

She stepped inside.

The room was empty.

Caitlin was still swathed in bandages. Only her face and hands were visible, but there was colour in her cheeks. She looked serene. Like a nun. Until she opened her eyes. Then Stefan could see the confusion. And the fear.

'Happy to see you're still with us,' Stefan said, smiling.

'Barely,' she muttered in a weak tone. She reached out and took his hand. 'I'm so glad to see you. What's going on in this hellhole?'

Stefan looked around. 'It doesn't seem that bad to me.'

'You know what I mean. Not the hospital. Cristobel.' She shuddered, then winced. 'Jesus, I hurt. Even my hair. Do you suppose they've put leeches on me? That's what it feels like.'

He smiled. 'I'm not surprised you're sore. You took quite a tumble.'

'An understatement.' She narrowed her eyes. Her grip on his hand was weak and he could feel it trembling. 'Do you know what happened to me?'

'I was hoping you could tell me.'

She closed her eyes. 'I've thought about it until I'm almost crazy. But all I can come up with is bullshit.'

'Like what?'

She pulled her hand away from his and began to fiddle with the edge of the sheet. 'Like someone told me to jump,' she whispered. 'I thought I was dreaming. A woman in a white dress told me to follow her and I did. Someone I knew but couldn't figure out who. And when she told me to jump, I did.' Her hand went limp. 'You're the shrink. Explain *that* if you can.'

Slowly Stefan shook his head. What Caitlin said made no sense, and yet it was exactly what he had expected. 'I can't explain a goddamn thing,' he said simply. 'But I'm not surprised.'

'Why not?'

'The same thing happened to Justine.'

Her eyes opened wide. 'What the hell are you talking about?'

Stefan told her about Justine's episodes. About the woman in white. 'That's why I came to Cristobel. To try to help her. She thought she was insane.'

'But she's not,' Caitlin said in a low voice.

'No. Neither is J.C. He's seen the woman too.'

Her breath came out in a long quiver. 'So what the hell is going on? Who *is* this person?'

A great weariness filled him and he shrugged. 'I don't know. I've heard her voice but I've never seen her.'

'Has Marcus?'

'No. Whoever she is, she has critically affected only three people. Justine, J.C. and you.' He hesitated, then decided there was no point in avoiding the truth. 'J.C. and Justine think she's a ghost.'

Caitlin's only reaction was a tightening around the corners of her mouth. 'A ghost,' she echoed. 'Why am I not laughing?' She looked at him out of the corner of her eye. 'Why don't I think they're both nuts?'

He thought for a minute. Then he said, 'Because you know there are things happening at Cristobel that defy the laws of reason. And so do I.'

A pause. Then she shivered. 'I guess I should consider myself lucky to have come out of there alive.'

'I think you should,' he said. 'Others haven't been so blessed.' He told her about August.

Her face stiffened. 'Do you think it was this monstrous woman who did it?'

'No.' He said it with absolute certainty. He wasn't sure how he knew, but he did. 'Whoever she is,' Stefan echoed, 'she had nothing to do with it.' He was silent for a moment, then changed the subject. 'Have you seen Marcus today?'

She managed to shake her head. 'No. He hasn't been here to see me at all.'

'He was here with me yesterday, but you were still unconscious. Anyway, Marcus and Justine are leaving Barbados the day after tomorrow.'

That was too much for her. She let out a low moan. 'You mean he's leaving me here all alone to rot in my own sweat?'

'Easy, Caitlin,' he said, taking her hand. 'He's made arrangements to fly you back to New York. I'm sure your doctor will be telling you all about it.'

274

She looked at him warily. 'Are you sure?'

'I'm sure.'

'How has he managed? He hasn't any money and he can't sell the place until the boys come of age.' She shuddered. 'Though I guess August doesn't count anymore.'

Stefan felt a flash of anger. 'No. As far as Marcus is concerned he doesn't count at all.'

'Well, at least the rest of them are getting away from that hellhole in one piece.' She seemed visibly relieved. 'So what about you? When do you get your reprieve?'

'I've already gotten it. I was ordered to leave the premises this morning. But I decided to stick around Bridgetown for a while. My brother may banish me from the old homestead, but he can't run me out of town.'

'What in hell would you want to stick around here for? I would think you'd be off this island on the next flight.'

He was silent.

'What's the matter, Doc? Who are you afraid of? The woman? Or is there something else?'

His thoughts were so tangled that for a moment he couldn't answer. Finally he said, 'I don't know what's happening, Caitlin. Nothing makes any sense. But I'm sure of one thing. Somehow, this woman, whoever or whatever she is, is not the only danger.'

A nervous look crossed her face. 'You're afraid for them, aren't you?'

'I am. But I don't know what I can do about it.'

A nurse came in and turned a valve on a machine next to Caitlin's bed. It made a cool hissing sound. After she left, Stefan said, 'I can see you're exhausted.

I'd better get out of here before I wear you out completely. I'll be back later.' He was already out the door when he heard her call. He stuck his head back in.

'I think there's something I ought to tell you,' she said and he could see that now it was a tremendous effort for her to speak. 'I've had a lot of time to think about it and the more I think, the more uneasy I feel.'

He came back in and sat down. He watched her fingers tracing small repetitive circles on the sheet. 'What is it, Caitlin? What's the matter?'

'You know I love Marcus dearly for all his faults. At least I used to. You do know that, don't you?'

'I do.'

'And I would still never do anything to harm him.'

He nodded.

'But after all that's happened at Cristobel, I'm beginning to wonder about something.' Her voice had sunk to a whisper and he had to lean over to hear her. 'Two years ago Marcus tracked me down. He sounded more distressed than I had ever heard him. Caroline had flown the coop and he hadn't any word from her in over a month. Not one word. Marcus said he was concerned for the boys. They hadn't heard from their mother and they were reacting badly to her neglect. It was affecting their schoolwork, their general health.' She took a ragged breath, then continued. 'That surprised me a little, I must admit, since I never thought they had any relationship with Caroline at all. You know what she was like. A tree is a better mother. But anyway, Marcus asked me if I would mind calling them from time to time and pretend to be Caroline. Just chatty little calls, so they wouldn't feel so abandoned.' She said the last in her perfect imitation of Caroline's voice, but this time Stefan didn't laugh. He didn't even smile.

The only sound in the room was the faint gurgling of the machine by Caitlin's bed.

'It wasn't Caroline?' Stefan repeated dully. 'You phoned them?'

She nodded. 'Over the past two years I've called maybe a dozen times or so. I didn't see what harm it could do. She was such a bitchy mother.' Her last words trailed off.

Stefan held up one hand. 'Now wait a minute, Caitlin. Let me get this straight.' He spoke his next words slowly, carefully, enunciating every syllable. 'At Marcus's request, you called the boys and passed yourself off as Caroline.'

'I did.'

'Do you know if Caroline ever phoned them?'

Painfully she turned her head to look at him. 'She never did. That's why Marcus kept asking me to do it. It sounds so weird when you think about it.'

'It sounds weird, Caitlin, because it *is* weird.' He felt numb. 'Why would Marcus ask you to do such a thing? Because he's such a caring father? Out of genuine concern for his sons?'

Their eyes met.

Something unspeakable touched the back of his neck and it made him dizzy with fear. Knowing Marcus, there was only one answer. Only one reason that made any sense. Stefan knew it and he could see from the look on her face that Caitlin knew it too.

Marcus had asked Caitlin to call because somehow he was certain that Caroline was never going to call again. But why? How did he know? Stefan stared past Caitlin towards the open window. *And does it have anything to do with what is happening at Cristobel right now?*

He stood up. He had only one choice. Confront his brother. Before it was too late.

31

There was no breeze. Even in the shelter of the trees the heat was suffocating. J.C. stumbled along behind his father and with each footstep he grew more apprehensive. After they left the house, J.C. had expected they would take the path down to the road. His father had said the car was waiting there to take them to Bathsheba. But once they stepped off the lawn and into the cover of the trees, his father changed direction and headed north, circling around behind the house, and it didn't take J.C. long to figure out that they were moving away from the road instead of towards it.

Marcus walked quickly, without speaking, and J.C. had a job to keep up with the man.

It wasn't until they reached the foot of the grassy slope that led up towards the cane fields that J.C. summoned the courage to speak. He moved up alongside his father. 'I ... I thought we were going to Bathsheba.'

'We are.'

'But ... but this isn't the way.'

Marcus stopped and looked down at him with such an angry expression that for one breathless moment J.C. thought his father was going to strike him. The boy drew back, cringing in anticipation of the blow, but when Marcus jerked his hand up it was only to wipe the beads of sweat from his own forehead. 'I have some things to take care of, Jean-Claude,' he said sharply. 'You just do as you're told. Now come along.'

'Yes, sir.' The words came out in a croak.

Marcus took one last look back toward the house, then turned away and they set off again. With a growing sense of dread J.C. realized that if they kept on in this direction there was only one place they could be going. Cane Cave.

J.C.'s mind raced. When they got there he had to be ready with an excuse so he wouldn't have to go inside the cave. What could he say? How could he avoid it? Maybe he could pretend to twist his foot. Or maybe he could get an awful stomach cramp and have to sit down to rest. That wouldn't be hard to fake. He already had a stitch in his side.

J.C. couldn't see past his father's body so he simply followed after him, keeping his eyes glued to the back of Marcus's legs.

They were almost to the palm grove when suddenly, without warning, Marcus stopped dead, his whole body stiffening. J.C. almost bumped into him but caught himself just in time. He stepped to one side. And then he saw her.

About fifteen feet ahead of them, blocking the way, her face grim, her eyes flashing, stood Amalie.

'Amalie!' J.C. darted around his father, intending to run to her, but Marcus grabbed him by the shirt and pulled him back. With an iron grip he held J.C. beside him.

'Don't you move,' he whispered in the quietest but most menacing voice J.C. had ever heard.

'Let the child go,' Amalie said and her tone was equally threatening.

J.C. felt his father grow tense, heard his muttered curse, as if seeing Amalie was the last thing he wanted. 'What the devil are you doing here?'

She answered his question with one of her own. 'Where are you taking the boy?'

'We were going to Bathsheba to meet you,' J.C. blurted.

Marcus's fingers tightened around the boy's arm. 'Silence!' he ordered.

'To meet me? In Bathsheba?' Amalie sounded amused, but J.C. knew she wasn't. 'This is not the way to Bathsheba.'

'I have business at Cane Cave,' Marcus said sharply.

'I think your business will have to wait.' Amalie took a few steps toward them, then stopped. 'I think it would be best if we all went back to the house so that you, Monsieur Leyland, can call the Inspector.'

It was his father's turn to sound amused. 'Call the Inspector? Whatever for? What could I possibly have to say to him that he hasn't already heard?'

Amalie paused, seeming to give a great deal of thought to his question. Finally she answered. 'I found Remus Hastings.'

'That's interesting,' Marcus said, 'but at this point it is hardly of any concern to me. I am leaving Cristobel today.' He took a measured step towards her, pulling J.C. along with him.

Her eyebrows arched. 'So you aren't planning to remain here to see justice done? To see August's killer apprehended?' On the surface she seemed merely curious, but underneath J.C. could hear something else. Something so ominous that he shivered with dread.

'Justice will be served with or without me,' Marcus replied sharply.

281

'I'm afraid not, Monsieur Leyland. You see, Remus insists that he had nothing to do with August's killing.'

Marcus threw his head back and laughed. 'What a surprise! I would have thought that at the mere sight of you he would have fallen at your feet, made a full confession, and begged for mercy.'

Amalie's response was controlled. 'Remus says he saw the killing.'

For the first time Marcus seemed thrown off balance. He loosened his grip on J.C.'s arm. 'Indeed?'

'I am sure the Inspector will be most interested to hear what the boy has to say.'

J.C. was suddenly conscious of a change in his father's posture. He coiled up like a spring, moving almost imperceptibly onto the balls of his feet. 'And what might that be?'

Amalie's eyes flashed with fire. 'Remus Hastings claims that *you* are the one who is guilty, Monsieur Leyland. That it was you who slashed August's throat. He was there. He saw you.'

J.C. stared, horror-stricken. What was she saying? Had she gone crazy? Surely she didn't believe such a lie. He squeezed a sideways glance at his father, expecting either an explosion of outrage or a shout of laughter. But Marcus did neither. He seemed intent on hearing her out.

'And I know why you did it. And why you have taken Jean-Claude. It is because you cannot sell Cristobel until they reach maturity. And therefore they must die.' Slowly Amalie's hand moved to her own throat and she held it there as if suddenly feeling August's pain. 'You murdered the boy, knowing full well that Remus Hastings would be blamed. And now it is Jean-Claude's turn.'

All the tension seemed to leave his father and he turned to look pensively at J.C. 'For once, Queen Amalie is right,' he said, nodding his head. 'But this will not be a murder. That would be foolish.' He looked back at her. 'My poor son is going to have a tragic accident. Playing by himself in his favourite spot. Such a careless, reckless boy. Falling to his death from the mouth of Cane Cave.' His voice went on in the same thoughtful tone. 'When they find his body, I'll have to fly back from New York. Grief-stricken but still capable, I'll make all the arrangements for his funeral. And then, of course, I'll sell Cristobel to the highest bidder.'

'Stop!' Amalie thundered. 'Say no more! Jean-Claude must come with me. Now. It will do you no good to harm him. No matter what, Cristobel will never be yours. Any day now Caroline will be home, and even if no one else believes you are guilty, she will. At the very least she will never allow Cristobel to be sold.'

Now the laughter came again, but this time it was soft, malevolent. 'You are a fool, Amalie,' Marcus said. 'In the past few days I have come to realize just how big a fool you really are. You still believe that Caroline is coming back to Cristobel. That somehow your spirits have summoned her to bring her home.' He shook his head in disbelief. 'How could I have misjudged you so badly? Even now, your stupidity astonishes me.'

Amalie's hand moved from her throat to the golden pendant around her neck, and J.C. held his breath, his heart pounding in his ears. He could feel the storm gathering. She's going to save me, he thought wildly. She is! She is! Now Amalie is going to turn my father into a toad!

But nothing happened.

'Your precious Caroline is never coming back to Cristobel,' Marcus continued, still smiling. 'And do you know why?'

Amalie waited, her eyes fixed on Marcus's face.

Marcus leaned forward as if he wanted to make certain she heard his next words. 'Your precious Caroline is never coming back because your precious Caroline is dead.'

Caroline is dead.

J.C. couldn't breathe.

Caroline is dead.

He opened his eyes wide and stared at Amalie.

She stood transfixed, her expression unchanged, but J.C. could see her chest rising and falling rapidly beneath the cloth of her dress. 'You are the fool, Monsieur Leyland, if you think I would believe such a preposterous lie. If Caroline were dead, I would know it.'

'You would know it?' Marcus laughed again, this time a sound that was full of genuine mirth. 'Even as my fingers closed around her throat, you, my dear Amalie, slept on peacefully in your bed only a few steps away. I slept very well that night myself, knowing that the bitch was gone forever, knowing that her body would never be found.'

What happened next was so unexpected, so horrendous, that the boy could only stare thunderstruck.

In one fluid motion, his father released his grip on J.C.'s arm and lunged toward Amalie. In the next instant J.C. saw a knife appear in his hand, saw the hand as it rammed forward, heard the dull *thunk* as it made contact with her stomach. His eyes started from their sockets. *His father had actually stabbed Amalie!*

J.C. saw her quick look of surprise. And then her

face crumpled up like a piece of tissue paper. She bent her head and looked down, incredulous. The front of her crimson dress was turning black with blood.

Without making a sound she dropped to her knees, then pitched forward on her face.

J.C. watched in abject horror as his father raised the knife high over his head to strike again. 'Amalie!' the boy shrieked and started toward her.

At the sound of the shrill scream, Marcus spun around, startled, as if he had forgotten the boy was there. Slowly he lowered his arm. 'Come here, Jean-Claude,' he said, his voice low, hypnotic.

J.C.'s ears filled with a thunderous roaring. He couldn't think. He couldn't move. And then through the din he heard a single whispered word. 'Run.'

In the next instant he was off, crashing through the underbrush, his father right behind.

32

Stefan paid the driver. He didn't wait for change. He ran up the shadowy path but this time it seemed to have no end. It rolled on in front of him, the black trees crowding close. In spite of the humidity he felt his mouth go dry. He had no idea what he was going to say or do once he got to the house. But it didn't matter. He had to make sure that Justine and the boy were safe. Then he would deal with his brother.

He stopped at the edge of the lawn to catch a quick breath, then ran the last hundred yards to the house.

The front door was closed.

He hesitated for only a moment before opening it, and stepped into the hall.

Justine was sitting at the bottom of the staircase, her arms clasped tight around her knees, a butcher's knife beside her on the marble floor.

'Justine?'

For a moment she stayed rigid, then relief flooded her face and she jumped to her feet, crossing the space between them, hurling herself into his arms with such force that she almost knocked him over. 'I'm so scared, I'm so scared, I'm so scared,' she kept repeating. 'There's no one here. No servants, no Marcus, no J.C.' She pulled away and stared at him. 'But what are *you* doing here?' Without waiting for his answer she hugged him. 'Oh, I don't care. I'm just so goddamned glad to see you.'

He put his arm around her and they walked back to the foot of the stairs. 'What were you planning to do with that?' He pointed to the knife on the floor.

She stiffened, her mouth a thin harsh line. 'I was going to stab whoever or *whatever* came at me.'

'I'm glad you didn't have to.' He suppressed an urge to put both arms around her, hold her tight. 'Where's Marcus?

She threw her hands up in a gesture of despair. 'I don't know, and I'm not sure I care. But I can't find J.C. either. He's gone, Stefan. He's not here anywhere. And I'm so scared for him because he would never have left the house by himself.'

'Maybe Amalie took him somewhere.'

She frowned. 'He would've said goodbye. I know he would. He knew Marcus and I were leaving this afternoon.'

Stefan felt his pulse quicken. 'You and Marcus? This afternoon?'

She nodded. 'He had a sudden change of plan.'

'And J.C. wasn't going with you?'

She shook her head.

'Why not?'

'Because Marcus said no.' She touched him lightly on the shoulder. 'Stefan? What is it?'

He shook his head. 'I'm not sure. But there's something urgent I have to talk to Marcus about.' He was filled with a sudden need to hurry. 'Right now. He must be somewhere in the grounds.' He took her hand. 'Maybe he's in the aviary. Let's go.'

Outside, the air shimmered with heat. They circled around the pool and were almost to the steps at the end of the terrace when Stefan stopped. A hazy figure had appeared at the edge of the lawn.

Stefan heard Justine make a small strangled sound in her throat that in the next breath became a sigh of relief. 'It's Amalie,' she said. 'I never thought I'd be happy to see her but I am.'

He squinted. The sun was dazzling bright, and as he watched, Amalie seemed to sway, mirage-like.

Then in slow motion she collapsed.

By the time they reached her she had managed to pull herself up. She staggered towards them with her hands held tight across her stomach, blood oozing from between her spread fingers. 'Marcus has killed me,' she whispered, dropping her hands to her sides so they could see the rent in the blood-soaked cloth of her dress. The remains of the fabric were stuck to the raw jagged edges of a murderous slash in her stomach.

'Holy Jesus,' Stefan breathed and grabbed her just as she toppled forward. As gently as he could, he lowered her to the ground.

Her eyes closed.

'Marcus did this to you?' Justine knelt beside the woman. 'That's impossible.' *Isn't it?* She could feel the bitter taste of bile in her throat.

'We've got to get some help,' she heard Stefan say. 'Go call someone. The police. Quick.'

'There's no time.' Amalie's voice was a barely audible whisper. 'Marcus has the boy. He means to kill him.'

Justine went weak with fear. Somehow she knew that Amalie was telling the truth. 'Where are they?'

Two faint words that neither Justine nor Stefan could make out.

Stefan bent over and put his ear close to Amalie's lips. 'Say it again, Amalie. Please. Try.'

Her eyes fluttered open. 'Cane Cave.'

Stefan turned to Justine. 'You go back to the house and phone for help. I'll find my brother.' He started to get up but Amalie's hand grabbed his and held it.

'Leave me,' she whispered. 'You don't know the way. She will have to show you. Now go.'

There was no alternative. Together he and Justine began to run.

In his blind flight to escape, J.C. had lost all sense of direction. His strength gone, he sank down in the shelter of a clump of frangipani trees and struggled to catch his breath. *Oh please God, don't let him find me. Please, oh, please.* Shaking all over, he squeezed his eyes shut and tried to think what to do. Somehow he had to figure out where he was. Then maybe he could get back to Justine before his father . . .

A sudden gust of wind blew through the trees, making a creaking sound, and J.C.'s eyes snapped open. He could see nothing stirring anywhere. In the smothering heat even the lizards seemed to be hiding.

He felt a faint stirring of hope. Maybe his father was lost too. Maybe J.C. could find his way back to the house before his father did. He drew a deep shuddering breath. On hands and knees he crawled out from the shelter of the frangipanis.

He straightened up and listened.

No sound.

Hitching up his shorts, he took two hesitant steps, then changed his mind and reversed direction. He hunched over to make himself as small as possible and began to creep through the dense foliage. Within minutes he found himself at the edge of the forest. Just ahead he could see the grove of wild orange trees.

Like a small animal he froze, listening.

No sound.

No movement.

He took one cautious step forward but before he could take another, *a hand reached out from behind and grabbed him!*

J.C. almost swooned but his father held him upright. He still carried the long curving knife, stained with Amalie's blood. 'Your time is up,' Marcus said softly.

He dragged J.C. through the grove and past the ruins of the old sugar house. J.C. offered no resistance. His father was going to throw him from the mouth of the cave but the only thing he could do was whisper the same two words over and over and over. 'Please don't please don't please don't.'

His father never looked at him nor did he stop until they reached the door in the side of the hill. Then with one quick motion he dropped the knife and with the next, he threw J.C. to the ground, knocking the wind out of him. Before the boy could recover, Marcus put his foot on J.C.'s chest, pinning him down. With both hands free, he unlocked the door, then moved his foot and yanked the boy to his feet.

As J.C. stared down the dark passageway, suddenly his terror exploded. 'No!' With a last desperate surge he tried to wrench away, but his father only tightened his grip, sending shocks of pain up J.C.'s arms. He felt the hot rush of urine run down his legs and into his sneakers and he went completely limp.

'You little fool,' his father said, hauling him to his feet. He left the knife where it was and dragged the gasping boy down the ramp, scraping J.C.'s knees raw on the rough stone.

By the time they reached the main chamber J.C. was only dimly conscious. He felt his father release him and he lay still.

Marcus bent over and twined his fingers in J.C.'s hair, snapping the boy's head back. 'Now, Jean-Claude,' he said quietly. 'Sadly enough, before you fall I must be certain you are no longer breathing.' And he slipped a smothering hand over J.C.'s nose and mouth.

J.C. heard a rushing in his ears and he knew he was about to die. But in that instant, echoing through the vast cavern came a soft mocking whisper. 'Marcus. Come here.'

Marcus let J.C.'s head drop and he whirled around. 'Who's there?'

A breath of laughter, low, vengeful.

Leaving J.C. almost senseless, Marcus began to inch along the back wall of the cave. He moved like a cat, his whole body poised to attack.

The boy stirred. He lifted his head. His vision was blurred but he could still see his father. A dark shadow moving across the floor of the cave.

And then on the opposite side, between the kegs of rum, *something else moved*.

With burning eyes J.C. saw his father freeze, heard his gasp of disbelief. Then a sudden flash of ghostly white as *she* stepped out of the shadow.

A single word came shrieking into J.C.'s mind. A word that brought him crashing to his feet. A word that sent him scrambling, clawing, crawling up the stone ramp in a last frenzied attempt to escape.

Mother!

Somehow J.C. managed to get to the open door. He pitched through it head first and lay panting in the tall grass, unable to go an inch further. Every ounce of his strength was gone and he lay dazed, defenceless.

And then from the depths of the passageway he heard footsteps. Someone was coming but there was nothing he could do about it. Panic-stricken, he rolled over onto his side. He didn't cry out. He knew no one would hear him.

Eyes shut tight, he didn't see her at first, but when he heard the sudden rushing of air, he looked up. The falcon came in low over his head, her talons thrust forward, and just as Marcus came rocketing through the door, she struck him full in the face. Marcus threw up his hands to protect himself but it was too late. With a terrible shriek of pain and shock he reeled backwards down the ramp.

Her powerful wings beating the air, the peregrine made a tight turn and followed Marcus through the open door.

For a moment there was silence.

Then J.C. heard his father scream. And scream. And scream.

Justine and Stefan ran up through the cane fields, not stopping until they reached the ruins of the old stone sugar house. 'The door that leads into the cave is just beyond that outer wall.' Justine pointed. 'What should we do?'

'We have no choice,' Stefan said, wishing he had some kind of weapon with him. He knew that Marcus had one. 'Let's go.'

They moved through the ruins and around a tangled

hedge of oleanders and in the next instant they saw him.

Barely conscious, J.C. lay on the ground beside the heavy wooden door. No more than a foot away from his head was a bloodstained knife.

Stefan knelt beside him.

J.C.'s eyes fluttered open and in the moment before he lost consciousness he whispered a broken sentence. 'He – he's in the cave – my father.'

Stefan gave him a quick once-over to make certain he was all right. Then he picked up the knife. 'You stay here,' he said to Justine. 'Hold him. Keep talking to him. He'll come around. In the meantime I have to find Marcus.'

'Oh God,' she whispered. 'Be careful.' Then she knelt and gathered J.C. into her arms.

After one last look, Stefan stepped through the door and stealthily made his way down the dimly lit ramp into the heart of Cane Cave. He had no idea how he was going to handle this, but he was certain of one thing. He did not want Marcus to see him first.

Inside it was cool but not damp, and the air smelled faintly of sickly sweet rum.

He listened.

He could hear the steady hum of the giant air conditioners and beyond that something else. A snapping sound. *Plip*. Like rubber bands breaking.

Plip.

Across the floor of the main chamber shafts of sunlight streamed in through the mouth of the cave. He felt the wall behind him and began to inch his way along, hiding in the darkness, circling behind the giant kegs of rum.

Plip.

And then Stefan saw him.

Marcus lay sprawled on his back in the shadow.

The falcon was perched on his chest. Each time she
bent her head to tear away another small piece of flesh,
it made a sound.

Plip.

There was very little left of Marcus's face.

Epilogue

The morning air was cool. Wisps of clouds tinted the sky with shades of pink and grey and a flock of birds rose high into the air, chirruping their displeasure at being disturbed.

The two black men strolled through the cane fields and past the old sugar house, walking rhythmically with long loose-jointed strides. One of them carried a toolbox. They seemed not to have a care in the world. But such was not the case. Neither John nor his companion was looking forward to the task ahead.

John liked his new employer. Mister Robert was a good man to work for. Fair-minded and reasonable, a man who showed concern for the people he employed. Not like the old mister. Not high and mighty like Mister Marcus.

John's dark knuckles knotted up. They did that whenever he thought of Mister Marcus. Strange how the man had died. They said it was a heart attack. But that didn't explain what the bird had done to his face. It had been savaged. Some of the servants had seen, and they had their own notions, some of which John was inclined to share. He thought that Mister Marcus must have died of fright. Maybe because of the bird. And maybe because of something else. Anyway, everyone agreed it was well deserved after the terrible things the man done.

And then there was all that ruckus trying to find Miss Caroline's body.

John felt his flesh crawl. He would have felt much better if after all their digging and ripping things up they would have found her. But they hadn't. There was a memorial service but none of the servants at Cristobel went. What good, with the body still unburied? With her soul still unshriven? Everyone knew it was unholy for a spirit not to have a final resting place.

He rolled his eyes to one side to make sure that Seton was still with him. Cane Cave was bad enough business *with* company. He most assuredly did not want to go in there alone.

He removed the padlock and pulled the door open and the two clattered down the long ramp to the cave, making as much noise as they could. 'Don't like this, mon,' Seton muttered. 'Don't like it one bit.'

'We be done before you know it,' John said loudly, moving across the floor to stand in front of Number Two keg. Yesterday the new owner, Mister Robert, had sent some of the boys to bring some cases of wine down to the house and to draw off some rum for a fancy party he was having next week to celebrate his first year at Cristobel. But for some reason they couldn't get any rum out of Number Two keg.

John knew it was at least half full. He had measured it himself years ago and to his knowledge nothing had been drawn off since. Mister Marcus hadn't liked rum. Strange man not to like rum, John thought.

John held a cup under the spigot and slowly turned the faucet.

About an inch of amber liquid trickled out.

'Humph,' John said. He drained the cup. The liquor burned all the way down. 'Fine rum,' he said. He turned to Seton. 'Hey mon, get me the length of wire out the tool box.'

He poked it into the spigot about three inches, then stopped. 'Something blocking it.' He frowned. He had never known the rum at Cristobel to have any sediment in it.

Seton was standing a few feet away, shifting from one foot to the other, clearly anxious to be done with this place.

'Get the ladder from the storeroom,' John ordered, pointing towards the rear of the chamber.

Seton shuffled out of sight and was back in a minute.

John leaned the ladder up against the keg and climbed up, carrying the long steel measuring rod with him. Maybe if he poked around he could loosen things up.

On the last rung he could just make out the top of the cork that sealed the filler hole. And as his eyes adjusted to the dim light he saw something else. Something that John found most peculiar.

Someone had cut a hole in the top of the keg, about two feet in diameter. The piece had been fitted back almost perfectly but the sawmarks were still visible.

With the tip of the measuring rod he prised the piece up. This was going to make their work a lot simpler.

'Hey mon,' Seton called from below. 'Hurry it up.'

John ignored him. Lifting the piece out, he gripped the edge of the opening and hauled himself up so that he could sit astride the keg.

He peered down into the hole but could see only blackness.

He stuck the stick down as far it would go, stirring the contents. He frowned. 'Something in there besides rum,' he muttered. Maybe their job wasn't going to be as easy as he had thought.

He slid forward cautiously and lay on his stomach, reaching his arm into the keg. The rum came up almost to his elbow. And then his hand closed around something. Something that felt like strands of wet cornsilk. 'What the devil . . . ?'

As he pulled the thing up, he could only stare in horror.

Caroline stared back, an expression of serenity on her ruined face, a dreamy look in her peeled sightless eyes.

John began to scream.

Tomorrow's Memories
Connie Monk

The Gowers of Denby are a picturebook perfect family. There is Tim, Jane, twins Richard and Liz just sixteen, and Hartley, almost one of the family. Even the onset of World War II can't touch them here in the safe haven of their Devonshire farm, or so Jane believes. In her thankfulness, she finds space and love to spare for two London evacuees and for Meg, a disturbingly beautiful young woman who arrives with a babe in arms.

But Jane is soon to find that no one is beyond the reach of tragedy, that no city, no village, no individual is untouched by war, that sometimes each new day can be a hurdle . . .

Tomorrow's Memories is the touching story of one family's war, of its relationships with one another, and above all, of Jane, as she holds on to memories of yesterday and looks towards tomorrow . . .

Fontana

King's Oak
Anne Rivers Siddons

Leaving behind a disastrous marriage, Diana Calhoun and her young daughter Hilary seek refuge in the comforting security of a small Southern town – Pemberton, Georgia, a close-knit, aristocratic community bordered by a primeval forest.

What she discovers, though, is not serenity but Tom Dabney, a magical, passionate man who has renounced his patrician heritage to live close to the land and who worships the wilderness surrounding Pemberton. Despite warnings from friends, Diana abandons herself to a fiery affair that releases within her unforeseen strengths.

She soon comes to realise that Tom will do anything to protect and preserve his world. When an explosive confrontation involving a sinister threat to his cherished wood pits Tom against even his closest friends, Diana must decide if she can follow . . .

'A wickedly good love story, one that soars'
New York Daily News

Fontana

Jewels of Our Father
Kristy Daniels

Sweeping from the bustling waterfront and gilded mansions of San Francisco in the 1920s to the intellectual excitement of de Gaulle's Paris and beyond, *Jewels of Our Father* is a vast dramatic tale that reveals the sins and secrets, passions and obsessions of a powerful newspaper dynasty.

Adam Bryant spent a lifetime forging the *San Francisco Times* into the most powerful newspaper in the country. His passion for journalism and his love for one woman helped him build his empire, yet bitterness and despair threatened to topple it. For on his deathbed, Bryant bequeathed control of the *Times* to his three estranged children.

And instead of uniting them, as their father had hoped, the legacy set the stage for a power struggle that would rage over a decade. Only Bryant's daughter, Kellen, shared her father's vision and could ride the turbulent wave of a new generation's passion and betrayal to save his failing dream . . . and fulfil her own tumultuous destiny.

Fontana

Fontana Fiction

Fontana is a leading paperback publisher of fiction. Below are some recent titles.

- ☐ GREEN AND PLEASANT LAND Teresa Crane £4.99
- ☐ KING'S OAK Ann Rivers Siddons £4.99
- ☐ THE EGYPTIAN YEARS Elizabeth Harris £4.50
- ☐ MAGIC HOUR Susan Isaacs £4.99
- ☐ THE RELUCTANT QUEEN Jean Plaidy £3.99
- ☐ TOMORROW'S MEMORIES Connie Monk £3.99
- ☐ WHEN SHE WAS BAD . . . Kate O'Mara £4.99
- ☐ THE CLONING OF JOANNA MAY Fay Weldon £3.99
- ☐ FORBIDDEN GARDEN Diane Guest £3.99
- ☐ KING'S CLOSE Christine Marion Fraser £4.95
- ☐ MEMORY AND DESIRE Lisa Appignasesi £4.99
- ☐ THE ROAD TO ROWANBRAE Doris Davidson £4.50
- ☐ SACRIFICE Harold Carlton £4.99

You can buy Fontana Paperbacks at your local bookshops or newsagents. Or you can order them from Fontana, Cash Sales Department, Box 29, Douglas, Isle of Man. Please send a cheque, postal or money order (not currency) worth the price plus 24p per book for postage (maximum postage required is £3.00 for orders within the UK).

NAME (Block letters)_____

ADDRESS_____